CROSSING THE DEADLINE

Sleeping Bear Press™
2395 South Huron Parkway, Suite 200
Ann Arbor, MI 48104
www.sleepingbearpress.com

Printed and bound in the United States.

10 9 8 7 6 5 4 3 2
10 9 8 7 6 5 4 3 2 1 (pbk)

Library of Congress Cataloging-in-Publication Data

Names: Shoulders, Michael, author.
Title: Crossing the deadline : Stephen's journey through the Civil War / by
Michael Shoulders.
Description: Ann Arbor, MI : Sleeping Bear Press, 2016. | Summary: Stephen,
an accomplished bugler in the town band, joins the Union effort in the
Civil War and endures trial after trial, from battle to Confederate prison
and the shipwreck of the steamboat *Sultana*, but through luck and fortitude,
Stephen survives.
Identifiers: LCCN 2015033876 | ISBN 9781585369515 | Pbk ISBN 9781585369522
Subjects: LCSH: Musicians—Fiction. | Soldiers—Fiction. | CYAC: United
States—History—Civil War, 1861–1865—Fiction.
Classification: LCC PZ7.S558833 Cr 2016 | DDC [Fic]—dc23
LC record available at http://lccn.loc.gov/2015033876

Cover art:
Stars and stripes graphic © pashabo/Shutterstock.com
Soldier graphic by Felicia Macheske for Sleeping Bear Press

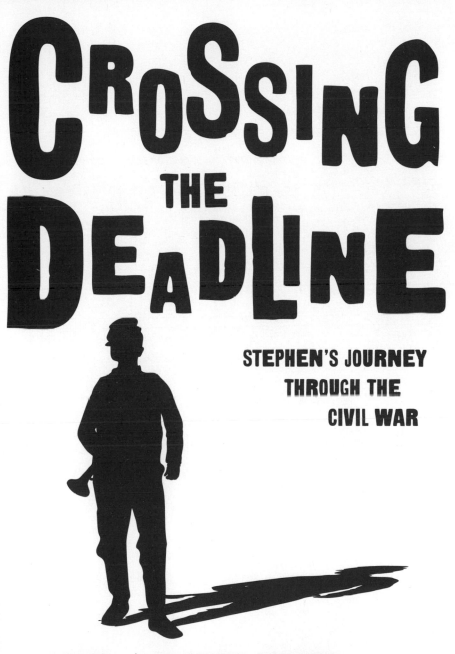

CROSSING
THE
DEADLINE

STEPHEN'S JOURNEY
THROUGH THE
CIVIL WAR

A NOVEL ★ BY MICHAEL SHOULDERS

For Debbie Shoulders

PROLOGUE

April 17, 1861

"You have to hurry, Stephen," my brother, Robert, called as he swung around the fence post and into the corral. He was out of breath from running to Clem's Livery, where I was mucking stalls. "Dad's going, and it's happening soon."

I'd been expecting that moment for days, dreading it. Dad had coughed up blood all the night before. The air in our room at the boardinghouse was filled with the stench from his soiled sheets. The doctor told us it wouldn't be long. I shouldn't have left the house when I did, but cleaning up after the horses for my uncle was better than having to watch it happen.

Robert turned and ran home, but I took time to scrub the pitchfork and hang it back next to the buckets on the wall. Scraping manure from my boots with a stick ate up a couple more minutes. I'd never seen anybody die, and Dad did not need to be my first. For months, consumption had slowly been eating his body like a flame chewing a candle.

Telegraphs from relatives in Pennsylvania and New York had arrived, expressing regrets of his pending death as if witnessing last breaths was as sacred as attending church. "Sadly, we're unable to accept the solemn honor of accompanying James at his death," an aunt wrote.

What honor?

On the way home, Paddy's Run, a creek just north of town, appeared on my right. It reminded me of the summer before and how we'd picnicked there every Sunday. Dad chased Mom with crawdads around trees, bushes, and into the creek. He threatened to let them pinch her. She shrieked like a train whistle, all the while knowing he'd never allow anything to harm a hair on her head. One time Dad fell asleep under a tree, and Mom offered a nickel to me or Robert, whoever came back first with a crawdad. Robert, seven years older than me, beat me and presented her with a large brown one. He pinned its tail on the ground while Mom squeezed its back between her finger and thumb. Lifting the crawdad with a firm hold, she placed its pinchers above Dad's lip until it found his nose and latched on tight as a tick.

I never heard Dad yelp so loud or Mom laugh so long.

When I arrived, the boardinghouse was quiet; a rarity since there were six rooms rented on the second floor. It was wrong, but as I closed the door I said a quick prayer asking God to have taken Dad during my walk home. I made my way past the large dining room, where we ate with strangers. Mother hated mealtime because we shared a table with renters who came and left with the wind. Most of the time we ate in silence as if everybody were wooden statues.

Mother had said many times, "Boys, one day we'll have a place of our own and a dinner table where we can talk and say anything without a care in the world."

But consumption took every penny my parents had put aside for a home. Dad hadn't worked in months—his weight melted away. Mom worried what she would do with two boys once Dad was gone. Lines she called crow's-feet appeared at the corners of her eyes, and she'd gaze into space for the longest time, as if in a trance. But I knew she was thinking, worrying, and wondering about how she was going to get by with three mouths to feed.

I climbed the stairs, opened the door to our room, and crossed to my bed. The doctor stood nearby, looking on, and Robert leaned against the wall, arms crossed. Dad's head was cocked back, almost facing the wall behind him, his eyes closed and mouth open wide like he were trying to catch snowflakes on his tongue. Beneath a blanket, his chest heaved and stalled for several seconds and fell back down. Over and over his body repeated the motion. Mom sat holding Dad's hand soft-like as if she had a butterfly between her palms.

Out of nowhere the smell of gardenias or honeysuckle filled the air, impossible in April, but I clearly detected a sweet scent. Dad's chest rose and fell faster and faster as the aroma grew stronger. If anybody else noticed, they didn't say. The blanket lowered, and I studied it like it were a fishing pole and we were waiting for a fish to take the bait. Then, as if somehow the doctor and the smell were tied together by an invisible thread, the aroma became overpowering and pulled the doctor nearer the bed, where he placed two fingers on Dad's wrist.

"He's gone," he pronounced quietly. Just as fast, the sweet smell left the room, and Mom began to weep softly.

It was mid-April, and our stay was paid up for the month. If Mother had figured out what she was going to do, she hadn't shared it with anyone. Dad was always the loving husband. As if he wanted to give her one last gift, he died with two weeks left in the month. Mother would have time to plan where the three of us would live come May.

The night of the funeral, after we went to bed, I heard Mom and Robert whispering. "I'm looking for work in the morning," Mom said. "You'll need to go ask your uncle Clem if he'll rent his spare room to us. We have to be out of here in ten days."

★ ★ ★

"I've moved a few things under the stairs and fit in an extra bed for the boys," Uncle Clem said, glancing at Robert and me. "It may be a bit cramped."

Mother looked down at the floor and said, "We'll make do, Clem. Won't we, boys?"

"We'll be fine," Robert said, smiling.

I squeezed Mother's hand. "Yeah, don't worry about us."

"Are you going to be able to pay every month?" Uncle Clem was more concerned with making money from the room than seeing to it that his brother's family was okay.

"Dutch posted he needed a servant to clean floors and carry coal and hot water to guest rooms," Mother said. "He offered me the job, and I begin tomorrow."

"You've never worked before. Can you handle it?"

"Well, there's no better time to learn," she said.

"What's he paying?" Uncle Clem pried.

"Five dollars a month, plus meals on the days I work."

Uncle Clem grunted in approval.

Through late spring and summer things seemed fine. Mother left home after putting breakfast on the table and stayed at Dutch's Mansion House until early evening. She came home and cooked for the four of us before dropping dog-tired into bed. But it wasn't long before Uncle Clem got an itch to get more money out of her.

"Weren't you paying twice what I charge when you were at the boardinghouse? It seems five dollars is practically giving my room away."

"You weren't getting anything for it sitting empty," Mother replied.

"That's not the point. It's what the room is worth that's important."

"I also cook and clean for you, Clem. So I think what I pay is more than fair."

Robert, with disgust wrinkled across his face, got up from the kitchen table to leave the room. My uncle raised his arm and braced himself against the doorframe, blocking

Robert's path. "Maybe the three of you'd be better off at the poorhouse, where they take in people who can't afford to live on their own."

Mother pursed her lips and left the kitchen through the side door that led into the yard.

"Stephen, I need to talk to your brother," Uncle Clem said. "Go down to the hardware and get a pound of nails. I need to work on the porch tomorrow afternoon."

That night, after they thought I was sleeping, Robert told Mother how he was tired of Uncle Clem complaining about how she was not pulling her weight. "I'm the man of the house now that Dad's gone," he whispered. "It's my responsibility to take care of you and Stephen. I don't want us living off charity."

"It's too dangerous," Mother pleaded.

"What skills do I have?" Robert asked. "I'm eighteen and can soldier for the Union Army. I won't gamble any pay away, so you don't have to worry about that. I promise I'll send as much home as possible."

Mother wept, knowing his mind was made up. "I don't know if I can do it . . . worry about you every day you're gone."

"Maw, the war's been going on for five months and won't continue much longer, maybe a couple months at most.

It will give us a chance to decide what to do. Besides, while I'm gone, you and Stephen will have a roof over your heads. Neighbors will pitch in if things get desperate," Robert reassured her.

A week later we said good-bye to Robert at the train depot. He dug into his pocket and produced a shiny gold object. "Here, Mother, I bought you something to remember me by." It was a neck brooch, the size of a dollar piece, with a quarter moon smiling at a sky of stars. "I want you to think of me every time you wear it."

Mother nodded and stared at the gleaming object in her hand. She turned it over and over, crying. She glanced at Robert's face but only for a split second. Her eyes darted back to the brooch. "It's beautiful," she whispered between quiet sobs.

Robert gently retrieved the brooch and with his right hand lifted her chin. He unclasped the pin and fastened it beneath her neck.

PART ONE

CENTERVILLE, INDIANA

CHAPTER ONE

"They should spell that piece of trash the W-E-A-K-L-Y," Richard Charman says late one afternoon, spying a copy of *Harper's Weekly* folded on the bench beside me. He glares at me with deep-set eyes. His brows, thick and wide-spreading as a robin's nest, give the impression that he looks out on the world from within a cave. Charman is Centerville's highest-paid lawyer for good reason. Arguing against him is fruitless and usually ends in defeat. It doesn't matter whether his clients are right or wrong. They almost always win with him on their side.

I'm sitting beside the front steps of the Mansion House, watching Conestoga wagons pass, when Charman spots my copy of the newspaper. He shakes a finger at me, squinting his eyes together like I've been bad. "That paper doesn't take a strong enough stand against slavery," he chides me, as if I personally wrote every line in the newspaper.

"Well, I don't know anything about that," I tell him. "I read it to know what's going on in the war."

"What good is the news if you can't trust the source?" he asks.

That's a good point, I think.

"They should be straightforward and call slavery what it is."

"Don't listen to him, Stephen," Jake Vandervite says, patting my shoulder. Everyone calls him Dutch because he emigrated from Europe a few years ago. He owns the Mansion House where Mother works. The hotel is a three-story oasis for travelers coming through town, most of them headed west. "Come inside," he says. "Got a fresh paper this morning for you." Travelers bring copies of the paper with them. They leave them in rooms or on tables after breakfast when they've finished reading them. Dutch saves them for me, and sometimes Mom brings them home with her. Ever since Robert left two years ago, I study anything about the war I can get my hands on.

When we reach the bar, Dutch says, "Pay Charman no-never-mind. He's got nothing better to do than stick his nose into everybody else's business."

Dutch is taller than everyone in Centerville, and stronger, too. He has to be in order to manhandle rowdies when they get too many drinks in their bellies. Once, he carried two men, one on each shoulder, out of the Mansion House's gambling room and dumped them smack on their haunches in the street.

I look up at him and notice light passing through his thinning blond hair like it's delicate lace. "I have something else for you besides the newspaper," he says.

"How many questions do I get this time?"

"Oh, this one will be hard to get, so I'll give you two extra guesses: an even dozen," Dutch says.

Besides newspapers, guests sometimes leave other items behind, and Dutch gives them to me if they're interesting. But I have to guess what they are.

I pause several seconds and stare deep into his blue eyes, trying to read his mind. "Is it candy?"

Dutch makes a fist and raises his thumb toward the ceiling. "One," he announces, starting the count. "It's not candy this time."

"A whistle that sounds like a train?"

"Nah," he says as he raises a finger beside his thumb. "You're not ready to guess yet, son. You need more clues. Narrow down the possibilities a bit."

"Is it man-made?"

"Now that's using your head, son. No, it's not man-made. Three."

"Is it a plant?"

"Yup, Mother Nature herself made it. Four."

"Does it grow up north?"

"Nope. You're not even close. That's five tries gone."

"I think I know. I'm sure of it this time."

"What?" Dutch interrupts me. "You think you know? You better take your time with more clues. You must guess it in twelve, or I give it to somebody else."

"Oh, I'll be right," I say. I scratch my chin, cock my head to one side, and ask, "Is it an orange?"

A slap on the counter rattles nearby glasses and bottles. "You cheated," he says, wagging his finger at me and grinning. "There's no way you got it with the questions you asked."

I double over in laughter.

Dutch turns around and looks at the bar mirror hanging on the wall. "No, really, did you see it in the mirror?" he asks. "It's impossible for you to have guessed it with those clues."

"I saw Mrs. Jensen trade a dozen eggs to one of your guests for an orange this morning," I confess. "I figured you'd end up with some of them, too."

Dutch reaches down behind the bar and tosses a perfectly round orange into the air. "You always were a sly one, Stephen."

I catch the fruit and roll it over in my hands several times. It's bigger than Dutch's fist, and that says a lot. "How did it get all the way to Centerville without spoiling?" I ask.

"By train, would be my guess. This beauty came all the way from a place called Saint Augustine, Florida." Dutch winks. "You might like to look at this, too." Dutch stretches his long arms three feet over my head and dangles the latest copy of *Harper's Weekly*. "Gotta jump for it."

I leap for the paper, and my shirt rises above my belt.

"My goodness, Stephen!" Dutch says, pointing. "How'd you get that bruise?"

I pull down my shirt. "What?" I ask.

"On your side ... there." he says, pointing again. "It's bruised something fierce. Your uncle Clem didn't have anything to do with that, did he?"

"Oh, no," I say, turning away. "I ... was ... ah ... shoeing a horse. He was favoring it and got spooked when I was checking it. That's all."

"Everyone knows Clem's temper is at the end of a short fuse. You sure he didn't have anything to do with it?"

"He's got a quick temper," I agree. "But this was from a horse."

Dutch nods, but he knows I'm telling a lie. "Okay," he says. "Well, you be more careful with those horses."

"Will do," I say. "I'll be more careful next time."

Dutch hands me the newspaper, and I turn to walk away, but he doesn't let go. "You need to learn to read people as well as you read words," he says.

CHAPTER TWO

I glance at the newspaper. "New York, Saturday, July 25, 1863" is printed across the top. A sketch of Major-General Ulysses S. Grant occupies the entire front page. "From a new photograph just received from Vicksburg" is written under his likeness.

I turn the plump orange over in my hand several times as I stroll to the southwest corner of the room. With a big window on each wall and two soft chairs tucked below them, it's the perfect spot for reading.

I sit and scratch the skin of the orange with the tip of my thumbnail. Sunlight illuminates the mist of juice as it explodes from the rind. A tangy, sweet smell fills the air.

From my spot in the corner, I can hear a group of older men chat at the hearth. One is a local fellow the kids in town call Possum Peckham. His real name is George Peckham, but his eyes sit too close beside an extremely long and narrow nose. Unless he looks directly at you, he appears to be cross-eyed. Folks in Centerville talk about how he left for the war with a full head of dark hair and returned ten months later crippled and gray.

Spinning yarns at the Mansion House is all Peckham can do since a rebel minié ball found his leg while he was down in Tennessee. He can't take a labor job of any kind. He claims a wad of flesh the size of a biscuit was ripped from the side of his thigh. I've never seen it.

Mom says the old fellow's true job is testing Dutch's ale for quality purposes. Occasionally, he drives a delivery wagon to Richmond, six miles east of Centerville. When pressed, he'll take a longer haul up to Fountain City.

Some of the men around the hearth sit backward in their chairs, chins resting on knuckles. Peckham's war stories hold my attention better than the preacher's sermon on Sundays.

"I tell you what, pards," Peckham says, "all them youngins who want to see the elephant, that's well and good until they stare it square in the face."

"The South is using elephants?" a man blurts out.

Peckham laughs. "'Seeing the elephant' means going into

battle for the first time. When soldiers hear that beast bellow like they've never heard before, then they change their minds. When they see the elephant once, feel it, smell it, nobody cares to wrestle the monster again. Our division had five thousand four hundred men, not a man less when we started. Three hours later, our numbers had dwindled to five hundred. If it hadn't been for the arrival of the Twenty-Third Missouri, every man would have been lost that day."

"Where was this?" someone asks.

"Tennessee . . . a place called Shiloh," I call out.

"That's right, Stephen," Peckham says, looking over at me. "Almost smack on the Mississippi line."

Peckham stands and removes a cracked, leather-bound book resting on the mantel. "Is your brother, Robert, still serving with Grant?"

"Yes, sir," I say proudly while showing the general's image spread across the front page of *Harper's Weekly*. "His last letter said his group is attached to the Army of the Tennessee down in Vicksburg, but we haven't heard from him lately."

He opens the book to reveal a tattered page of a newspaper pressed between the pages. "This here's a drawing of the battle of Shiloh. Gotta give it to 'em. They got the battle drawn mostly right, too."

I'd seen Peckham share the same drawing many times.

"And you were there? And saw it all?" a tall man asks, staring at the image. Peckham nods in silence and passes the picture to a man with a pipe hanging from his mouth. The man takes the picture, looks at it, shakes his head, and passes it to the man sitting to his left.

I rise from my chair and approach. "Can I give it a look, sir?"

He nods and hands the faded yellow paper to me.

The picture shows two groups of men in a clearing, facing each other in rows. Their lines stretch across the open field. Those clustered near the bottom of the picture have fixed bayonets ready for hand-to-hand combat. Thick smoke billowing from cannons blocks much of the center of the scene. Two men carry a fallen comrade past a dead horse.

Peckham continues. "There was one place where bullets flew so thick, we called it the Hornet's Nest." He leans forward and taps one man on the arm several times. "Imagine if you take a piece of hickory and whack a hundred wasp hives. Then try to fight off every last one of 'em with that stick." He pauses for a couple seconds and in a low, serious voice adds, "That's what it sounded like. Angry hornets. We thought it'd never end." Peckham rubs the upper part of his right thigh.

"That's when Johnny Rebel's minié ball found my leg."

The man with the pipe says, "Unbelievable. Simply unbelievable."

"There was a small pond near a peach orchard," Peckham continues. "Not large at all, maybe as wide as from here to across the road out there. After the battle, when both sides were claiming their dead, the water in the pond looked like a pot of stewed tomatoes."

"At least it was another Union win," a man with a red beard says. "That's what counts."

"I don't know 'bout that," I correct him. "The Union had thirteen thousand men wounded, dead, or missing, while the Butternuts only lost eleven thousand."

"You're pretty young to know so much about the war," the man says.

"That's more than the War of 1812 and the Revolutionary War put together in just two days of battle," I say, looking again at the worn page from the newspaper. "A copy of *Harper's Weekly* 'bout a year ago showed the eleven generals who were at Shiloh. Sherman, Buell, and there, square in the center of 'em all, was Ulysses S. Grant. 'The Heroes of the Battle' the paper called them."

Peckham nods. "Stephen's right. Grant was there."

I hand the picture back to Peckham. "Thank you, sir, for letting me take a look at it."

"Your brother served at Shiloh when Peckham was there?" the man with the pipe asks.

"No," Peckham and I say at the same time.

"He's with General Grant now at Vicksburg. Last we heard." As I walk back to my chair, all the talk about soldiers killed in the war reminds me how much I miss my brother. I remember how Robert teased me about girls and how, late at night, Mom yelled for us to "quiet down up there so you'll be worth something to the world in the morning." That only made us laugh harder.

The paper called the generals "Heroes of the Battle," and Grant gets his likeness put in papers all the time. But I know what a real hero is, and it's not the generals. Robert's a hero.

CHAPTER THREE

September 28, 1863

The first frost of the year coated the ground last night, so it's cold as I set out for the train depot. "On your way to play for the governor?" Miss Amanda Gates calls from her porch. She and Margaret Peckham are rocking and tying American flags onto thin cedar rods. "I see you have your horn."

"Yes, ma'am," I reply while pushing open her gate. "Mr. Wilson gave me a solo to play. We'll see if all my practice pays off."

Margaret drops a flag into a large wicker basket as I place one foot onto the top step. "You'll do fine, Stephen. I have no doubt," she says. She pulls her quilt tighter around her waist. "Late September has brought a chill to the air."

"Yes, it has," I reply. "That's a lot of flags you've made for the recruitment rally."

"We've collected scraps for weeks," Miss Gates says. She motions with her finger for me to come closer. I lean in, and with a hushed voice she says, "Even Mrs. Loggins, who's meaner than a cottonmouth cornered in an outhouse, surrendered a swatch of white from a piece of bedding."

Mrs. Peckham laughs. "Not that she gave up much. Looked like it hadn't been washed in seven years."

"Margaret!" Miss Gates says.

"I'm just tellin' the truth, Amanda. I'm only tellin' the truth."

"I'm sure everyone will love your flags," I say.

Miss Gates nods toward Margaret. "She made the stars. She wound white thread around her needle three or four times, held the knot in place, and pushed the needle back through the same hole it came from. White dots the size of tomato seeds."

I smile at Margaret. "Miss Betsy Ross herself would be proud."

"We don't want the governor of Indiana to be embarrassed by his hometown," Margaret replies.

Miss Gates lays the fabric in her lap and shoots a sideways smile at her friend. "Horsefeathers, Margaret. How could Governor Oliver Morton not be proud of his own hometown?

We're family. When he sees these flags waving, he'll have to be wallpapered not to be impressed."

Miss Gates holds up her latest creation. "Stephen, does this look crooked to you?"

She's fishing for a compliment. "What on earth are you talking about, ma'am?" I say. "The seams appear straight as rails. They're expecting a couple hundred people to hear the governor. Do you think you have enough flags?"

"They'll go as far as they can go," Miss Gates says.

★★★

Two hours later I see the ladies carrying their baskets through the crowd at the depot. Their hands retrieve one flag at a time as if they're delicate dried flowers. They nod to each man and hand a flag to each lady. Sherry Ball stands next to me. She runs her fingers over a row of French knots.

"Every single flag has exactly five rows of seven stars, Sherry," Margaret assures her. "There's no need to count 'em all. One star for each state. The thirty-fifth star is West Virginia's. It was official on July fourth."

"Should only be twenty-four stars on your flags, ladies," Richard Charman butts in. When the war started, Charman hung a flag from his front porch. But he cut one star out for every state that left the Union. "Seceshes' stars should be taken off every Union flag," he says with venom in his words.

Margaret raises her voice. "You may call any state who seceded a Secesh, Richard Charman, or whatever else you like. But this is an American flag." She stares him dead in the eyes, daring him to blink. "What you do with your flags, at your house, sir, is your business. These are my flags, and I worked hours to put every dadblamed star on 'em. I thank you very kindly to keep your comments to yourself."

"It's a very beautiful flag, indeed, Mrs. Peckham," I interrupt.

"Thank you, Stephen," she says, fighting back tears. She walks away, then stops. After taking several seconds to collect her thoughts, she turns and looks back. "Stephen, your brother, Robert, is fighting for all of this flag, every red and white stripe and all thirty-five stars. His efforts are not for a cut-up and tattered flag with some stars missing."

That brings a smile to my face and a lump to my throat.

CHAPTER FOUR

A train whistle draws everybody's attention west. I look down the tracks and see pillars of smoke swell from a locomotive's engine. The train's "welcome whistle" blows, and Mr. Wilson waves his hand to get the band members' attention.

Our director has taught music for twenty-five years in Centerville. A year ago he formed the Community Band with boys too young to enlist and men who returned from the war wounded. When the train whistles, he pushes his spectacles up the bridge of his nose and taps his baton against George Peckham's tuba. There are no signs of Mother. But with the band sitting on chairs so close to the platform and the crowd so thick, I can only see past three or four people.

Mr. Wilson says I know more about music than anybody he's ever taught. "Stephen, you take to the bugle like a flame takes to a candle," he said one day. More than anything in the world, I hope Mother's here to hear me play my first solo.

I refocus my gaze on Mr. Wilson. He puts one finger against his lips to indicate we are to begin softly. "We'll build the music," he said in practice. "We'll whip the crowd into a frenzy."

We begin "Battle Cry of Freedom" on the downbeat. As the train nears the depot, Mr. Wilson keeps the beat with his right hand and motions with his left hand for the music to swell. As the train slows to a crawl near the depot's platform, the music reaches a loud crescendo.

When the train screeches to a stop, four porters pull boxes painted red with white stars from the side of the grandstand to create steps from the train.

The doors open, and a hush falls over the crowd as if this all had been practiced a hundred times. A rotund man, dressed sharply in a dark suit, a watch fob hanging from one vest pocket, steps into the doorway. He grips the metal bar on the side of the train with one hand and waves to the crowd with a black walking cane tipped with a gold sphere. He waddles down the steps and onto the platform. Governor Morton receives a deafening roar of approval. He tugs on his goatee and bows his head to the crowd.

The governor lifts both hands and says, "Thank you." Nobody can hear his words above the ruckus. He strokes his thick black mustache and raises both hands again, calling for silence, but his gesture has the opposite effect. The cheers grow louder. Men remove their hats and wave them in tight circles over their heads. The words "thank you" are said again and again, paired with nods of his head. "Thank you. Thank you," he says louder.

When the crowd finally settles, George Peckham lowers his tuba and shouts, "Welcome home, Governor!"

"It's good to be home, George," comes the answer. He strolls to a podium decorated with pressed bunting of red, white, and blue stripes.

"The good folk of Centerville certainly know how to wake snakes," he says.

Another chorus of cheers erupts from the crowd.

"Who's that up there?" a shrill voice yells when it's quiet enough for her to be heard. "All I see standing behind that podium is plain ol' Oliver Hazard Perry Morton." The comment brings a roar from the crowd.

"Yes, Miss Amanda Gates, it's just me," the governor confesses.

"Why, I remember when you had a full head of hair and

were thin enough to hide behind a buggy whip," she says. "What happened to you?"

Governor Morton laughs politely at her comment. "Well, as you can see now, it's reversed. My belly is full and my hair is thin. It would take an entire barrel of whips to hide me now. And"—he wags his finger—"I'm not leaving town until I've had a slice of your famous pumpkin pie."

Miss Gates shakes her finger back at the governor and says, "I thought so. I got two pies cooling right now. Just stop by and take a whole one home with you."

CHAPTER FIVE

As the laughter dies, Governor Morton pulls several notes from inside his coat pocket. "Friends, this war has taken too many of the Union's finest; some from right here in Centerville. Many said it would be just a summer conflict. But here we are, three summers past. We will not rest, we will not bend, because our cause is the right cause."

Governor Morton points to a tall thin man leaning against the train, his arms folded against his chest. "Bill Robbins came to Centerville seven years ago and opened a hardware store. Bill, would you have worked as hard as you have to see all you've earned given away to somebody who did none of the work?"

"Not in this lifetime," Mr. Robbins says.

"But that's what slavery is. People working hard for no

reward. That is wrong, and we can't allow it to continue. Where is Dutch?" Governor Morton asks.

Dutch is near the platform, hidden from view by the podium. He waves his hand in the air. "Down here, Governor."

"This gentleman traveled a long ways from Europe and built a business along Main Street. Does he give all his sweat so that one hundred percent of what he reaps will be handed over to others?"

"No, sir!" Dutch yells. "I work hard for what I have."

"Exactly. You do the work." The governor pauses. "And you reap the rewards. Slavery, folks, is unrewarded work."

"But we're sick of this war!" a woman yells from the back of the crowd.

A chill flashes up my spine, and the hairs rise on the back of my neck. Was that Mother? Did she come to the rally to challenge Governor Morton?

Governor Morton nods in agreement. "I know you are." He pauses several seconds and opens his mouth to talk, but stops.

I turn to Sherry Ball. "Who said that?"

"It's Richard Charman's wife," she says.

The governor pulls forward on his goatee with his left hand and taps the side of the podium with his right. "We're all downright sick of the fighting," he finally says in a lowered voice. "The separation from fathers, brothers, and sons is a pain we can't put into words. But there is a larger call. That's why I'm here today, in my own hometown of Centerville, Indiana, to remind you, my friends, that this war is a crusade, and we must continue to do our part to preserve the Union.

"I see a time in the very near future when we will once again have one flag representing all of the United States of America.

"Show me a man facing battle with fear and yet staring it smack in the face out of a sense of duty to his country. Then I'll show you a hero.

"I speak about two of our own bravest: Robert Gaston and John Robbins." People turn to stare at me. I feel my face turn flush.

"Those two boys did not leave Centerville, family, and friends to fight for glory. Robert's mother, already a widow, has sacrificed in his absence while he is serving his country.

"President Abraham Lincoln, who is a good friend of mine, said to both houses of Congress on July 4, 1861, 'having thus chosen our course, without guile and with pure purpose, let us renew our trust in God, and go forward without fear and with manly hearts.'

"Residents of Centerville, I came here today to ask you to continue to join our president and go forward without fear and with manly hearts to fight the battle to heal this great nation."

Governor Morton folds his papers and tucks them into his coat pocket. He waves to the assembly and says, "Thank you, Centerville, for welcoming me home today."

Mr. Wilson waits for the ovation to subside before turning to me. I quickly rub the sweaty palm of my right hand on my pant leg so my bugle doesn't slip, and play the first four bars of "Battle Cry of Freedom" alone. The notes spring loud into the air, and I hope Mother is listening somewhere hidden by the crowd.

When the rest of the band joins in, the governor raises his hands. "Mr. Wilson, Mr. Wilson, one moment please," the governor interrupts. "Stephen Gaston, I almost forgot. If you'll come over to the house later, I have a little something I'd like to give you. George Peckham, I have a package for you, as well."

The governor points to Mr. Wilson to continue the song.

Yes, we'll rally round the flag, boys. We'll rally once again.

Every time the words "rally round the flag, boys" are sung, men remove their hats and wave them over their heads. A spine-tingling sight, though, is the sea of tiny red, white, and blue flags waving back and forth.

Shouting the battle cry of Freedom; We will rally from
the hillside,
We'll gather from the plain, Shouting the battle cry of
Freedom.

The band plays to a crescendo, and the crowd joins in on the chorus.

The Union forever, Hurrah, boys, hurrah. Down with
the Traitor, Up with the Star;
While we rally round the flag, boys, Rally once again,
Shouting the battle cry of Freedom.
We are springing to the call for
Three Hundred Thousand more,
Shouting the battle cry of Freedom, And we'll fill the
vacant ranks
Of our brothers gone before ....

CHAPTER SIX

Mom places a bowl of fried chicken on the table as I set three plates. "Did you come hear me play my solo today?" I ask.

"No," she says almost in a whisper.

"It seems like the whole town was there."

"The last place I saw Robert was on that train platform."

"I know, but Mr. Wilson picked me to play. . . . "

Mother stabs a spoon into the bowl of potatoes so hard, I'm surprised the glass doesn't shatter. "Stephen, we rarely hear from your brother or know where he is on any given day. He said he'd be gone for a few months, and it's been two years. This war's turned into an ugly scab that refuses to heal. If I show my face at a rally, it means I support what's going on. And I'm just not ready to do that."

Uncle Clem opens the back door, and a gust of cold air fills the kitchen. He removes his jacket and walks to the basin to wash his hands. He glances at Mother in the mirror hanging on the wall.

"What's wrong?" Uncle Clem asks.

"Chicken may be a bit overdone," Mother lies.

★★★

Throughout dinner Mother, Uncle Clem, and I stare at our plates, only looking up to reach for a bowl of food. The clanking of forks against plates breaks the silence. Not another word is spoken at dinner until Uncle Clem clears his throat. I hope a piece of chicken or potato is lodged, but when I look up, I see he is trying to get my attention. He pinches a piece of biscuit and tosses it into his mouth. He nods at my mother, sitting to his right.

"Ma, can the apple pie wait until later, after I see what the governor has for me?"

Mother sees the uneaten pieces of squash scattered around my plate, then narrows her eyes. "What is that supposed to mean?"

"Who knows?" Uncle Clem answers quickly. "Governor

Morton said he has a package he wants to give Stephen." He shoots a look at Mother, and then back to me. "I guess it's not every day you get an invite to the governor's house now, is it? I'm sure it's something important. Don't you think?" he asks her.

Mother stares down at the table in Uncle Clem's direction but doesn't make eye contact. She glances at the pie, and then smiles at me. "The pie can sit right where it is until you get back," she relents. "Go on."

My feet barely touch the ground as I race out the side door. I run through the narrow arch that connects our courtyard to Main Street, wondering about the package. Why didn't the governor give it to me at the train depot? He'd said he had a package for Mr. Peckham, too. Maybe "package" means something altogether different. Is it the same thing for both of us?

My feet fly across the cobblestone on Main Street lined with Conestoga wagons parked for the evening. Ever since I can remember, hundreds of them have passed through Centerville like rain in downspouts. Every one of them headed west, stopping in Centerville only long enough to rest or get supplies.

I go by one with a bed frame strapped to the side.

Another has a barrel cinched with a rope as thick as my wrist. As I round the back end of one of the wagons, my shoulder catches a chair leg strapped to the sideboard. It yanks me back as my feet fly out from under me.

"Hey, watch where you're going, pard," a man calls down to me. He's standing beside the wagon, working on a wheel he's removed from the axel.

I stand up and dust myself off. "That wheel's taller than me," I say, admiring its size.

"And four inches wide." The man gives a tug on one of the spokes. "They sink right down in the muck if the wheels aren't wide enough."

I pat the wagon's side like it's a horse's flank. "It's a whale on wheels," I say. "I want one of these to take me to Texas one day."

"Why there?" he asks.

"Don't know. Guess because it's not here."

"Well, you're young," he says. "Got plenty of time to make that happen."

★★★

It only takes me two minutes more to make my way to the governor's house. It sits on a small rise, like a pedestal. The yard slopes gently up to his front door. Tonight I think it's odd that the governor's shades are drawn. He invited me to come by, yet the house appears empty. I knock on the door just before dark.

CHAPTER SEVEN

I knock a second time and hear feet shuffle inside. I throw my shoulders back and lift my chin, trying to stand a bit taller, a little straighter. *It's not every day the governor invites you to his house.* A door slams inside, and all goes quiet. The front door opens a few seconds later.

Lucinda, the governor's wife, greets me wearing a purple evening gown. Gold bands of trim on her skirt look like braids of rope. Her face is narrow and delicate, in sharp contrast to her husband's.

"Good evening, Mrs. Morton," I say. "I'm here to see your husband."

"Yes, I know," she says, opening the door and motioning with her head for me to come in. As I walk by Mrs. Morton, the sweet flowery smell of her perfume reminds me of Dad.

It is almost like the smell I caught when he died.

"Hello, Stephen. Welcome." The governor, leaning slightly on his cane, shuffles from behind a green tufted sofa and extends his hand.

"Hello, sir," I say, trying my best to deliver a strong handshake.

A small package, wrapped in brown paper, sits on an end table next to the sofa. I wonder if that's my package.

"How are you?" he asks.

"Fine, sir, just fine," I reply.

"I'm glad you were able to stop by. I have something for you." He studies my face hard for a couple seconds. "Did you know that I've met Abraham Lincoln?"

"I heard you say 'a good friend of mine' when talking about the president this morning."

"Oliver's met President Lincoln several times," his wife says. She's sitting by the fireplace. Waxy pomade in her hair allows the light from the flames to twinkle on her head. "He telegraphs Oliver quite often," she adds.

"I can't imagine what that was like ... to meet the president, I mean."

"He shook my hand the same as you did," Governor Morton says. "Your handshake might have been a tad firmer," he adds.

I laugh. "Amazing," I say. I steal a second glance at the package, and Governor Morton notices.

"Did you know that the president is a voracious reader?"

"Yes, sir, I'd heard that," I say.

"Just like you, from what I've been told."

First I'd been surprised when the governor of the whole state of Indiana called my name at the train depot. Now he's telling me he knows how much I like to read. "Who told you that?" I ask.

"President Lincoln told me," the governor says.

I nearly faint. I must have the oddest look on my face because Mrs. Morton quickly says, "No, no, no, not really. Oliver P. Morton, stop pulling this young boy's leg."

Governor Morton laughs and pats me on my shoulder. His mood turns serious. "Your brother, Robert, told me, Stephen." The room falls quiet as a January night.

"How do you know Robert?" I ask.

"I met him at the training camp in Indianapolis. Recruits come to drill there before heading south."

"Well, the *Weekly* reported Indiana has sent more soldiers than any other state to the war."

"Almost as many as Delaware," the governor corrects me. "I make it a point to talk to as many of the Centerville boys as I can when they're in Indianapolis training. Robert and I talked for nearly an hour one day. You know what he talked about most?" he asks.

"The war?" I guess.

"No. We hardly mentioned that. We spent most of the time talking about you. He said you like to sit in Paddy's Run Creek and call birds. He said you can call a bobwhite to within ten feet. Is that true?"

"When my lips work right, I can."

"He also said you like to read."

"Yes, sir, I do. Mother read to Robert and me since before I can remember. She taught us."

The governor leans over the sofa and picks up the brown package from the table. He smiles broadly as he lifts it toward me.

My feet feel nailed to the floor.

"Take it," the governor insists. "I brought it all the way from Washington, D.C., just for you."

I slowly raise my hands and take the package. I stare at it a few seconds and peel back the paper. "A book," I whisper.

"Not just any book. It's *David Copperfield*," Governor Morton says. "It's by Charles Dickens. President Lincoln recommended it for you."

I look at the governor in disbelief.

Mrs. Morton rises, leans in toward my ear, and whispers, "This is when you're supposed to say, 'Why, thank you, Governor, it's very kind of you.'"

"Ohh! I'm sorry, sir. Thank you so very much, Governor. It is very kind of you," I say. "It's just ... I ... "

"Don't need a speech. 'Thanks' will do just fine." The governor laughs. "I know I don't have to tell you how much you mean to your brother, Robert."

"Well, thank you, sir. He means a lot to me and Mother," I say.

"And it's no coincidence I'm here in Centerville today."

"It's not?"

I recognize a sharp change on the governor's face. His smile and laughter evaporate. He purses his lips, but not in an angry way. "Your brother seemed to be an honorable man."

"He is, sir. Robert's never cheated anyone out of a nickel."

The governor pauses and looks me over from head to toe. "I bet you're cut from the same cloth as your brother."

"I am. Mother and Dad raised us both the same."

"Then you can keep a secret, Stephen," the governor says more than asks.

I search his face for a clue to see if he's serious or if this is headed to be another joke. He stands stoic, almost wooden. "Yes, sir. I can keep a secret. I promise, I can."

CHAPTER EIGHT

Governor Morton looks at Lucinda and nods toward the kitchen table in the adjoining room. She gathers her skirt in both hands and joins her husband at a pine chest along the wall. They grab black handles on the ends of the chest and drag it several feet, revealing a small door leading under the stairs.

Uncle Clem's house has a similar small space. He stores winter clothes there in summer along with household items seldom used. The governor swings a metal latch and opens the door cautiously, as if some wild animal might escape. I tilt my head to one side and try to peek around the door, but I can't see into the dark alcove.

The governor motions into the blackness with his thick finger. No response. He reaches his hand under the stairs.

A shape the color of coffee grounds emerges from the darkness and rests on the governor's palm. It's a hand.

A barefoot boy, dressed in mis-fitting pants and shirt, steps out from the darkness. He's exactly my height, but thinner. His hair, although cropped short, curls tightly against his scalp. His eyes are dark and flash with fear as they dart quickly around the room, taking in his surroundings, especially me.

"This is Clay," the governor says, bringing him farther into the room.

"Hello, Clay," I say, extending my hand.

Clay averts his eyes to the floor. "*Bonjour, Ami*," he whispers.

"What are you doing under the stairs?" I ask.

No reply.

"Can he speak English?" I ask Governor Morton.

"Ask him," the governor insists.

"Speak English?" I say slowly, enunciating each word. Clay looks at the governor and shrugs.

"*Parlez-vous Anglais?*" the governor translates for Clay with a wink.

"*Naturellement, je vivais dans Louisiana,*" he says.

"My goodness. What did all that ... ?"

Clay interrupts me before I finish, "Of course, I do. I'm from Louisiana." He smiles.

I look at the governor and then over to Clay. The pair slap their thighs and laugh together, proud of the trick they've played on me.

"You knew what I was saying?" I ask Clay.

"*Naturellement.*" Clay nods. "Naturally."

"How do you do that?"

"Do what?" Clay asks.

"Is that French you're speaking?"

"*Oui.*"

"How do you do that?" I ask again.

"Don't know how I do it. Been doin' it since I was born near New Orleans fourteen years ago on John Burnside's plantation along the mighty Mississ—"

"No, no, no," the governor interrupts. He waves his hands back and forth quickly. "No names, Clay. Remember?"

Clay closes his eyes and bows his head, ashamed of his mistake.

Governor Morton grabs Clay and pulls him close for a hug the same way Dad hugged me when I did something wrong and was sorry for it. "It's okay," he assures Clay with a pat on his back. "It's okay."

A slight smile returns to Clay's face.

"What's the Mississippi River like?" I ask.

"They don't call it the Mighty Mississippi for nothin'," Clay responds.

"Cotton is big down there in the South, isn't it?"

"*Non, sucre*—sugar where I lived. Brings in more money than cotton. We worked the sugarcane fields from 'can to can't,' " Clay says.

"Can to can't?"

Governor Morton explains, "Slaves work from when they *can* see the sun until they *can't.*"

Two loud knocks on the front door send Clay scrambling to the small space beneath the stairs. He dives in and quickly pulls the door shut. The Mortons scoot the chest back in place along the wall. Lucinda walks to the door and glances over her shoulder at the governor. She stands patiently, waiting for his signal. Governor Morton looks toward the chest, places his fingers against his lips, and nods to his wife that it's okay to open the door

CHAPTER NINE

George Peckham steps into the house. He's alone. He looks at the governor, tilts his head back and arches his eyebrows. The governor nods back at him. Mr. Peckham peers into the darkness and motions with his hand for someone outside to come in. Seconds later, Margaret Peckham and a dark-skinned lady enter the room. George closes the door quickly behind them.

Margaret stands with one arm around the lady's shoulders, comforting her. The lady sobs softly. Mrs. Morton crosses to her side and drapes a shawl over her shoulders. Governor Morton advances slowly. He tenderly lifts the woman's chin, forcing their eyes to meet. A smile spreads across his face, revealing teeth between his mustache and goatee. He nods ever so slightly.

"Ohhh, Lord," the lady says, choking on her words. She stamps her left foot against the rug multiple times as if trying to knock a hole through the floor. Tears stream down her face. Mrs. Morton collects a hankie from her sleeve and places it in the woman's hands.

The lady covers her mouth in disbelief. Governor Morton puts one finger against his lips and points to the pine chest beside the stairs. He walks over and motions for her to follow. The governor points to the handle on the chest, and together, they drag it away, revealing the small door.

The governor gestures at her and then to the latch, indicating that *she* is to be the one to open the door. She grasps the latch softly, as if the slightest jarring might break it. Her trembling hands cause the metal to rattle. She rotates the fastener, swings the door open on its hinges, and peers into the darkness.

A second later, Clay lets loose a blood-chilling scream and leaps from his hiding place into his mother's arms.

Mrs. Morton catches a sob in her throat. It sounds like a hiccup, but I know better. She produces a second hankie, this time from the other sleeve, and covers her mouth and nose.

"Mama," Clay finally says. "Mama, is it really you?"

"*Oui, mon cher, c'est vraiment moi*," she says. She presses Clay's cheeks between the palms of her hands. "Yes, child, it's really me."

We stand quiet as the moon, save for sniffles and the rustling of hankies, for several minutes.

Clay's mother looks at Governor Morton. "Four years, Governor," she manages to say between sobs. "Four *long* years."

"I know," he assures her. "I know. And we'll do what we can to reunite you with the rest of your children," he says. "Give us time."

Clay's mother lets go of her son, walks over to Governor Morton, grabs both of his hands, and kneels to the floor.

"No, no, no," the governor insists. He pulls her off the floor and pats her hands softly.

"You don't understand." She reaches for Clay's hand and draws him next to her. She wraps her arms around him and kisses the side of his head. "We always worked hard. We rose before the sun. We did what we had to do to make it through. Whatever Master said, we did. Then he sold us off like we mattered less than cottonwood seeds blowing different directions in the wind.

"But you know what, Governor? We all need a reason for living. My children are my reason for putting one foot in front of the other every day. One day Master began selling off my children. He never told us where they was going. I didn't know where any of them would end up."

Governor Morton nods. He begins to say something and pauses, thinking better of it.

"When I said good-bye to each of my six children," Clay's mother continues, "I thought for sure it was the last time I'd ever speak to any of them again. Never thought the day would come when one of 'em would be in my arms again."

Governor Morton pats her arm. "George, you better head on over to Fountain City now. You can drop Clay and his mother off at Levi Coffin's house. He's expecting *packages* around midnight."

"Come," Mr. Peckham calls to Clay and his mother. "We'll have to hurry." So Clay was the *package* the governor said he had for Mr. Peckham this morning.

Clay's mother, unable to control herself, wraps her arms around the governor's neck and squeezes. And then, just as fast, Mr. and Mrs. Peckham whisk their two packages into the darkness toward Fountain City.

CHAPTER TEN

The governor, his wife, and I glance at one another, no one able to speak. Governor Morton and I stand in utter silence while Mrs. Morton walks to a nearby chair, sits, and wipes at her tears. I am shocked by the incredible joy Clay and his mother just experienced. But I can't imagine the depths of her sorrow that she still does not know where five of her children are.

Finally, Governor Morton speaks. "That is, in large part, what the war is about, Stephen. That's what Robert is fighting for. The president often reminds me how much the Union depends on Indiana. He says, 'Every person makes a difference. Everybody counts.' Do you agree, Stephen?"

"Yes, sir, I do."

"Do you remember when the Confederates fired on Fort Sumter?"

"Two and a half years ago. April, 1861," I say, not needing a moment to think about the answer.

"Lincoln called for volunteers to restore order. Within two weeks, I had twelve thousand men in Indianapolis ready for the cause. They became the Ninth Indiana Infantry under General Robert H. Milroy."

"Shiloh," I say. "Mr. Peckham was there with Milroy, wasn't he?"

"Indeed," the governor replies. "We're mustering in the Ninth Indiana Cavalry Regiment soon. That's why I'm home, Stephen. I can't ask towns across the state to do their part on the war without asking my own to do the same."

I shuffle on my feet, feeling uneasy. "I'm glad you asked me to come here tonight," I finally say. "After seeing Clay and his mama and the struggles they've faced, I want to join. Besides, Mother could use the extra money."

"How old are you?" he asks.

"Thirteen. But I can do an awful lot. I can ... "

Governor Morton raises his hand for me to stop. He rubs the back of his neck several times. "Thirteen, huh? You're a tad bit too young, Stephen."

"I'll be fourteen in less than three months. I can do a lot. I shoe horses at my uncle's livery every day. Mr. Wilson said he never saw anybody take to the bugle as fast as I did. I can ride a horse. . . . "

"Wait a minute," the governor says. "Was that you playing the bugle today at the depot?"

"Yes, sir. I played the solo this morning."

"Your brother, Robert, mentioned you played in the band, but I wasn't sure what instrument."

"A bugle's been in my hand every day since I was nine. I've been playing five years now."

"I can count, Stephen." The governor rubs the back of his neck again. "Well, I'm just thinking out loud now, Stephen. Officers need strong buglers to relay order to the soldiers. What I heard from you this morning was impressive."

"Thank you, sir."

"Buglers wake the men in the morning, tell them when it's time to eat, and when to extinguish their lights for the evening. Do you think you can learn fifty different bugle calls?" he asks.

"I can learn a hundred," I say quickly.

"I have to leave for Indianapolis first thing in the morning. Your mother will have to sign for you, since you're underage."

"I understand," I tell him. There's no way my mother will

sign for me, so I don't say another word. I stare at him, no emotion on my face.

"I'll tell you what I'll do," the governor says as he crosses to a rolltop desk in the corner of the room. He raises the slats and pushes them up and back into the rear of the desk. He reaches for a piece of paper and takes the quill from a jar of ink. "I'll write a letter to your mother, stating I recommend you to be Major Eli Lilly's personal bugler."

Governor Morton writes on the paper as he speaks. "Dear Mrs. Gaston, Major Eli Lilly is in need of a top-notch bugle player such as your son. If you'd be so inclined as to allow Stephen to enlist, I'll see to it he's kept in good care. The major is a brilliant druggist from Indianapolis and a personal friend. I consider him one of the Union's finest soldiers. Your son will be in good hands."

The governor signs the bottom of the note with a flourish and folds it in an envelope. "Show this to your mother, Stephen."

I nod to him but can't bring myself to say the words "I will."

"Ohh, and one more thing," he says. Taking the copy of *David Copperfield* out of my hands, he taps the book against my chest several times. "If your good mother signs for you and you enlist, I want you to personally bring this book back to me when you return home. I've had little time for reading since working in the capital. I look forward to borrowing it from you when the war's over."

"I'll do that, sir. I promise I'll return the book to you."

Governor Morton slips the envelope into the middle of the book and hands them to me.

★★★

I rush into the house to tell Mother what the governor of the entire state of Indiana said about Robert and to show her what he gave me. There's an envelope on the kitchen table addressed to Mary Gaston. The letter has fallen to the floor, so I pick it up and glance at the last line and see it was sent by John Robbins, son of the hardware store owner who mustered in the same day as Robert.

In Camp with TN 115th Regiment Infantry
near Lexington, Kentucky

September 16, 1863
Mrs. Gaston,

It is my duty to put pen to paper to inform you Robert met his Maker today, September 16, 1863, in Nicholasville, Kentucky, as our regiment encamped nearby. Robert was the finest soldier I know and was a friend to every man he met.

He died bravely preserving our Union. If financial circumstances prevent you from claiming his body, I want you to know he will be buried with several Indiana men, side by side, in a beautiful spot overlooking the Kentucky River.

Robert spoke often of you and Stephen and loved you dearly.

Your dutiful servant,
John Robbins

Mother did not leave her room for weeks.

CHAPTER ELEVEN

November 12, 1863

After thinking about it for two months, I decide to tell Uncle Clem my plan. It doesn't take much talking to get him to see it my way. He leans against a stall rail, his arms folded, and never says a word as I explain what I want to do. I've never seen him so quiet. He ponders it for three more weeks, and then his only condition is I can't tell Mother. "Leave a note for her," he says.

★★★

Ice crystals form on my lips as Uncle Clem and I ride due south toward Moores Hill to enlist me into the Union Army. I stretch a woolen scarf over my mouth and nose, and that helps a bit but not much. Tucking the ends under my coat collar holds it in place so it doesn't fly off. A thin slit, just below my hat, provides an opening for me to see where I'm going. One saving grace is that it's not snowing or sleeting.

Occasionally I tilt my head and look straight down at the saddle horn and use the top of my hat like a shield to cut the wind. Finally the cold becomes unbearable. I lean forward and tuck my head against the horse's mane. His neck feels warm like a thick blanket.

Most of the trip is covered in silence. Cold winds whip us from every direction. As we come out of a slow bend in the road, a tavern appears on the right. Thick smoke rises from the chimney. Uncle Clem sees it too. "I'm cold," I say, hoping he'll stop.

"Are you, now?" he replies.

"Can we stop to warm up?" I ask. "Just for a little while? My hands are turning numb."

Uncle Clem nods rapidly. "Yeah," he says. "Let's stop and thaw out."

We tether our horses and rush in. Six tables sit off to the left of the room, gathered near a roaring fire. The blaze heats the tables enough so that the men playing cards have discarded their coats. They stop their game and look up at us, then quickly go back to what they were doing. A long wooden bar, chest high with stools, covers the right half of the far wall. Uncle Clem walks to the fireplace, then presents his hands to the flames and rubs them together.

"Your mother makes five dollars a month as a laundress for Dutch," he says when I step beside him. "That doesn't pay for the food the two of you eat, boy. You should thank your lucky stars I was there to take the three of you in when your father died."

I nod but don't say anything.

He turns to face me, which puts his back to the card players. "Keep your mouth shut when we get to Moores Hill, and I'll get you signed into the army. You send me seven dollars from each paycheck, and your mother has a place to stay. Do what you want with what's left. Spend it, gamble on cards like these guys, I don't care."

A paunchy man walks up to the table nearest us, wiping his hands on an apron along the way. "What'll you two men be having today?" he asks.

"Whatever you recommend," Uncle Clem says with a smile.

"I got pork and roasted potatoes ready right now," he says.

"If it's hot and good, I'll take it."

"Drink?"

"Anything you bring will be fine."

When the man walks away, Uncle Clem says, "If I don't see seven dollars a month, you can collect your mother at the poorhouse when you get home."

"Mom has nowhere else to go. Dutch doesn't pay her enough to get a place of her own."

"Dutch?" Uncle Clem snarls as he says the name. "He's taken a shine to you, hasn't he?" he asks.

"Yeah, Dutch has been good to me and Mom."

"And I haven't?" Uncle Clem raises his fist to hit me. I put both hands over my face to block the coming blow. If the men were not nearby, I'm sure I'd feel his knuckles against my nose. Uncle Clem leans so close, I feel his breath against my ears. "You went crawling to Dutch and told him I beat you, didn't you?" he asks.

"No," I answer.

"I say you did."

"I swear I didn't say anything to him." I put my hands down and walk over to sit in a chair.

"Liar," he says. "Dutch came to the livery and told me so. He said if another bruise appeared on you, he'd make sure it would be the last."

I shrug like I don't know what he's talking about.

"I don't have to worry about that anymore, do I?" Uncle

Clem pats his coat pocket. "The letter the governor wrote will see to it you're gone and out of my hair."

The food arrives, and Uncle Clem smiles as the chubby man sets two steaming plates in front of us.

"Drinks?" he reminds the bar owner, and shovels a fork of meat and potatoes into his mouth. "Giving this letter to me instead of showing it to your mother was the smartest thing you've done in a long time."

"She would have ripped it into a million pieces and tossed every last one of them into the fire," I say.

"I know," he says. Then he laughs. "I'd love to see her face when she sees the note telling her you decided to run away and look for work in Ohio."

"She won't believe it."

"I don't know about that. Your mother's not that bright, and she won't care. She barely notices that you're around most of the time."

"That's not true," I say, feeling myself getting flush. I want to spit in his face.

Finally, when I calm down, I decide to ask something that's been on my mind for a long time. "Did Robert send you money?"

"What?"

"When he mustered in. Mother said she never knew what Robert did with his army pay. She never saw any of it."

My uncle chuckles. "You had a roof over your head, didn't you?"

I can tell by the grin on his face that what I suspected was true. Robert sent all his money to Uncle Clem. And he kept it all for himself. "Why do we have to go to Moores Hill?" I ask. "Why couldn't I have joined in Cambridge City or Richmond?"

"Too many people know us there, boy," he explains. "Can't take the chance they'd ask too many questions. They'd want to know why your widowed mother isn't signing you up, you being thirteen and all. You keep your mouth shut when we get to Moores Hill and let me handle it. Got it?" he asks.

Two glasses are set on the table in front of us. Suddenly I feel shame for leaving home without telling Mother the truth about why I was leaving or where I was going. I pray when she finds out, she'll understand that it's up to me, the man of the house, to do something to make life better for the both of us and for families like Clay's.

With bellies full and bones warmed, we ride the last hour south. A banner, stretched across the street and tied from the roofs of the saloon and bank, greets our arrival:

THE UNION MUST AND SHOULD BE PRESERVED!

We stop at the livery to stable the horses before walking across the street to a cluster of tents. Posters dot the town:

ELI LILLY, DRUGSTORE OWNER, FORMING AN ARTILLERY.

In This Great Emergency Our Government wants Men! Men with stout hands and willing hearts, men who will fight manfully for our just and holy cause.

RALLY! RALLY! RALLY!
MEN OF INDIANA!

Respond nobly to this last call as you have done to others. Listen not to those who would deter you from going: they will approach you in a thousand ways; heed them not; they have oily tongues but are

TRAITORS AT HEART

The undersigned has been authorized by His Excellency O. P. MORTON, Governor of Indiana, for Eli Lilly to raise the 9th Indiana Cavalry

PAY FROM $13 TO $23 PER MONTH HEADQUARTERS, MOORES HILL, IN

Captains, Lieutenants, Sergeants, and 2 Buglers per company

"Send me ten dollars per month, boy," Uncle Clem says when he sees the sign.

"You said seven before," I remind him.

Uncle Clem grabs the hair sticking out from beneath the back of my hat into his fist. I wince, and he yanks my head back and tilts it up so I'm forced to look him dead in the eyes.

"You're hurting me," I say through gritted teeth.

"I don't care. It was seven dollars before I saw the sign. I had no idea they'd pay that much for somebody to blow a stupid horn. The deal's changed. Ten dollars."

I nod, as much as I can with him holding my hair in a vice. He lets go and heads across the street toward the recruitment tent. I follow him, feeling like a whipped pup.

CHAPTER TWELVE

It's not hard to find the recruitment tent. A gray canvas banner hangs between two trees beside it with the words:

HEADQUARTERS 9TH INDIANA CAVALRY

Uncle Clem opens the flap to the tent and motions for me to go in. "His father's dead," he tells the man sitting behind the table.

"Captain Northam," the man says calmly.

"Beg pardon?" Uncle Clem asks.

"I have a name, sir," the man says. "It's Captain Northam."

"Yes, sir," Uncle Clem says quickly. "Captain Northam, this boy's father is dead."

The captain slides his spectacles down the bridge of his

nose a bit and glances at Uncle Clem. He looks at me, lays down his pen, and rubs his hands together to warm them. Cupping his hands and breathing into them tells me he's as cold as we are. During all this time he never takes his eyes off me. His pleasant, peaceful manner, along with his gray beard, seems more the makings of Saint Nicholas than a war recruiter.

Captain Northam sits in silence, simmering as quietly as a stew. He stares at me until the silence grows too thick for Uncle Clem. "I'm his guardian. His uncle. I'll be signing for him today."

The captain turns and spits in a tin can resting on the ground by the table leg. Slowly, he wipes his mouth with his sleeve. Again, he turns his gaze to me. "What about your mother?" the captain asks. "Why isn't she here?"

Uncle Clem puts up his hand and says, "She's unable to be here to sign him up, so I'm here in ... "

Without taking his eyes off me, the captain puts his hand up to stop my uncle from speaking. "I asked the boy a question. Your mother?" the captain asks again. This time he adds a warm smile. "What about her, son? Where is your mother?"

I have to think quickly. I don't want to anger my uncle,

but I have to answer the captain's question. His stare and silence cause me to shift my weight several times. "She's ...ah ... She couldn't come today," I say. That *is* the truth. *Think!* I say to myself. "She ... is ... ah ... "

"Gravely ill," Uncle Clem says. "In this last year, the good Mrs. Gaston has lost her husband and her oldest son to the war."

That's a lie because Dad died two and a half years ago.

"Is your mother okay with you joining?" Captain Northam asks me.

Uncle Clem points to the banner strung across the street. "She supports the president's cause to preserve the Union but cannot travel here to sign her son into the army. My good man—"

"Captain. Captain Northam," he corrects my uncle again.

"Sorry. Captain it is," Uncle Clem agrees. "Captain, she, like all good patriots, believes that the Union must be preserved."

Captain Northam hasn't looked at Uncle Clem since the conversation began. He stares at me with a warm smile. I get the feeling this very scene has played out many times, and he has sent every underaged boy home.

"Is that true, son?" Captain Northam asks.

"My father and brother both have met their Maker. Yes, sir. My brother, most recently, near Lexington, Kentucky." Technically, I told the truth. I didn't say they both died in the war. I said they both died and that Robert had died in Kentucky. If the recruitment officer thinks they both died in battle, that's not my fault.

Captain Northam removes the tobacco plug from his mouth and tosses it into the spittoon. His thumb and forefinger are stained with tobacco juice. He wipes them on the underside of the table.

"He's a bugler, just slightly underage," Uncle Clem says.

"How old are you, son?"

"Fourteen," I say. Now I am lying, but just barely. I won't be fourteen for another three weeks.

"And Governor Morton assured his mother the boy would be away from the front lines ... back with Major Lilly... when she allowed him to join. He's to enlist as a bugler. Show the captain your horn," Uncle Clem commands.

I open my leather case enough for the captain to see. "Take it out and play something for me," he says.

"Now?" I ask.

"No time like the present," Captain Northam says with a smile.

I look at Uncle Clem. "Go ahead. Do what the good captain says."

I take the instrument from the case and press it to my lips. The frigid metal stings and shoots pain through my mouth. I blow slow breaths into the horn to warm it up.

Captain Northam folds his arms across his chest and buries his fingers into his armpits.

I take a deep breath and begin the melody from "Battle Cry of Freedom." The notes come crisp and clear just as they did the morning I played it for the governor. The confines of the tent make the horn sound louder than I expect. It startles me. Midway through the first verse, men from nearby tents come in to see who's playing. After I finish one verse and a chorus, a round of cheers erupts.

Captain Northam stands and claps the loudest. "That was absolutely wonderful," he says. "Just wonderful."

Uncle Clem reaches into his jacket pocket and pulls out an envelope. "Here's a letter stating that Stephen's to enlist as a bugler." He lays it on the desk and pushes it across to the captain. "It's written by Governor Morton. He knows of the family's situation."

Captain Northam opens the envelope and snaps the paper crisply to unfold it. He reads the note carefully and looks up at me. "You know Governor Morton?"

"Yes, Captain," I say. "The governor and I talked about the war in his living room just a while back."

Captain Northam folds the paper and hands it to me. He dips a pen into a bottle of ink and asks for my name.

"Stephen M. Gaston," I say.

Captain Northam writes my name in the ledger with "Bugler—Company K" beside my name. "Sign here," he says, spinning the book around. "You're Major Lilly's personal bugler. Welcome to the war, son."

CHAPTER THIRTEEN

Captain Northam hands me a slip of paper and explains I'm to get on the morning train to Indianapolis. "Give this ticket to the conductor. We send rosters to Major Lilly on a daily basis. He's in the capital, training men as we speak," he says. "You'll arrive the same day as he gets his new list of names."

Uncle Clem grabs the shoulders of my coat and pulls me close. He hugs me as if seeing me leave is the hardest thing he's done in his entire life. He's never hugged me before, so I know it's a show for the captain's benefit. He fishes in his pocket and hands me a dollar. "I can't stay and see you off in the morning, so use this to get a room for the night."

★★★

We walk to the livery, and I watch my uncle mount his horse. "Give the man a dollar for taking care of the horses," he says.

I take the same coin he gave me ten minutes earlier and hand it over to the man at the livery. Uncle Clem grabs the rein of my horse and heads toward Centerville without so much as a look back or a good-bye.

I collect my linen duffel bag and bugle case and head to the saloon. The cost of a soda water is a bargain in exchange for a few hours of warmth until it's time to sleep. There are a few dollars in my pocket, enough to get a room for the night, but I don't want to spend it on that. I need to save every penny I can to send home to Mother. Knowing I'm providing a place for her to live so she won't have to take charity from the poorhouse brings a wide smile to my face.

I don't want to take a chance on missing the morning train for Indianapolis, so just after dark, I walk to the train station. Few people are on the street at this time of evening, and the depot's empty. The trains have stopped running for the night. There's a place in the back, facing the tracks, where two wide walls come together to form a right angle. I sit on my blanket and lean against the wall.

I open my bag and eat a piece of salt pork, bread, and a slice of apple pie that Mother baked last night. After I finish eating, I lie down with my back to the wall and use my bag for a pillow. The blanket doesn't keep me warm enough, so I sit up, pull all the clothing out, and put on anything I can wear. Multiple layers plus the blanket do the trick. I finally drift off to sleep.

I have a horrible nightmare:

Sweat runs down my forehead and off the tip of my nose like it did on August afternoons at the livery. I swipe my face quickly with the sleeve of my shirt, only now, my white shirt has been replaced with a blue Union uniform. Water covers my bare feet. I'm standing in the middle of Paddy's Run, a gun in my hand. Lifeless forms, stacked like cordwood four-, five-, six-deep, cover the creek's banks. The war hasn't made its way north to Centerville, Indiana, has it?

Four men in Confederate uniforms carry limp bodies toward Crown Hill Cemetery. I stand perfectly still, exposed and unable to move, hoping they don't notice me. The soldiers go about their work, oblivious to a Yankee standing close enough to see the ranks on their coat sleeves. Why am I invisible to them? A cannon rings out from the west, causing the ground beneath my feet to rattle.

The blast wakes me from my dream. It takes several seconds, but the realization hits that I'm sleeping at the train station. The sky's a seamless black, and there are no sounds coming from the city streets. Swells of blood pound in my neck, and the throbbing in my wrists is like the constant beating on a bass drum. Short breaths, in and out, slow my heart rate to normal.

As soon as my eyes close the nightmare returns.

I raise my gun and point the barrel downstream. My eyes dart from bank to bank. My right forearm quivers and taps my rifle stock, making it sound like telegraph code.

The creek flows clear as windowpanes, but I can't feel the smooth rocks at the bottom of the stream, only the coolness across the tops of my feet. I walk downstream and end up past the cemetery and out of town in a shallow pool near Governor Morton's home. The pool sinks to waist deep at one end here before rippling out the west side of town.

More piles of men lay dead on the banks. Body fluids pour from their mouths and nostrils. Organs spill from wounds, and flies smother every cut like apple butter on bread. Blood cascades over dirt and rocks and mingles with creek water, turning it red as a cardinal's wing.

Mother stands stoic beside Uncle Clem beneath a barren oak tree. She's wearing a flowing black mourning dress with crinolines. A widow's cap rests snugly on her head. Light bounces from a piece of golden jewelry. It's a brooch with a quarter moon and stars and is clipped near the base of her throat.

Suddenly something catches Mother's eyes, and she points frantically to a body being carried to the cemetery. To my horror, I realize the next soldier to be buried is my brother, Robert. His eyes are open and blinking. He struggles to free himself but is unable. In desperation, he turns his head toward me and yells at the top of his lungs, "You have to save me, Stephen!"

Noise from a gathering crowd wakes me. Mothers, fathers, and girlfriends have come to say good-bye and wave handkerchiefs to loved ones. Some men mingle around the platform, shake hands, and tell one another they're from Rushville, Batesville, or Connersville. Watching them hug family and friends makes me wish I had said a proper good-bye to Mother. "I'm so proud of you," one father says as he shakes his son's hand.

I take off the extra clothes I wore for the night and pack them and my blanket into my bag. There are few open seats when I make my way down the aisle of the train. As I scout for an empty seat, I overhear one fella talking about how he got his first kiss from his sweetheart just before boarding the train. Those not talking about their sweethearts talk about how quickly the 9th Indiana will end the war.

I notice a shiny leather horn case in a compartment with one empty space nearby. "Is that seat taken?" I ask, pointing.

"Naw, help yourself," the man in the seat says as he turns my way. It's August Smith, a fellow bugler from the Centerville band. "What are you doing here?" he asks, jumping up to give me a hug.

"I knew you were joining, and I thought the Ninth needed a good bugler," I say with a laugh.

"Well, it's good to see you," August replies. "I can't believe you joined."

CHAPTER FOURTEEN

December 21, 1863

As we pull into the station, my stomach rumbles as much as the train. A shield of dull gray hangs above the city, and a foggy haze sits on everything. It looks like snow will fall from the sky at any moment, but the promise holds off. The smell of thick smoke and steam ambushes us as we step down from the train.

A man wearing a dark blue overcoat is waiting on the station's platform. His mustache is cut short to end above the corners of his lips. His chin and neck are shaven clean. Charcoal-colored hair hangs below the edges of his cap. He's thin and walks parallel to the train in measured, crisp steps, almost in a strut. He points through the smoke toward a double gate nestled into a two-story-high wall and yells, at no one in particular, "When you get inside the camp, go past the tents on the right. There's a platform nearby. Gather there."

As I pass, the man grabs my shirt collar. "Hold on, young man," he says, pulling me back to his side. "Kinda young-looking to fight a man's war, aren't you?" he asks.

Golden oak leaves sit on his shoulder straps. Major, I think. I wonder if he's Major Eli Lilly.

"Well ... actually ..." I catch my answer before it slips out. Robert wrote home of some boys, as young as twelve, trying to muster in the army. Many wrote the number eighteen on a piece of paper and tucked it into the heel of their boots. When enlistment officers asked, "Are you over eighteen?" young recruits could honestly say, "Yes, sir, it's a fact. I'm over eighteen and that's no lie."

I recognize I have paused too long and need to say something. "Save it," the major says. "I bet you're 'Over eighteen'! Right?"

"Yes, sir," August Smith answers for me. "We're over eighteen, and the Ninth is gonna help end this dadblamed war," he assures the major. "As soon as we're trained, the Ninth's gonna end this fight in double-quick time."

The major eyes me up and down, points his chin toward the gate, and says, "Get inside."

As we walk away, August looks back over his shoulder. "Pleasant fellow," he says. "Stephen, if you wait until you're eighteen, the war will be over."

Large wooden gates open to reveal a city within the city bustling with activity. Immediately off to the left of the entrance, a man is yelling. "You're going to be shot five times before you can get your powder in the barrel." He snatches the musket from a soldier and continues his rant. "You should be able to fire three rounds per minute. Whoever loads faster, you or Johnny Reb, determines who will live. Watch the steps as I go through them again."

The instructor reaches into a black container strapped to his waist and pulls out an object the size of his thumb. "Retrieve cartridge from box and tear the paper with your teeth. Pour the powder and minié ball in." He demonstrates.

"Ram the powder and ball into the barrel, and replace the ramrod."

He reaches into another container. "Prime the weapon with a percussion cap, and you're now ready to cock, aim, and fire."

Beyond the men learning to shoot, in a field large enough for all of Centerville to fit in, men ride horses. The riders all make their horses gallop on command then stop suddenly. They trot and walk in patterns.

With so many people, the training camp must have a larger population than most towns in Indiana.

August nudges my shoulder and points to a building opposite the main entrance. "I can hear my stomach growling. Maybe we can get something to eat there." Along the far wall, smoke pours from several chimneys attached to a long building. "It's gotta be the dining facility."

"The major said we're to gather around the platform," I remind him, pointing to a wooden stage.

"Don't worry. I'll be back in time," he says, heading in the direction of the mess hall.

A series of buildings that appear to be barracks run along the edge of two walls. Men, their hands planted in their armpits, dash in from the cold. White tents, too many to count, sit just yards from the barracks and stretch beyond, past what I can see.

CHAPTER FIFTEEN

Men stroll along, carrying bags and an occasional bugle case. All my worldly possessions are stored in one sack: the clothes I packed, a blanket, a copy of *David Copperfield*, ten pages of writing papers, envelopes, a pencil, stamps, a Bible, and my bugle.

A towheaded man sits under a walnut tree, polishing a bugle. He looks to be about my brother's age, maybe twenty. "Cold, huh?" I ask.

"Not bad," he replies.

"I'm from Centerville."

"Rushville," he replies.

"I'm Stephen Gaston. What's your name?"

"Henry."

"Just Henry?" I ask.

"Dorman," he adds.

"Are you a bugler?"

"Company K."

"Hey, me too," I say. Getting him to say more than a word or two is as tough as using pull-offs on a horseshoe. He wipes his horn with a cloth.

I sit and lean against the tree. "Excited?" I ask. "About going into battle and about seeing the elephant for the first time?"

"Naw," he says, shaking his head. He lowers his voice and leans closer to me. "I can't play it," he whispers.

"What do you mean you can't play it?"

Dorman shrugs.

"You mean you can't play very well."

He hands the bugle to me. "It sounds like a goose when I blow it."

"How'd you join as a musician?" I ask.

"I lied," he says. He tucks his lower lip between his teeth and clamps down. "I told 'em I could play, and they never asked to hear me blow a single note. I need work to feed my wife, Sarah, and my son. I saw they needed buglers, and I don't want to get shot. I figure this is the safest place to be in the army."

"Yeah," I agree. "Back with officers, sounding their orders."

A light breeze lifts a tuft of his thin hair, and he reminds me the world of Dutch.

"I'll teach you to play," I promise.

"Is it hard?"

"Naw, as long as you practice, you'll do fine. And make thirteen dollars a month as you learn," I say.

"I've got to send every penny home to the wife and new son. He's three months old."

"Yeah. I know what you mean. It's just me and my mother, so she needs every penny I can send her."

Taking Dorman's bugle and turning it over in my hand reveals it's covered with scratches and dents.

"I stole it from a cousin," he says quickly. "I figured if the recruitment officer saw I owned a horn, they'd believe I could play it."

"I bet it sounds beautiful. You'll pick it up fast," I assure him. "We won't head south for a while. There's lots of time to learn to play between now and then."

"I just hope we're safe with these," he says, gesturing to our bugles.

"Hey, fellows," August says, coming around the tree. "Did you know prisoners are being kept three blocks north of here at Camp Morton?"

"That close?" I ask.

"Yeah, three thousand prisoners from places like Lexington and Fort Donelson. I'd give anything to get a good look at 'em."

"Hold on," I interrupt. I can't believe what I'm hearing. Lexington is where Robert was killed. "Did you say prisoners from Lexington are three blocks away?"

"Yeah, Gaston. Clean out your ears."

A bugle sounds, and the recruits who were on the train with me rush to an open section of the field near the center of the camp. The major I had met earlier climbs the steps to a shoulder-high platform. He strides to the front edge and waits for silence.

"Men, my name is Major Eli Lilly of the United States Union Army. The two hundred of you who arrived today join eight hundred men already in camp to form the Ninth Indiana Cavalry. As of now, you are the eyes of the army. It's our job to keep commanders informed about enemy movements. That's not an easy assignment."

"We're up to it, Major!" August yells.

A whoop erupts from the crowd as men remove their hats and wave them in the air.

"We'll see," Major Lilly says. "It takes two years to properly train cavalrymen. From looking at you, it'll take three. Hell, the war may be over by then, and we want to get in there and do our part. I can tell that you're a sorry lot, but we are going to get this training done in four or five months. By early summer we'll head out of Indianapolis."

Five months? That seems so far away. Yet, at the same time, too soon.

"Where are my musicians?" Major Lilly asks.

Henry Dorman, August, and I raise our hands. Two other hands go up nearby.

Major Lilly points to a building off to his left. "Report to Private Alfred M. Thornburgh inside the building with the smokestacks. He's Indiana Ninth's chief bugler, and he's waiting for you there. You'll be under his care for the next few weeks. Buglers only, dismissed!" he shouts.

I gather my belongings and head to the far side of the camp with August and Henry.

★★★

Private Alfred M. Thornburgh, nearly as wide as he is tall, greets us in a well-heated room. He's so round that if he lost his balance at the top of a hill, he'd roll all the way to the bottom before stopping. "When I call your company, say your name so I'll know you're here," he instructs. "Company A?"

"Charles Evans, sir."

"I'm not a 'sir,' Evans," Private Thornburgh says. "Call me Chief. Who's the second bugler with Company A?"

"William Peacock, sir.... I mean ... William Peacock, Chief."

Thornburg glares at Peacock. "Company B?"

"John W. Sherill!" a man yells.

"August Smith."

★★★

I study the faces of the men around me and wonder how many will return home alive. William Peacock is strapping strong and looks like he could handle himself real well, even in hand-to-hand action. His shoulders are square, and his chin looks strong enough to be on a statue. Most of the men have full bushy beards. Although I'm tall, I feel naked without scruff on my face; I haven't shaved yet.

"Company K?"

Henry Dorman elbows me in the side.

"Who is the second bugler from Company K?" Chief yells.

"Stephen M. Gaston," I say, coming out of my daydream.

After calling roll, Thornburgh points to a cabinet off to the side. "If you brought your horn, use it. If not, get one from that cabinet."

Several men retrieve horns and return to the group. "Men, you have all the power in the army. You wake soldiers in the morning, tell them when to eat, how fast to march, when to drill, and how to drill. Bugles are a camp's timepiece...."

For the rest of Thornburgh's talk my mind drifts from bugling to Camp Morton and the prisoners there. I begin thinking of a reason to make my way to the prison and see those responsible for taking Robert's life in Kentucky. I want to look them in the eye and tell them what they did to my family. I want them to know that they are the reason I have to go off to war so Mother has a room to sleep in and food to eat.

CHAPTER SIXTEEN

December 22, 1863

Buglers from the same company are assigned to sleep in the same tent. Late the next afternoon, Dorman and I are settling into our two-man tent. I take a pair of documents from between the pages of *David Copperfield* and lay them side by side on the ground. Then I tap Dorman's leg and ask, "What do you think? Take a look at these."

He turns and crouches to study the letters, his eyes darting back and forth between the two pieces of paper. "What do you mean what do I think? They're two letters from the governor is what I think. What are you doing with them?"

"Do the signatures look the same to you?" I ask.

"Yeah, exactly the same. Why?"

I shake my head, afraid to tell him that I forged one of the documents this morning. The bogus letter states that at the governor's request I am to speak to a hometown prisoner who left Centerville to fight for the Confederacy. I hope it gets us into Camp Morton, but the less Dorman knows right now, the better. "Hurry up. It'll be dark in an hour," I plead.

"I'm almost done," he says while pushing a button through the last hole in his shirt. Where are we going anyways?"

"You'll see. Just hurry," I insist. "It's my rotation, so I have to be back in time to play taps."

Henry tucks his shirt into his pants.

"Stop frettin' with your gall-darn shirttail, Henry, and put on your coat. We're not going far."

We walk briskly out the gate, turn north, and cover the three blocks in silence. We approach a stern-looking man at a gate. A sign, in three-inch-high letters above the gate reads, CAMP MORTON.

"Let me do the talking," I say in a low voice.

A man with a dimpled chin raises his hand to stop us. The two gold stripes on the side of his arm represent the rank of corporal. "Where do you two think you're going in such a hurry?"

"Yes, good afternoon..." I begin. The words sound awkward, over-rehearsed. I may not have planned this out enough. "Governor Morton sent us to talk to ... talk to ... a prisoner. ... " My voice trails off. I reach in my pocket and pull out the forged piece of paper. "John Williams," I say, looking at the forgery. "Yes, that's who we need to see."

"Governor Morton sent the two of you to talk to one of the prisoners here?"

"Exactly," I say, handing the paper to the guard. I think of Uncle Clem and hope he has taught me how to lie well enough to get inside.

The guard scratches his dimple with his finger as he studies the paper. "The governor sent the two of you?"

I nod.

Henry stands beside me, wide-eyed.

The guard reviews the paper and turns it over in his hand to look at the back. "Why would the governor send you two to speak to Mr. Williams?"

I glance at Henry, who looks as lost as a goose in a snowstorm. His vacant stare tells me I'm on my own. "He sent us ... because Williams ... uhh ... the name on that paper, is a no-good Secesh." I spit on the ground.

"He's a copperhead," Henry chimes in, and spits on the same spot.

"Williams is from Centerville, where the governor, my

pard here, and I live," I say. Now Henry knows something is up, because he's from Rushville. I hate to drag him into the lie without him knowing, but there is no way I'm going into a prison camp alone. And I know he never would have come along if I had told him earlier. "Williams lived in Centerville and ended up fighting for the South down in Tennessee. The governor wants me to ask him something."

The guard raises both eyebrows. "Ask him what?"

"I am not at liberty to tell you that," I say. "I'm just doing what I'm told to do. What the governor asked me to find out is between Governor Morton, John Williams, my pard, and me."

There's a moment of silence as the guard looks down at the paper again. I reach over the edge. "That's the governor's signature right there," I say, tapping at the bottom.

"I know what the governor's signature looks like," the guard growls. "I've seen it hundreds of times." He shouts over his shoulder to a man talking to a lady near the street. "Sergeant Whitson!"

"And that's his signature," I say, tapping the paper again.

"The governor sent you?" the guard asks Henry, whose eyes are now the size of silver dollars.

"Ahhh, yes, sir. He sent me, indeed. I mean . . ." He looks

at me. "The governor, that is, sent the two of us. He sent the two of us to find, ahhh, Williams."

"Why did he send you?" the guard asks.

I have to bail Henry out. "I told you. Because I know John Williams. . . . Well . . . I know of him. He's a tad bit older than me, and we went to school together . . . well . . . at the same time. . . . Him being older than me, I don't really know him. Look, I don't have time to explain all this to you. It's right there on the paper, and it's an order from the governor for me to come here to find Williams and ask him one simple question. And it's almost dark," I insist.

"And you know Williams?" the guard asks Henry.

"Ahhhh, no, sir, I don't know him at all. Never laid eyes on him . . . ever," Henry answers.

"*I* kinda know Williams," I say, stressing the word "I." "*We* went to school together. Look, nobody likes him on account that he's a no-good copperhead." I spit on the ground. "The whole family's a bunch of copperheads." I spit again.

Henry shakes his head quickly. "No-good copperheads," he repeats, and spits, appearing a bit more confident, too.

"Actually, I know the governor better than I know Williams. Governor Morton invited me to his house back in

Centerville to give me a gift," I add for dramatic effect. "Lovely house he and Mrs. Lucinda have."

While the guard looks down to examine the paper, Henry taps me on the shoulder and points to a sergeant approaching.

"I'd hate to be in your boots if I don't see Williams and get his answer back to the governor before dark," I say in a rush.

The guard folds the paper, hands it back to me, and waves off the sergeant. "I've got it taken care of, Sarge."

"When you walk in, don't stop before crossing the deadline," he warns.

I look at Henry, then back to the guard. "Deadline?"

"There's a line on the ground twenty feet from the wall," he says. "You'll know it when you see it. Anytime somebody is between the wall and the deadline, the guards have authority to shoot. They may give a warning shot … but odds are they won't. It doesn't matter if you're a prisoner or Governor Morton himself—you're liable to wake up dead."

"Wake up dead. That's funny," I say to the guard. "I like that."

The guard does not react. "When I open the gate, walk quickly into the compound. Don't stop until you've crossed the deadline."

"Crossed the deadline," Henry repeats, nodding.

The guard walks back a few steps to the wooden gate. He raises the latch, and we walk into Camp Morton.

★★★

Once inside, we take twenty quick paces before stopping just past a white line on the ground.

"You never said we were going inside a prison camp," Henry says sternly.

"So, what are you 'fraid of?"

"Afraid of?" he says in disbelief. "Stephen, we're inside a prison."

The enclosure is surrounded by a plank wall as tall as a house. Nearby, a long line of crude buildings that look like they were built as sheds extends away from us. A small ravine, narrow enough to throw a rock across, slopes down and ends at a shallow stream. The slope rises on the other side to another row of buildings. The wooden structures and a few randomly placed tents keep us from seeing how far the prison goes beyond that.

Henry stares out at the sea of people. "We'll never find what's-his-name. There's got to be a couple thousand men in here."

"Don't worry, Henry," I say. "There is no John Williams."

"What do you mean?"

I shake my head. "There's no John Williams."

"Are you crazy? What about the paper you showed the guard?"

"It's a forgery. I made all that up."

"Did the governor sign the paper?"

"No. Governor Morton doesn't know we're here."

"How did his signature get on the paper?"

"He signed a book for me. A gift. I studied his hand. It's not exact, but close enough, I guess. It fooled you and the guard."

Henry stares at me and shakes his head slowly.

"What?" I ask.

"I can't tell when you're lying or telling the truth," he confesses. "What are we doing here, then?"

"Gotta see somebody."

"But not Williams," he says, catching on. "Who?"

I clench my fist and furrow my brow. "The men who killed my brother."

CHAPTER SEVENTEEN

Henry Dorman and I walk toward a group of five men gathered near the edge of the ravine. They're thin, dirty, disheveled, and inadequately dressed for a northern winter. They encircle a small fire, keeping their backs to anybody approaching. "Soldiers, I'm looking for men from the Army of Kentucky," I announce.

Without lifting his head, a tall man with sharp fingers motions toward the stream. He says in a frail voice, "Kentucky men are on the other side." The man wipes his mouth with the back of his hand.

The two of us make our way to the bottom of the ravine, weaving past groups of men clustered around fires, some with their palms out, catching elusive warmth. We step across a thin stream of filthy water and climb the other bank. We pass men sitting frozen like carved figurines. Their empty stares reveal their bodies are in Indianapolis, but their minds are elsewhere. Henry skims their faces and asks, "This is what we'll be fighting down South? They look near death."

"Dorman, I doubt they mustered in looking like this."

"My God, this is what prison did to them?" he asks.

Prisoners had constructed clotheslines at the top of the west bank and draped blankets across much of the lines. Just beyond the blankets, five wooden barracks resembling horse stables stand end to end.

"Which one we going in?" Henry asks.

"One's just as good as the next," I reply.

After opening the door, we step into almost total darkness. The air is thick with moisture. It smells like rotting cattle and manure. I gag so hard, I feel my stomach trying to come up into my throat. I hear Henry do the same. I use the collar of my coat to cover my nose from the stench and wait for my eyes to adjust.

Along each side wall, a row of beds stacked four bunks high reach from the ground to the eaves. The bottom bunks are inches off a bare earthen floor. Rags stuffed between planks of wood in the wall keep out some of the wind. Men press so close around an object in the middle of the room that it's hidden from view. A pipe leads from the center of the men to the roof. A stove.

If the meager fire warms the men standing by it, it does little to heat the ends of the building. Too many rags have fallen out, allowing the cold to sweep inside. It's as frigid where Henry and I stand as it is outside. A moan to the left draws our attention. Although dimly lit, the shape of men huddling under blankets in a bed catches our eyes.

"Look how they're lying together, trying to keep warm," Henry whispers. "There's five or six men under a couple of blankets."

I walk over to the men on the bunk. "Where you soldiers from?" I ask.

One man raises his head to see who's asking. "Alabama," he says.

I kneel down beside his head and see it's crusted with layers of filth and dirt. "I'm looking for soldiers from Kentucky," I say.

The man lifts one finger and points outside. "Tents," he says.

"The tall tents outside?" I ask.

He nods and lies back down.

★★★

Henry and I rush outside and shut the door behind us. It's a relief to be leaning against the outside wall, and we take deep breaths to clear our lungs of the stench.

"That was horrific," Henry says. "My eyes are watering."

"My uncle Clem's livery was cleaner," I tell him. "Even when it needed to be mucked, it smelled better than that."

I pull open the flap to the first tent we come to. Again, beds line both sides of the canvas walls, creating a pathway down the middle. There's barely enough room for two people to pass. I walk slowly down the aisle, looking from left to right. I pass each bed slowly, gazing at the men.

Many prisoners shiver beneath blankets, some violently. I lift my nose into the air and flare my nostrils. Henry tilts his head too. "What do you smell?" he asks, almost in a whisper.

"There's a sweet smell in the air," I say, remembering the overpowering smell of gardenias as Dad died.

"I don't smell anything sweet," he answers. "It's foul in here, too." Henry tilts his head down and pulls his coat over his nose.

"There's a sweet smell mingled in," I insist. "Concentrate. Can you smell it?"

Henry lifts his head and sniffs several times. "No. The only smells I'm getting make me want to vomit."

"I can tell by the scent, Henry," I tell him. "Death is here. Somebody's dying here, right now."

Henry hits me hard on the shoulder. "Stop it right now, Stephen. You're scaring me."

"No, it's true." I say.

"You're lying again."

"No, I'm not lying this time. When my father died of consumption, I smelled this exact smell. Nobody else in the room mentioned it then. But this is the same smell I noticed just as Dad passed."

I look at a man lying on a bed to my left, then bend over him, our faces inches apart. "You from Kentucky?" I ask.

The man doesn't open his eyes or raise his head. He nods slightly.

★★★

I stare at the man, nose to nose, unable to take my eyes off him. I wonder: *Was he the one who pulled the trigger?* Did he take Robert from us? Is he the one putting Mother through unbearable agony? I wait for hatred to come to the surface, like waiting for water to boil, but it doesn't. I want every ounce of my pain to turn to joy in seeing him suffer in squalor, thinking of him dying a slow painful death. I want it more than I've ever wanted anything in my life. But neither hatred nor joy appears, so I stand up.

"This has to be the worst way to die, a slow death like this," Henry whispers. "Can you imagine the pain? When I go, I want it to be fast."

I walk past Henry and lay my arm against a set of empty bunks. I lean my head against my arm and cry.

"What's wrong?" Henry asks.

"These boys killed Robert, and they are going to meet him again real soon. I thought I'd feel better about seeing them suffer. But I don't."

CHAPTER EIGHTEEN

January 21, 1864

Dearest Mother,

I'm sorry for leaving a note instead of speaking to you in person when I left, but good-byes are too difficult. With Dad and Robert gone, I feel I should make my way in the world. Uncle Clem took us in, so I don't worry about you having a place to live. That's comfort far more than I can express.

Several months ago I heard a lady say we must all have a reason for living. I know what she meant. We can't go on living like we are with Uncle Clem. I have found my reason for living, and it's to get us out from under his roof.

The truth is, I'm not in Ohio. I've joined the Union Cavalry as a bugler. The one time I mentioned mustering in, you asked, "Do you think Robert and your dad need your company in the graveyard?" I pray God agrees they do not, but that remains His decision. Perhaps I'll learn a trade along the way. I'm not proud of how I left, but what's done is done, and I can't take it back.

I thought I could send more money home, but things come up. I make a little extra from soldiers. Many of them never learned to read and write. A couple of them pay two cents a letter if I write home for them. It's easy spotting fellows writing home to girlfriends. They cover their letters and don't let anybody peek over their shoulders. I'll send what I can from my pay but will have expenses to meet. Don't expect much.

Time is different at training camp, Mother. When we drill, time creeps as slowly as a slug. The first thing we do in the morning is drill. When we finish that, we have a short time when we drill. Once our drilling is done, it's time to drill. When there is no drilling to be done, we drill some more. Sometimes, we drill between drillings.

We call the bugle instructor Chief because he's in charge of the rest of us. He rotates us through the calls while soldiers walk through the motions. We do the calls over and over so that one day they will be a part of us, like a leg or a hand.

"It should be natural. Like breathin'," Chief says. "You don't think about breathin', do you?" he yells at us.

I know most calls clean now and only have a hard time with a few of 'em. Chief picked me to play taps for the entire camp the first week I was here. When I play that song, everybody has to extinguish their lights and go to sleep. Guess I'm further along than most. One bugler couldn't play a note when he arrived, so he and I leave camp and go to a nearby cemetery for extra practice. Nobody there complains when he sounds bad.

When we play, Chief says to sing words in our head. It helps make sense of what we're playing.

We sound reveille at six every morning to wake the soldiers. The Chief taught us to sing in our heads:

You got to get up, you got to get up, You got to get up this morning.
You got to get up, you got to get up, Get up with the bugler's call.
The Major told the Captain, The Captain told the Sergeant, The Sergeant told the bugler, The bugler told us all.
You got to get up, you got to get up, You got to get up this morning.
You got to get up, you got to get up, Get up with the bugler's call.

We've been here for weeks and haven't trained with horses. We were told we won't get them for a long time. Not enough to go around. We head south in a couple months, with or without mounts.

I read David Copperfield *when I'm not plum tired. I see why President Lincoln likes it so much. It's not about America, but in a way it is. The powerful have control over the poor. I think of slaves as the poor people in* David Copperfield. *Southern slaves are slaves, not from flaws in their minds like some think, but because of unfairness toward them. Did you know some slaves speak French? You can't be dumb and do that, I don't think.*

Send my love to friends. Save a share for yourself,
Stephen

PART TWO

THE SOUTH

CHAPTER NINETEEN

Friday, September 23, 1864, 2:30 p.m.

When the officers declared we were ready, we boarded trains in Indianapolis and headed south. Three days later we arrived in Nashville, a large southern city firmly under Union control and heavily fortified. We cooled our heels there in May, June, and July. We fought a lot but not against Johnny Reb. Instead, we battled mosquitoes and the heat all summer. The air felt thick, and my uniform was constantly soaked with sweat. The only rebs we saw were on trains headed north to prison camps. While we waited, Henry Dorman's bugle playing improved, and our supply of horses trickled in. We didn't get enough for every company in the Indiana 9th, but several were completely covered.

Major Lilly let me pick my mount. I chose a nice smoky black gelding and named him Texas. His back is shoulder height and he leads with a strong, steady head. His short ears pivot fast as a wink. I'm sure he can hear a fly land on a log twenty feet away. And I swear I can read his eyes and know what he's thinking. His sleek muscles run from his knees up through his shoulders and along his neck.

Now it's September, and we've been assigned to guard the railroads in a southern Tennessee town called Pulaski. After lunch, some of the soldiers request a song. I ask, "Does anybody know the tune 'Can I Go, Dearest Mother?'"

Sergeant Joseph Survant, a soft-spoken fellow from my company says in a deep voice, "I do."

I begin the first few notes of the song, and soon his voice blends in sweet as sugar added to coffee:

> *I am young and slender, Mother, they would call me yet a boy, But I know the land I live in, and the blessings I enjoy;*
> *I am old enough, my mother, to be loyal, proud, and true*
> *To be faithful to my country I have ever learned from you.*

Men who were lying on their backs sit up and take notice.

> *But the faithful must not falter, and shall I be wanting? No!*

Bid me go, my dearest mother! Tell me, Mother, can I go?

Out of the corner of my eye I catch William Peacock lowering his head between his knees and wiping his eyes with his sleeves. I don't look back at him again because if I do, I won't be able to finish the song. It's not my playing that's reaching his heart; it's the words and Sergeant's beautiful voice. I look up at the sky and at the trees and think of the next notes I have to play. Major Lilly's standing beneath one of the trees, watching the men listening to the tune.

After the song, Henry taps me on the knee and points. Major Lilly's walking toward us, purpose in his stride. He isn't coming for pleasantries. We stand as he approaches.

"Sir," we say together.

"Dorman, call assembly in fifteen minutes...," he begins. "General Starkweather has ordered some of us to head south this evening. Pack your gear; we may not be back for a long time. We ride at dusk."

"Sir, you said, 'Dorman, call assembly.' Did you mean to say Gaston?" Dorman asks.

"No, I said what I meant. I want you to do it. I rely enough on Private Gaston, and you're sounding better on that piece of tin every day."

"Thank you, Major," he says, smiling.

"Who's going, sir?" I ask.

"Only mounts from the Ninth and Tenth," he answers. "We're headed to the Elk River Bridge on the Alabama-Tennessee line."

"Alabama?" I say joyfully. I don't mean for excitement to spill into my words, but at the thought of getting closer to a fight, it bubbles out.

"Alabama," Major Lilly repeats. "Forrest is wreaking havoc on the rails in northern Alabama. We need those rails to move troops and supplies. It's our assignment to protect them."

We'd heard reports of General Forrest's exploits ever since we got to Nashville in May. He entered the war as a lowly private. He captured a Union battery at Fort Donelson and fought at Shiloh. By the summer of '62 he was a general. Moving south increases our chances of seeing him, and, maybe, capturing him will help end the war.

As the major walks away I call after him, "Sir, do you think he's in the area?"

"General Forrest?" Major Lilly asks.

"Nathan Bedford Forrest," I say.

Major Lilly walks back to us. "When Colonel Spalding came into camp on Tuesday, he brought five prisoners with him."

"Forrest's men?"

"Exactly. Recent reports from spies put him in Alabama. Last week he struck a railroad four miles south of Athens. The telegraphs went dead between there and a railroad bridge called Sulphur Branch Trestle. Reports say his brother, Colonel Jesse Forrest, is around too. So my best guess is yes, he's close. We're taking the five hundred men with mounts. The other seventeen hundred stay here. Dorman, blow assembly in fifteen minutes."

CHAPTER TWENTY

Major Lilly leaves, and I turn to Henry and William Peacock. "You know what that means, don't you?"

"No, what?"

"If only the mounted troops are going, they expect action. We'll be moving fast. No infantry to slow us down."

"You're way too excited about all this," Henry says. He tucks his lower lip between his teeth and bites gently.

"What are you worried about?" Peacock asks.

"What do you mean?"

"Henry, I've been your tent mate since we enlisted," I say. "You only bite your lip when you're fretting over something."

"Like learning to play the bugle," Peacock says. "It took you a long while to catch on. You worried they were going to reassign you, and you nearly chewed your lip off the entire time. Right?"

He nods.

"And now the major's requesting that you call assembly," Peacock says, putting his arm around Henry's neck. "You learned all those calls and got worked up for nothing. This may be our best chance yet to finally see the elephant. We've been through Indiana, Kentucky, and Tennessee and haven't as much as shot at one dadblamed reb."

Henry pushes his hair back across his ears and speaks in a hushed voice. "I'll be honest, fellas. I don't care to see any fighting." He looks around to see who's in earshot. "I know we trained hard and all three of us bugle real good, but I don't mind telling you ... I'm scared." There's a quaver in his voice I've not heard before.

"There's nothin' to be afraid of," I assure him. "We've trained for this, and we have the best soldiers in the US Army." I pat the side of Henry's arm. "Major Lilly's the best there is. We'll be fine." I think better and correct myself. "You'll be fine."

"I'm all my wife's got left. My son hadn't taken his first step when I left. If something happens to me ... " Henry's voice breaks off.

"I lost four brothers to the war, pard," Peacock says.

"Four?" I ask.

"Mom and Dad buried four. They didn't want me leaving." Henry and I look at him, shocked.

Henry drops his head and clears his throat. "If something happens ... to me ... will one of you get word to my wife?"

I nod.

"Tell her I said, 'I love you to the moon and back.' If you tell her that, she'll know I said it. She'll know it for sure."

"Why you talking crazy?" Peacock says. "Everything's going to be fine."

"I don't know which would be worse, dying in battle quickly or a slow death in a prison. Stephen, you saw how those fellows looked in that prison we snuck into in Indianapolis. I can't do that. I can't go to prison."

Henry shakes his head and doesn't say another word. He stops blinking and stares toward the base of a tree. His face has the same look that Mom's face had when she stood on the porch, watching black clouds head toward Centerville. *How bad is this storm going to be? Will it grow into a tornado and rip everything into a pile of rubble or peter out and just leave a good soaking?*

The three of us finish our coffee in silence. Henry does a

fine job sounding assembly, and as we pack to leave, I think of what he said. "I love you to the moon and back." My load seems heavier than it did yesterday.

A quarter moon provides little light as we ride. Often we travel near open meadows. Just as often, the trail ducks into forests of old growth. Under trees, it's barely possible to see past the horse's mane. My eyes dart from side to side, looking for Forrest's picket lines. Once, in a clearing, I see Henry glancing toward the sky for several seconds.

"Whatcha looking at?" I ask.

"Sarah and I promised to look at the moon as often as we could while I'm away," he says. "It's our way of connecting with each other."

"I like that," I say. I don't know what else to tell him to put his mind at ease.

"It's like, when we are both looking at the same thing at the same time, we feel connected," Henry looks at me. "Don't laugh. I know it doesn't make any sense."

"No, no, no . . . ," I insist. "I think it's a nice way to stay in touch, to stay connected. How do you know when your wife's looking at the moon?"

"I don't. But I pretend she's looking every time I'm looking, and I worry less. It makes me feel good." Henry smiles and glances up at the moon again.

"I bet she's looking right now," I say.

"Ya think so?"

"Yeah, that's exactly what I think. Sarah's looking at the moon right now and thinking of you. You know, my mama always told me, 'Don't worry about trouble till trouble comes.'"

It's good to hear Henry laugh. "Yeah, I guess she's right."

CHAPTER TWENTY-ONE

The hooves clattering on the ground cause my mind to drift back to Centerville. I wonder how many horseshoes I've replaced on horses pulling wagons west. How many nails did I pound into hooves? I want to wrap Mother up in a blanket, set her on a wagon, and ride to Kansas or Texas, far away from Uncle Clem.

At midnight, a fog creeps in and shrouds what light is coming from the quarter moon. Major Lilly orders us to slow our gait. The railroad remains to our left as we make our way toward the Elk River. A water station appears, and we're ordered to stop and rest awhile.

I dismount and reach for Major Lilly's reins. He doesn't give them to me. "Sergeant Survant, take our horses and give them some water," he orders, and climbs down. After the horses are pulled away he asks, "How are you doing, son?"

I'm taken aback. Major Lilly has never called me "son" before. "Fine, sir. I'm doing fine," I say.

"That's a nice horse you have there," he says.

"Thank you, Major. His name is Texas."

"He's a beaut," he says. "Are you scared, Stephen?" he asks.

"No, sir," I answer. "Not really."

"Not at all? Not even a little bit?"

I clear my throat. "Well, maybe some, I guess."

Major Lilly laughs. "Smart man," he says. "Back in Pulaski, when I told you that we were heading out, you seemed giddy."

"Somewhat," I confess.

"Only a fool goes into battle unafraid, son."

I don't know if he can see in the dim light, but I nod nonetheless. "I heard Governor Morton say that once, sir."

"Part of Forrest's strategy is to disrupt the movement of supplies along the railroads. I think there's a ninety percent chance we'll meet the gentleman real soon," he says. "We'll need you more than ever when that time comes."

"You will, sir?" I ask.

"*We* will," he says again. "It's your job to raise the spirits of our men in battle. When I came to tell you we were leaving Pulaski, I waited for you to finish the song you were playing for the men."

"The song was 'Can I Go, Dearest Mother?'" I say.

"Yes. I didn't get to be a major without noticing important details, Stephen. The men had tears in their eyes."

"I didn't mean to upset the men."

"They weren't sad, Stephen. You reminded them of why we're here. Don't underestimate your contribution to the regiment," he says. "Governor Morton told me about you. 'The boy's special,' were his exact words. I saw that last night. Your horn connects with these men."

"Yes, sir," I say. "I understand."

"I'm not sure you do," he says. "I didn't hire you to blow a horn. I can train a goose to do that. Your style lifts their spirits and gives the men confidence more than any speech I can make." I can't quite see the major's face, but his tone tells me he's a bit concerned, too. "Do your job well," he says. "The men need you. You are a valuable part of this unit." With a nod, he says, "Dismissed, son."

"Yes, sir," I say.

★★★

The sun burns off the fog by midmorning. The closer we get to the Elk River, the more tree stumps we see. Obviously, the trees have been used in the construction and repair of the bridge and blockhouses over the river. We arrive at Elk River at noon. The camp's commander informs Major Lilly that we are a little over a mile away from the Alabama line.

"Union troops have captured the bridge called Sulphur Branch Trestle, a few miles into Alabama. They are in need of help," he says. "We're in the middle of a Confederate hotbed, and we need to hold that bridge. I'm ordering you to take two hundred of your men there," he says. "Rest an hour or so and head out when you feel the horses are ready."

★★★

Riding through northern Alabama is like riding on an unmade bed: lots of flat places, but wrinkled here and there with shallow valleys and short, steep hills. We ride a few miles into Alabama and through a place called Elkmont. Just south of town we get a view of Sulphur Branch Trestle, and I can see its importance. The massive structure connects two hills and is long enough to support seven flatcars at one time. One slip from the center of the trestle means a fall the height of a full-grown oak tree. Wooden blockhouses sit beside either end of the trestle. An earthworks fort sits at the top of the southern hill close to the tracks.

Major Lilly leads us down a steep slope, and we ride to the base of the hill at the far end of the bridge. "Stephen, once we walk up this hill into the fort, you and Henry stay near me," he orders. "I want you within earshot at all times." We pool our horses in the ravine and scale the hill on foot to the fort. This embankment is the first line of defense and is too steep for horses to climb.

A rifle pit, deep enough for a man to stand in, rings the outside walls of the fort and provides the second line of protection. We enter the fort through two wooden doors wide enough for one man to pass each way. Two blockhouses sit inside the fort.

A man with muttonchops walks quickly to us and salutes. "Colonel Minnis," he says. He blinks rapidly as Major Lilly introduces us. The colonel waves his hands excitedly and hurries us over to a pit in the ground. "Here's our magazine. I'm afraid it's pitifully stocked with ammunition for a couple hundred men. There are only two frame buildings inside." He points to one. "That one is set up as a hospital, and the other is a command center."

The fort is much smaller than I expected. I am astonished by its lack of size.

"Over here," Colonel Minnis says, walking quickly to a small window on the western part of the fort. "This side was built close enough to the tracks that the cross timbers can be touched by men in the rifle pit. Just beyond the tracks, the hill falls away to a field of dried cornstalks."

Major Lilly asks, "Can troop advancements be seen coming through the field?"

"Certainly," the colonel replies. "That's not a concern at all. But over there," he says, pointing to the opposite side of the fort, "is another story. A deep, narrow ravine to the east creates a natural boundary preventing a *mounted attack*. However, that ground rises quickly to a hilltop higher than this fort." Colonel Minnis points to trees outside the fort. "The trees you see there are on the far hilltop, less than sixty yards away."

Major Lilly shakes his head. "Perfect for a Confederate artillery strike. The possibility of being attacked from that side is one hundred percent."

"Exactly."

I turn to Henry and speak low enough that he alone can hear. "I can't believe we stayed three months in Nashville, the most fortified town in the South, to end up at Sulphur Branch Trestle, Alabama, with no protection at all."

Henry nudges me on the arm and points to the eastern hillside. "We're like ducks sitting on a pond, waiting to be shot," he says.

I nod and Henry bites his lip.

CHAPTER TWENTY-TWO

"Your two hundred men bring our total to one thousand," Colonel Minnis says.

Major Lilly shakes his head in disbelief. "Even with those numbers, two twelve-pound howitzers are not enough to defend an attack from the east." His voice is raised, clipped with anger. He points toward the ridge. "How far away are those trees, Stephen?" he asks.

"Sixty yards, seventy at the most," I guess.

"And how far do howitzers shoot?"

"Up to one thousand yards, sir," I answer.

"What's the problem with that?"

I glance at the top of the hill—the answer is easy. "It's like stirring a cup of coffee with a shovel," I say. "Our cannons are too large of a weapon to protect the fort from the nearest and most obvious threat, that hilltop."

Major Lilly nods. "He's fourteen and sees the problem. We don't have the right tool for the job, and the fort is built in the wrong place. Why aren't our men on that hill?" he asks.

"There's no protection up there. It would be putting my men up there with their backs to a cliff."

"Well, what good are howitzers when the enemy is looking down at you from less than one hundred yards away?"

The colonel throws his hands into the air. "I agree, but it's all we've got. And we only have sixty rounds per howitzer."

Major Lilly squints like he's staring into the sun. "One hundred twenty rounds?" he asks. "My God, can it get any worse?"

The officers stand and stare at each other. Major Lilly massages both temples with his fingers. "I say we turn the western howitzer to face east. If we get hot fire from that hilltop, it's going to be hard to stop. But maybe we can scare them to death."

Colonel Minnis nods. "An advance from the west can be handled with guns. We have the upper ground there," he says.

"I have another concern," Major Lilly says.

"What's that?"

"Who's leading the Negro troops?"

"Colonel William Lathrop. They're the One Hundred Eleventh Negro troops, and he has several hundred men."

"We don't want another Fort Pillow on our hands."

"What do you mean?"

"Forrest is in the area, right?"

"Correct."

"Word is he took Fort Pillow's white soldiers as prisoners but lined the Negro troops up and shot them like rabid dogs."

The idea makes my stomach lurch, and my chest feels like it's being squeezed in a vice. "We can't let that happen," I mutter to Henry. It's hard for me to catch my breath.

"We'll worry about that if the time comes," Colonel Minnis says. "Forrest overran Athens, five miles south of here earlier this week. He's picking off small forts one by one like he's going down a row of corn."

It's decided that Major Lilly will take fifty men and follow the railroad south toward Athens to have a look. Just before sunset I sound the boots and saddles call, and we mount. We leave the corral with a squad and eight additional men who have been at the fort for several weeks and know the area. We ride quietly until we face a small rise in the flat terrain.

"That's called Hay's Mill," a private says.

Major Lilly stops the line and orders the private and Sergeant Survant to ride ahead. Near the top of the rise, they stand high in their stirrups. Sergeant Survant turns and motions for the rest of us to advance. Far ahead, we see small pockets of flames, too numerous to count. They span a wide swath of land.

"My God," Major Lilly says in a low tone. "We've found the rebels."

"How many?" somebody asks.

Major Lilly tugs on his mustache. "Several thousand, I'd say."

We sit in silence, scanning the orange horizon. "Mother calls that color of sky Indiana sunset," I tell the major.

"It's not the sun painting that orange wash along the bottoms of the clouds. It's fire," he says.

"Can small fires cause the clouds to glow like that?"

"No." Major Lilly shakes his head. "Campfires, even that many, won't reflect that high. My guess is Athens is burning."

"Where are the rebel picket lines?" I ask.

"They're not worried about us," Major Lilly says. "Not now."

Tree branches snap, and suddenly pops ring out from the

direction of the fires. But a safe distance ahead. It's the first time I've been fired at.

"There's your answer, Gaston," Sergeant Survant says.

"Have you ever been fired at, sir?" I ask the major.

"Many times," he says slowly.

Knowing we are totally outnumbered and sitting ducks in the fort makes my face feel flushed. With a battle looming, I no longer want to see the elephant when it attacks in full force. "Why would they shoot from that far away?" I ask.

"Someone wants us to know they see us. They know we won't attack. There's too many of them. Let's head back before they decide to get close enough to do harm," Major Lilly says.

We ride back to the fort, store the horses in the ravine, and climb the hillside. It's nine p.m.

★★★

"How will the Negro troops perform if fighting turns thick?" Major Lilly asks Colonel Lathrop when we return.

The colonel twists his head to the left as if he's hard of hearing. "I don't understand. What do you mean, *How will the Negro troops perform?*"

Major Lilly's struck a nerve, but he keeps pressing. "I estimate over two thousand rebels perhaps three miles south of here. We'll need every able-bodied man to defend the fort and trestle. What is your level of confidence that your men will perform when the fighting starts?"

"Major, their lives are on the line, more so than yours or mine. Every man under my command has trained like any other Union soldier. Their dark skin doesn't mean they'll perform any differently than your men."

Major Lilly smiles and nods. "That's what I wanted to hear, sir," he says. "I'm sure we'll all make Forrest's acquaintance sooner than later."

★★★

Twenty minutes pass, and Colonel Lathrop requests Major Lilly to join him along the western wall, where the Negro troops are stationed. "From that vantage, Forrest's sharp-shooter can pick us off one at a time," he says.

Major Lilly agrees. "That's going to be problematic. The only cover for your men is the hospital. When it starts—and it will—make sure your men stay out of the line of sniper fire from the hill. Don't worry about advancement from the cornfield."

Major Lilly turns to me. "Stephen, tell the Ninth to assist the Eleventh for the rest of the night. Build an earthworks anywhere on this side of the fort that can be seen from the hill. Logs, thick branches, large rocks, anything you can get your hands on need to be here for them."

★★★

Henry Dorman and I carry rocks from the creek and lay them to create a crude wall extending from the corner of the hospital. William Peacock and a fellow nearly seven feet tall make several trips with us. The two of them are strong as bears and carry the largest boulders. I hear others call the taller fellow Big Tennessee. After several trips we collapse for a rest. Henry stares at the half-moon, and I watch his lips move slowly.

I look up at the moon as well. "Maw, I love you to the moon and back," I say loud enough for Henry to hear.

CHAPTER TWENTY-THREE

Sunday, September 25, 1864, 12:01 a.m.

Henry Dorman, Big Tennessee, and I are sitting, our backs against the southern wall, when, without warning, a cannon shot sails from the eastern hilltop, over the fort, and lands in the cornfield to our west. The explosion is close enough to make lanterns rattle against the fort's walls. Soldiers who had fallen asleep fumble for their guns and peer out from their stations into the darkness.

"That shot didn't miss the fort by much!" somebody yells from the eastern wall. "Recalculation will bring it closer."

Colonel Lathrop runs from the tiny building used as the command center. "What do you see?" he asks Major Lilly.

"Nothing. It's hard to see 'em with darkness and trees giving them cover."

"How could they miss the fort?" I ask.

"They didn't miss. It's a warning shot."

I clench a gun with one hand and my bugle with the other and stare into purple darkness, waiting. Each minute seems like an hour. Everybody sits in silent anticipation for a second shot.

After a long wait, somebody says in a loud whisper, "What's going on?"

"They want us to know they've arrived," Colonel Lathrop says. "They're playing with us like a cat plays with a mouse. Remember, we have forty rounds per man, so make every shot count."

My hope sinks. We're fish in a barrel, low on ammunition, and outmanned by several thousand.

★★★

Through the wee hours of the morning we sit clutching our guns and wait. Just before dawn, Colonel Minnis decides a picket needs to slip out of the fort to the west and into the cornfield. "Scout an escape to the west," I hear him tell the squad of eight. "I'm sure Forrest has moved troops around to the north and is now in charge of the railroad between us and the Tennessee line. So that route is out of the question."

I turn to Henry Dorman. "Forrest has plenty of troop strength. The idea that he might have left us an escape route is wishful thinking. He would be an idiot to leave the west flank unguarded."

★★★

Fifteen minutes later, as dawn breaks, gunfire erupts from the far side of the cornfield. "They've gotten into a skirmish," Major Lilly says. "They'll be headed back our way. Forrest has us covered on all sides."

I can't see the cornfield, but the gunfire grows louder. There's enough light to see men at the western wall in ready position, muzzles aimed through thin slits between planks and bricks. A cool breeze brings a waft of gunpowder mixed with dried cornstalks across the field. It floats up the hill and over the fort's walls. So the elephant is getting closer, and this is what it smells like.

★★★

Full daylight arrives slowly. Sergeant Survant calls for Colonel Lathrop to come to the northeastern wall and look out a tiny window called the embrasure. To protect the cannon and men, only the barrel sticks out the embrasure. When the colonel reaches the spot, two men pick up the handspike, while four others roll the cannon back until its barrel is fully inside the fort. One private points to the top of the hill across the ravine.

Colonel Lathrop removes his hat and sticks his head through the opening. He turns and yells toward the center of the fort. "Colonel Minnis, two ten-pound Parrott guns on the eastern hill!"

"Troop movement approaching from the south!" William Peacock yells from the wall near where Henry and I are crouched, our backs against the fort.

Private Dorman grabs his gun and nuzzles against the fort. "I'm scared, Stephen," he whispers.

"That's okay, pard. You're not alone. Everybody is."

Colonel Lathrop walks away from the cannon and toward Colonel Minnis to discuss the situation. At exactly the same time, a shell sails over the eastern wall and strikes the ground inside the fort. Timbers, bricks, and earth fly into the air and rain down upon soldiers. The explosion is so powerful, debris reaches my area. I have to turn toward the ground and cover my head with my arms. When rocks stop falling, I can see that a jagged hole, large enough for a pair of horses to run through, has appeared in the northern wall. There are five, maybe six, men lying on the ground, motionless.

Uninjured men nearer the explosion dive closer to the eastern side of the fort to use the wall for protection. One man scampers behind the wall of the hospital. Another hops to safety, dragging what appears to be a useless, mangled foot behind him, like a sack of horse feed.

A soldier lies on the ground, writhing silently in pain. I throw down my gun and bugle and rush to help him. Blood trickles from his left ear and he snorts red bubbles out both nostrils. It's Colonel Lathrop. "Nurse!" I yell. Several Negro soldiers sprint to help drag him into the hospital. He's conscious, but barely.

Colonel Lathrop grabs the sleeve of a black soldier and pleads, "Don't surrender the fort." As he utters his last words, Colonel Lathrop's hands and arms go limp, and the smells of gunpowder, dirt, and gardenias swirl through the air.

I hurry out the hospital door and back to the southern wall. "Was that the colonel?" Henry asks.

"Yeah," I say.

"How is he, Stephen?" Peacock yells over to me.

I shake my head. "He's gone. I was holding him when he died."

"I'm sorry," Henry whispers.

Henry begins rocking back and forth, clutching his bugle. "We don't stand a chance against cannons firing down on us from higher ground."

"I know," I say. "It's one thing to be brave in a fair fight, but it's lunacy to fight a useless battle."

"No. And they won't storm the fort with infantry," Henry says. "They'll use big guns to do as much damage as they can from afar. Wear us down like boot heels."

★★★

I hear the squad in the cornfield retreating in full gallop back toward the fort. Because of the huge gap in the wall, I can hear when they race under the trestle and to the corral.

"They're safer in the cornfield," Henry says. A minute later they're running back inside the fort.

"Caleb Rule!" Colonel Minnis yells. "Take nine men back down into that ravine and guard those horses," he orders. The soldier called Caleb, a farrier from Tennessee, hastily gathers a team of men. They crouch low along the eastern wall and leave. They're gone only minutes when a cannon shell, fired from the north, strikes the ground near the horses. Caleb's squad reappears almost instantly at the hole of the fort.

As soon as they are inside the fort, tufts of sod kick up around their feet. Minié balls, fired from trees on the eastern hillside, strike one of the men and he falls like timber. Other shots kick up pieces of ground as the men run for cover. Caleb makes a zigzagged path until he's put the hospital between him and the snipers on the hillside. A few men dive toward the safety of the eastern wall.

Caleb peeks out from behind the hospital, using it as a shield from the snipers. He looks our way, steps back several feet, leans forward, and sprints from behind the hospital toward us. Two shots hit the ground, sending a spray of dirt into the air just behind his heels.

A Negro soldier hurries from his position near the western wall to behind the hospital. He peeks around the corner, kneels, and loads his gun. The building provides perfect cover. After waiting for what seems like forever, he pulls the trigger. In the quick silence following the shot, I hear a splat from the hillside followed by the breaking of large tree limbs as a body falls from a tree and tumbles through dried leaves down the hillside.

Caleb's out of breath but hasn't lost his sense of humor. "Sharpshooters ... in ... trees at the top of that ravine," he says, and laughs. He stands up and cups his hands around his mouth. "We got sharpshooters, too!" he yells up into the trees. A shot is fired, and he dives for the ground. When he looks up, he says, "What's that blood on Henry's chest? Was he hit?"

CHAPTER TWENTY-FOUR

I look over my right shoulder. Henry's sitting, his back against the wall, cradling his bugle with both arms, rocking back and forth as if in a trance. I hear soft, muffled moans, and he's biting his lip so hard, his front teeth have sliced all the way through. Blood's running down his chin and pooling onto his shirt.

I slap Henry on his shoulder. "Stop biting your lip!" I yell.

He stops rocking, but his stare is fixed somewhere distant. "Stephen, I ain't going to prison," he says. "I'd rather die here and get it over with fast."

But I know Henry's wrong. I pray, for both our sakes, a Confederate bugler sounds the call requesting our surrender. At least we have a chance to survive a prison stay, but zero odds if we continue fighting. The call for surrender doesn't come.

A speck of sun finally appears in the eastern sky, and another man limps in from the cornfield. He's favoring his right leg, where his britches have a gash the size of my palm. The pant leg below that spot is soaked in crimson red. I watch him grab a piece of splintered wood dangling from the wall of the fort. The plank comes loose in his hand, and he falls like a quail shot to the ground. He pulls himself up, uses the plank as a crutch, and starts toward the hospital. He hobbles to the building, but, as he reaches the door, a shell whizzes past his head. The building looks like a snowdrift hit by a locomotive engine. Debris flies in every direction. Nobody inside can still be alive. Timbers, bedding, and surgical equipment rain down over the fort.

The ground feels alive, breathing and beating. I don't see the Negro sniper who used the hospital as a shield. He must be buried beneath the building's rubble.

I turn to the wall and peer through an opening barely wide enough for the barrel of my gun to fit. I see soldiers move from tree to tree, but they are too far away to take a shot. Moisture runs down my thigh. I fear I've been hit by a bullet or a plank from the hospital. I look down. Thank God, it's not blood. I've only wet myself.

The occasional shot fired from our rifle pit stops the

progress from the south, but we all know they won't advance much closer from that direction. They are not there to attack the fort. They're there to prevent us from escaping. Attacks grow more intense from the north and east as the day goes on. Time crawls, and the ground never stops shaking. Not a minute passes that somebody doesn't scream out in agony or yell to God for mercy.

By nine p.m., snipers from the hill have driven off all the Negro soldiers from the western wall, and they're now dispersed among all the troops ringing the inside of the rest of the fort. One fellow squeezes between Henry and me.

A shell explodes near Colonel Minnis, and he falls to the ground. The hospital's a wasted heap of smoking rubble, so soldiers carry the colonel to the underground magazine, where munitions are stored.

Major Cunningham takes command and hurries toward Major Lilly. He's a few feet from us when a minié ball shoots through his back and comes out of his chest.

Major Lilly takes command and, through the roar of explosions, yells at me, "Stephen Gaston, sound cease-fire!"

I bring my bugle to my lips, stand, and point the barrel toward the eastern hillside. I sing the words in my head as

I play the notes as loudly as I've ever played before, "C-ease Fire. C-ease Fire. C-ease Fire."

Our men stop firing, and soon, so do the rebels.

"Major Lilly," somebody calls. "We are close to running out of munitions. We have a pile of Smithfields, but they're too large of a carbine to use."

Major Lilly surveys the destruction to the interior of the fort. Gaping holes sprinkle the western and northern walls. The hospital's gone. Major Lilly thinks for a minute, then stands. "The lead is soft enough to pare. Whittle the Smithfields down to fit." He sounds angry. "If that's all we have to use, we'll have to use them."

Can't he see the situation is hopeless? He's said so from the moment we arrived at the trestle.

"Men, hold your fire until they're close to the fort. Then make every shot count."

The rebs must have thought they had waited long enough for a sign of truce from us, because an explosion near the center of the fort sprays dirt over every part of me. The shell explodes with so much force, it blows the bugle plum out of my hand. A golden glint of metal flies up and away from me.

I spit dirt for several seconds and feel that something has me pinned to the ground. At first I think it's a log from the redoubt. But then, whatever it is, slowly moves on its own. It's not made of wood at all. It's the giant fellow called Big Tennessee.

"Keep your heads down, boys," Big Tennessee says to Henry and me. "It's going to get real bad now."

I'm still confused and dazed from the explosion as Big Tennessee drags me closer to the eastern part of the fort. "Stay close to the wall so the snipers can't pick you off," he says.

Henry looks at me and stands up. "Do you remember when we snuck into the prison in Indianapolis and saw those men at death's door?" he asks.

"Yeah," I say, half dazed.

"I can't do it, Stephen," he says. "I'm not going to die a slow death in prison."

Before I understand what Henry's doing, he's standing and facing the center of the fort. He takes two steps into the open line of firing. Big Tennessee tugs his arm to pull him back to safety, but Henry yanks loose and looks back at me. "Stephen, remember, I love my wife to the moon and back," he says calmly, and walks farther into the open. He stops, bends over, and retrieves a shiny piece of metal from the dirt. It's my horn. As soon as it's in his hands, a shell explodes just beyond his feet. I duck, but not before seeing him tossed ten feet into the air. The force throws him against the wall of the fort. Bricks come loose and fall on top of him.

I rush over. He's facedown. I pull jagged bricks off his back. Blood pumps from his neck like water from a spring. "Henry! Henry!" I yell. I reach for his shoulder to turn him over and notice he's still clutching my horn in his hand.

"Don't!" Big Tennessee shouts at me, and reaches for my shirttail. I pull away so hard, my shirt rips in his hand.

"Stephen, don't move his body!" he screams at me. "He's gone."

Big Tennessee is right. I should have listened to him. I never should have turned Henry over.

CHAPTER TWENTY-FIVE

Sunday, September 25, 1864

At eleven a.m. the elephant rests. All sense of time stops. Soldiers hug their guns and look around. I have not been ordered to sound retreat, so this is just a break in the fighting. The rebs are giving us another chance to think about surrender. For the first time, I hear men crying without shame. Moans echo from every corner of the fort. The one nurse, lucky enough to be out of the hospital when it exploded, goes from body to body, doing what he can. Red mud clings to his boots like spurs. Soldiers stare at friends lying near the center of the fort, frozen, unwilling to venture into the open to aid comrades in their last minutes of life.

The ground's a plowed field of guts, bones, and bloody mud.

Through the cries and sobs, an unusual sound develops. Major Lilly raises his hands, signaling for silence.

Ever so faintly, we hear why the rebs have stopped firing. From the north, perhaps a mile away, we detect the muffled sounds of firing. An engagement. Cheers ring out from several men in the fort. Reinforcements from Pulaski have arrived. Major Lilly manages a slight smile.

Perhaps this means the onslaught on Sulphur Branch Trestle will end soon.

Over the next hour, the sounds of gunfire from Forrest's troops positioned to the north grow fainter and fainter until they disappear altogether.

"They're being driven back," says Big Tennessee.

★★★

At noon, a Confederate bugle sounds cease-fire from the area of the trestle. Major Lilly goes to the north wall and looks out. A Confederate soldier, standing in the middle of the bridge, waves a white flag of truce. But Forrest isn't surrendering to us. The white flag is a sign he's giving Major Lilly the chance to end the fighting and talk things over.

Major Lilly turns back to the center of the fort and leans

against the wall. "How many . . . ?" Major Lilly's voice trails off. In ten months I've never seen him like this. He seems weak, spent, unable to finish his question. He clears his throat with a deep cough and looks down at the ground. "How many dead from the Ninth Cavalry?" he shouts.

"Nineteen of our two hundred," Sergeant Survant reports.

"One Hundred Eleventh Colored Troops?" Lilly asks.

"Over thirty-five," someone says.

"Sir, there are over one hundred dead," somebody calls in a somber voice.

Major Lilly slumps to the ground and buries his head in his hands.

★★★

There's an uncomfortable silence in the fort as I walk over to him. He doesn't look at me but glances back out at the white flag still fluttering at the trestle. Wrinkles carved deep into his face show the shame he's feeling. I sense what's he thinking. *How will this play out from here? Now it's a chess game with Forrest, and I have to think several moves ahead.*

Everyone studies the major's face and waits for his response. We're down to the last handful of bullets. What will more fighting accomplish? Won't we only lose more men and the battle end the same?

Major Lilly slowly raises his head. "Stephen, sound retreat."

★★★

I look toward the dark faces scattered among the white ones—they've fought together for six hours. "Sir," I say. "What about the Negro . . ."

"Damn it, Stephen, the order was for you to sound retreat."

★★★

I walk over to William Peacock and place my hand out, palm up, and ask to use his bugle. There's no way I can take mine from Henry's hand and play it.

After the last note is blown, Major Lilly stands and places his hands on my shoulders. "Come with me and listen carefully. You're young, and you'll be my second pair of eyes and ears. Make a memory of all you see and hear."

I nod.

"We need somebody from another state to go along too," Major Lilly says.

"Big Tennessee?" I suggest.

The three of us exit the fort and walk across the trestle to the far end. An officer sitting on a horse motions for us to advance.

"I'm Major Strange," he says as we approach. He unfolds a paper curtly and begins reading aloud. "General Forrest demands the immediate and unconditional surrender of the United States forces, with all materials and munitions of war, at Sulphur Branch Trestle. In case this demand is not instantly complied with, General Forrest cannot be held responsible for the conduct of his men."

Major Lilly shakes his head several times. "What kind of general do you follow? One that 'cannot be held responsible for the conduct of his men'?" he asks.

Major Strange does not answer. He folds the note, leans forward in his saddle, and hands it to a private. He, in turn, walks it over to us and, with his arm outstretched, presents the paper inches from Major Lilly's nose. The private stands for several seconds before Major Lilly waves him off with a flick of his hand, refusing to accept the offer.

"Let me say it another way…," Major Lilly begins. "I'd

never surrender any fort under such unprofessional insults. If General Forrest can't *control his soldiers*, he doesn't deserve his command or your respect." Major Lilly turns and motions for us to walk back to the fort.

A lump the size of the state of Texas rises in my throat. Is he bluffing? *We're all going to die now*, I think.

When we're halfway across the trestle, I hear footsteps approaching rapidly from behind. "Major Lilly," a voice calls out. "General Forrest wants an interview."

"Just as I hoped," Major Lilly says low enough for Big Tennessee and me to hear.

CHAPTER TWENTY-SIX

General Forrest is sitting outside a tent on a supply box when we approach. Elkmont, the ghost of a town we'd ridden through the day before, is visible off to the west. Forrest's face is thin—too thin, I think. A pipe protrudes from his mouth under a dense mustache. A long, wavy beard covers much of his neck. He has the darkest eyes I've ever seen. They sit deep beneath thick eyebrows. As we approach, he unfolds himself to reveal a height of well over six feet with wide-spreading shoulders. A patch of gray on each temple and a receding hairline are the only signs of aging.

"So, you have problems with my terms?" the general begins.

"I do, sir," Major Lilly says.

"What are your worries?"

"We are still able to inflict much damage on your troops," Major Lilly answers. "My men are willing to carry on the fight if the alternative is to surrender under the conditions you laid out."

General Forrest laughs slightly. "Go on?"

"It is strange, General, that you say you are *unable to control your troops...*," Major Lilly begins. "It's curious to me that you'd put that sort of thing in writing, where others might read it later. I, on the other hand, am confident that the soldiers under my command will follow every order given. If your troops won't follow your commands, it makes me worried about the well-being of my soldiers upon surrender."

"How so?" Forrest asks.

"I have Negro troops," Major Lilly says in a calm voice. "I want them treated the same as every other soldier under my command."

"What makes you think they won't be?"

"Your demands said you 'can't control your soldiers' if we don't surrender. So why would I think you could control them otherwise? Would a competent general question his leadership abilities?" Major Lilly asks.

"Here is what I'm prepared to offer," General Forrest says. "Officers retain personal property, horses, and sidearms. My men will escort officers to Mississippi for an eventual exchange to take place in Memphis. Other soldiers retain any personal property, but no sidearms or horses."

"All soldiers?" Major Lilly asks.

"Only soldiers," General Forrest says cryptically. I know what he means by that. He doesn't see Negroes as soldiers but property, like a sack of sugar.

"General Forrest," Major Lilly says, "every man in that fort wears the letters 'US' on his belt buckle."

"Only soldiers," General Forrest repeats but slower this time.

"*Every* man in that fort has an eagle on his buttons," Major Lilly insists, pointing toward the fort. He's near tears, but he realizes the fight's over. Now I understand he's on a mission to save every life he can, and he needs Big Tennessee and me here to witness the agreement. Major Lilly clears his throat, trying to regain composure. "I need your assurance, as a general, that you *will* control your troops and *will* give my soldiers ... *every* soldier ... the dignity they deserve."

General Forrest thinks for a moment, takes the pipe from

his mouth, and pounds it upside down against a tree. After the ashes finish dropping to the ground, he nods ever so subtly in agreement.

Back in the fort, Major Lilly asks me to blow assembly. When our remaining troops have gathered, he explains the conditions of surrender. At the end of his talk, the major dismisses everybody except the 111th Colored Troops. "I promise you'll be safe," he tells them.

"Major, how can we be sure he'll keep his word?"

"I wouldn't concede the fort until General Forrest promised me you'd be treated like every other soldier under my command."

"But maybe that's just him talkin'?"

"I took two witnesses to hold him to his word. You have no reason to doubt his promise."

"Sir," an older soldier says, "most people wouldn't have done that for us."

One after another, every Negro soldier salutes and shakes Major Lilly's hand. When he's finished, he turns to me. "Stephen, I'm sorry," he says.

"For what?"

"I promised Governor Morton I'd keep you safe and alive."

"And you have, sir."

"Don't make me out to be a liar," he says. "You're alive, but you're not safe. You've got to make it back to Indiana and your mother. That was an order Governor Morton gave personally to me."

★★★

Ninety minutes after meeting with Forrest, the few remaining officers mount horses and ride under armed escorts west toward Memphis. The Negro soldiers are corralled on the edge of the cornfield. We're told they'll be taken to Mobile. The rest of us begin walking south to Athens to catch a train bound for a prison near Selma. Behind us, flames lap the sky, and Sulphur Branch Trestle burns to the ground.

CHAPTER TWENTY-SEVEN

September 28, 1864, 9:45 a.m.

Under heavy guard, we ride the train for two days before arriving in the town of Beloit. The Alabama air is humid and filled with uncertainty. We're told we have to walk the last three hours to Cahaba, and immediately many of the men shed their shirts and toss them into the ditch.

"Your stomach's growling," Big Tennessee says as we make our way.

"The piece of salt pork and hardtack they gave us in Athens is long gone," I say. I turn and look back on the line of prisoners stretched behind me on the narrow road and see a cloud of dust rising into the sky.

"Don't look back, soldier," a man shouts from the side of the road. "Keep your head and eyes forward."

Big Tennessee's hand smacks the back of my neck. He

twists my head so I'm facing the front. Since our surrender, we don't travel by squads. We meander piecemeal, however we want, in a controlled mob. "Don't get us in any trouble before we're even in the prison," he says with a laugh.

"We're not in enough trouble now?" I ask.

"I guess you're right about that," he says.

The nickname Big Tennessee doesn't do him justice. Giant Tennessee is more exact. He's the tallest man I've ever seen. "How tall are you?" a man asks as we march.

"Let me just say Ole Abe himself would have to look up a tad to stare me square in the eyes," he answers.

Big Tennessee has a barrel for a chest. His upper arms could serve as legs for most men. He puzzles me in many ways. Men cower from him and keep their distance as if he has a disease. But on the train, he shared his meager portion of rations with several of us. He speaks softly and never takes the name of the Lord in vain. He says "thank you" and "please."

"Don't leave my side till we are at the prison, son," Big Tennessee whispers to me as we walk. "Most townsfolk are probably not too happy to see us here."

★★★

The people in Cahaba gawk at us from front porches and behind window curtains. A woman grabs children from her yard and hurries them inside when she sees Big Tennessee approaching. Doors slam. Shades are pulled as we pass. One lady, wearing a black armband, walks up to the row of soldiers and spits twice on prisoners walking by. Big Tennessee grabs my shoulders and pulls me to his left, out of her range.

"Big oaf," she calls out when she sees Big Tennessee. "Not so big now, are you?" she says, pointing a thin finger toward him. She throws her head back and spits hard in his direction. Big Tennessee nods to her as if to say, "Good day, ma'am."

Spit runs down his neck and shirtsleeve. He doesn't touch it. Several steps down the street, Big Tennessee wipes himself with his sleeve but keeps looking straight ahead as if nothing happened.

At the next corner, another lady watches us pass. She stands in silence and studies each person traveling by. She's wearing a dress of sky blue partially covered beneath an apron of white. Her head's covered with a matching bonnet trimmed in lace. My mother has one just like it. Our eyes meet as I approach. The lady stares, not at Big Tennessee but at me, and never stops looking my way until we pass.

★★★

Our lines slow near the banks of a river. The smell of muddy water and fish fills the air. Five tents are set up in a row, and one man at a time walks inside. I think of that day eight months ago in Indianapolis when I entered Camp Morton with Henry Dorman and saw a multitude of men knocking on death's door. I knew I'd be leaving the prison that same afternoon. Today, I don't know what to expect. How long will we be confined? A day? A month? A year? Will I smell the scent of death in the air like I did the day my father died and again when I spoke with the prisoners from Kentucky?

When it's my time to go into a tent, a man inside barks at me, "Everything out of your pockets and on the table." His voice is gruff and displeasing. He has a strong chin and is clean-shaven save for a thick mustache sitting above a pair of thin lips.

"Yes, sir," I say.

"Lieutenant Colonel Jones to you, Sunday Soldier," he says. He's standing beside the table, a private seated to his left. A box filled with large envelopes rests on the table between the private and me. Boxes cover much of the ground inside the tent, most filled with bulging envelopes.

"This is my pocket watch and two dollars." I lay them gently on the table.

"Name?" the private asks.

"Gaston."

"First name?"

"Stephen."

"'V' or 'P'?" The private asks without looking up.

"What?" I'm confused.

He looks up at me and taps his pencil on the desk. "How do you spell your first name?" he asks impatiently. "With a 'V' or with a 'P'?"

"Oh, sorry. S-T-E-P-H-E-N."

He writes my name across the envelope with the date, October 5, 1864, under it. "Drop everything in here," he barks.

I place the money and watch in the envelope.

"That book, too," the colonel says, pointing to the copy of *David Copperfield* tucked under my arm.

I'm overcome with fear. Certainly they'll let me keep the book with me. It can't be used as a weapon. How will I spend time in the prison? Why do they want it?

"The book, too, Colonel?" I ask to make certain. "Can't I keep it?"

"You'll get it back when you leave. *If* you leave," the colonel says, and laughs.

I take one final look at the book and lay it gently on the table, sure that this is the last time I'll ever see it. I think about what the governor said to me in his living room. "Personally, bring this book back to me." Personally.

"Anything else in your pockets?" the private asks.

"N-n-no," I stammer. "That's everything I have. My knife was taken back near Athens."

"Well, I can't do anything about that," the colonel says. He's trying to rub it in a little. "Git out of here." He points to the backside of the tent. "And welcome to Castle Morgan."

I remember the prison camp in Indianapolis had a similar name. Is that a cruel coincidence? A bad sign? Perhaps Henry was right. Maybe we will all experience a slow death like the prisoners we saw in Indiana.

Big Tennessee's waiting outside. Together, we drift toward the prison gates. The river flows off to the left, no more than a stone's throw away. A narrow walkway, maybe ten feet off the ground, is built into the outside walls of the prison. Armed guards, spaced around the wall, pace back and forth. From their position they have a clear view of the inside and outside of the prison. The guards stare at us as we walk beneath them on our way into Castle Morgan. One guard, chewing a plug of tobacco, spits from his perch. A long line of brown tobacco juice lands on Big Tennessee's head with a splat.

"Nice shot," another guard calls to his friend. "If you was that good with bullets, you'd be up in 'Ginny right now."

★★★

The call of "fresh fish" echoes through the prison as our group enters—I guess that's us. My first surprise is the sheer number of men crowded into such a tiny space. As soon as we pass through the gate, men surround us and all speak at once, each talking over the other.

"Where were you fighting, pard?"

"How's the war going, pard?"

"Any sign of it ending soon?"

"Where's General Grant?"

Pockets of men fan out, answering rapid-fire questions as best they can. Not that we have much news to give. I'm left alone. Nobody thinks someone as young as me might be in possession of any important information.

I stare in wonder at what lies before me, disturbed by the

number of men confined here. Castle Morgan's shockingly tiny and can't be as wide as the National Road passing through Centerville. It won't take a full minute to walk from one end of the prison to the other. Men are crowded in so thick, there appears to barely be enough room to stand. It must be impossible for everybody to lie down at the same time. How is this space going to handle the extra men coming from Sulphur Branch?

A bald-headed fellow approaches me. "What's your name?"

"Stephen Gaston," I say.

"Grisby's my name," he tells me. "I'll cut your hair for part of your rations." He looks slightly older than me, but without hair, it's difficult to tell. His red eyebrows are stretched tall above his unblinking eyes.

"My hair's fine," I say, turning away.

He taps me on my left shoulder. "Not for long. Come see me when you're ready. My pocketknife's sharp enough to cut your hair clean off without nicking your skin."

"No, thanks," I insist.

"I can't take care of all the graybacks for you," he says. "They're everywhere. I can get them out of your hair, though, but it'll cost you some food."

Most of the men in the prison have very short hair. It's easy to tell who just arrived and who's been here awhile by looking at heads. Most are shirtless and so deeply tanned that their skin has turned to leather with deep-set wrinkles.

"Don't worry none with Grisby," a deep voice says from behind me.

I turn around. "Excuse me?"

"Grisby doesn't have a knife. We think he's lost his mind. He's been here too long, but he's harmless, really."

"What are graybacks? He said they are everywhere here."

"Well, he does have a point there," the man says. "Graybacks are lice. We call 'em that cause we like 'em about as much as we like the gray-coated rebel guards. If you spread your shirt out on the ground, it'll nearly crawl across the prison. Graybacks will be in your hair thick as bees in a hive by morning," he says. "Nothing you can do about it, either."

He reaches down on his pant leg and grabs something almost too small to see.

"Can you see him?" he asks, pointing to a small speck on his palm.

I see a tiny critter crawling toward his thumb. "Yeah."

"You probably got 'em on you already," he says. "How old a boy are you—sixteen, maybe?"

"Fifteen, in three months." I try to stand a little taller.

"Haven't even shaved yet, have you?" he says, and laughs.

"Don't guess that's what makes a man a man, is it?"

"Settle down. Settle down. No need to rile up and take offense."

A loud explosion causes all the bald-headed men to sit down on the ground. They motion for the fresh fish to do the same.

"Men, if at any time you hear gunfire, like you just did," yells a booming voice, "you are to drop immediately." The words are coming from a man standing above the gate on the outside ledge. He's visible from the waist up. "My name is Lieutenant Colonel Jones, commander of what we affectionately call Castle Morgan."

Some of the guards chuckle when he says "Castle Morgan."

"Roll call is at seven thirty a.m. and five p.m. daily," the colonel continues. He points to a line on the ground parallel to the prison wall. "That there is the deadline. Cross over the deadline and you'll be shot." He pauses for dramatic effect. "No warning will be given. The guards shoot to kill."

Deadline. I had heard those words before at the prison in

Indianapolis. Colonel Jones adjusts his glasses. "This prison is nearly two hundred feet long and over on hundred feet wide." He paces a few steps to his left and then back to the right. "Today, we brought in a lot of men from northern Alabama. It will be crowded, but we will make it work. Fall in for roll call."

Men move with no sense of urgency into groups. Nobody tells the fresh fish where to stand, so we wait to see what part of the compound will hold us. I meander around, looking for men of the Ninth. I notice Big Tennessee standing at attention. It's hard not to see him; he's towering over everyone.

"The Ninth is near the gate," Big Tennessee says, pointing in the direction of Colonel Jones.

I hear Sergeant Survant calling my name. "Where's Stephen Gaston?" I move toward his voice, but men are standing at every turn. I hustle around one group of people, along an open space nearby to get to my company—the only open route I see. A deafening shot rings out. Dirt springs up and pelts my face. I dive for the ground. Everyone in the prison does the same. When I open my eyes, the white line on the ground is directly beneath my face. The shot was fired toward me.

A hand grabs my trouser leg and pulls me back across the deadline. "Pay attention," Big Tennessee whispers angrily into my ears. "Always know where you are and what is around you."

CHAPTER TWENTY-EIGHT

September 28, 1864, 3:00 p.m.

The crazy fellow, Grisby, who greeted me when we first entered Castle Morgan, stands nearby in formation. He points in my direction. *You cook*, he mouths silently to me.

"What?"

He shakes his head rapidly and then squeezes between two men to get closer. "Stephen, you cook tonight," he says, pointing at me, then heads back to his place.

I have no idea what he means until the end of roll call when we have to form squads of ten and designate a cook to prepare dinner. The guy's out of his mind, but when it's time, I offer to prepare the meal for my squad.

Guards let the cooks leave prison to collect firewood. Grisby yanks my arm to join him as we pass through the gates to gather firewood. He shows me where to collect a handful of twigs beneath an oak tree. You don't need much. With as many fires as we have to build, the more we burn, the farther we have to walk to get wood the next time.

"Get some of that dried grass, Stephen," he says, pointing to tufts of brown near a fence post. "Dried grass is plentiful, and it helps catch the wood on fire."

He motions with his head to return to the prison. As we walk back he says, "Wood that is rotting smokes and won't heat, so don't use it. Fresh fish always go for that because it's big and round. Don't use pine, either, unless the oaks and hickories haven't dropped any limbs. Pine doesn't burn hot enough for a low fire," he warns. "Most of all, remember coals are hot, flames are not. So don't get flustered when the flames die out."

★★★

We reach the inside of the cooking area through a small door in the middle of the north wall. This area is surrounded on the other three sides by a board fence. "Rations vary from day to day," Grisby says. "Often the meat seems unfit for dogs. Don't worry; it's fine. All you have to do is roll it in the ashes and brush it off. What's left adds flavor and makes it almost bearable," he says. "Best part, the ashes hide the smell."

Grisby points out the pots and rations and helps me build my fire. "Always begin with leaves or dried grass for kindling, not wood. Flames from the grass will catch dry wood pretty fast."

"You're pretty smart. Somebody told me you were crazy."

"Yeah, that's what I want 'em to think," he says. "They leave you alone if they think you're touched in the head."

Soon the cook yard is filled with low fires and smoke. At times, it's impossible to see from one wall to the other.

After our fires are going and we have our rations cooking, Grisby says, "With how little meat they give us, it won't take long for this to cook. Walk near the fence with me."

He sees my apprehension and adds, "Don't worry. There's no deadline in the cook yard. It's hardly guarded at all."

We walk over to the fence, and Grisby stands, his back to the guards.

He points to a hole in the fence. "See that hole that's about the size of a small apple?"

"The one at eye level?"

"Yeah. Look out that hole," he says.

Looking through the opening, I can easily see the river off to the right.

"That's the Alabama River," Grisby says. "The crapper on the far end of the camp empties dead into it." He starts laughing. "Some guys escaped out the crapper and into the river about a month ago. I'd advise against that. They were back in four days."

"You can see the town from here," I say, pointing to the left.

"Stephen, look at that first house," he says. "It's about two hundred feet slightly to the left."

"Yeah. It's very close."

"Belle lives there."

"Who?"

"Belle. Belle Gardner. If there's heaven on Earth, it's Belle Gardner. Purty as flax in spring."

"You don't say."

"Oh, I do say. I cut that hole in the fence myself with my pocketknife."

"I was told you don't really have—"

"Have a pocketknife?" he says, finishing my sentence.

"Yeah."

"What do you call this?" he asks, producing a piece of

folded metal from his pocket. "That hole started as a rotten knot. I cut a little more every time they let me cook until it finally got that big. Sometimes the smoke is so thick in here, you can't see your hand in front of your face. That's when I started whittlin' on it."

"Nobody noticed you?"

"How could they? I could barely see what I was doing myself."

When we're done cooking, Grisby points to the ration table. "Take your pot back there, and we're almost ready." He helps me divide the mess into ten equal portions. "Split 'em as equally as possible. Then ask every member in your group if they're satisfied with the portion sizes. Have a man turn his back to the food. You point to a single portion and ask, 'Who gets this one?' The person calls a name to whom that portion is given, and there's no appeal from his decision. Do that every time until the food's all given out."

On the first night it's obvious that not everyone sleeps at the same time. There is not enough ground to hold this many men. Bunks have been placed in one corner of the compound called the roosts because men resemble chickens in a coop when it's full. The planks, stacked six tall, with barely enough room to scoot in between each level, are the only covered area in the prison. When it rains, it's the lone place to keep dry.

All the men on a single plank lie on their sides, facing the same direction when they sleep. They look like spoons in a drawer. From time to time a member of one roost yells, "Switch!" and everyone on that plank rolls over at the same time and faces the opposite direction. A spot on the ground near the roosts will do fine for my first night in prison. It's not long before I discover there are more unwanted guests in Castle Morgan than there are humans. I scratch my head and try to go back to sleep. But whatever it is grows in numbers because, soon, both sides of my scalp feel like they're on fire. Then the rest of my body. I rub my legs against the ground to relieve the itching on my thighs. I flail my arms and wiggle my toes.

"Cut your hair in the morning, boy, so we can get some sleep," a man says. "Vermin here are thicker than blackberries in July."

He's right. In the morning, not only is my hair full of lice, so are my clothes. Sergeant Survant gets shears from a guard and soon has a line of fresh fish waiting to get their hair trimmed. When the last snips are done, my hair feels like short bristles on a rough board against my fingers. Sweat skids off my head and cascades down my neck, but at least my head doesn't itch constantly.

Somebody else in my squad cooks lunch the second day while I stay in the main prison compound. Grisby rushes to me after delivering the food he's prepared for his group. "Gaston, when you arrived, did you walk through town beside the tall fella named Big Tennessee?"

"Yeah, why?"

"Were you carrying a book with you?"

"Yeah, a copy of *David Copperfield.*"

"Mrs. Gardner wants to see you at the hole," he informs me.

"Who?"

"Mrs. Gardner. Belle's mother, for crying out loud. She said she wants you to meet her at the hole this evening. Be sure you volunteer to cook."

"I don't know her."

"Doesn't matter. Just be sure you're the cook tonight."

The only thing to think about all afternoon is why this woman wants to speak to me. Reasons turn and grind in my brain as to why, but my mind's as empty as my stomach. Late that afternoon, following roll call, I volunteer to cook again.

I get no argument from the other men.

Once we've gathered our firewood, I build a small fire. I keep one eye on Grisby and the other on the hole. Nothing happens for the longest time. He flashes his palms at me as if to say, "Slow down, be patient." The few vegetables are about finished heating when Grisby calls, "Now, Stephen. Go over to the fence now."

Whoever's on the other side has stuck a bent spoon into the hole. It's a signal.

"Yes?" I ask peering through the hole. Nobody's there. "Mrs. Gardner?"

"Yes. How old are you, Stephen?" comes an urgent female voice. The lady steps back a couple feet and raises her head enough for me to see a face.

"How did you know my name?" I ask.

"Grisby told me."

She's the same woman who had stared at me on the street the day we arrived. "You're the lady in the blue bonnet, aren't you?"

"Yes," she says. "Now that we have that out of our way, my question was, how old are you?"

"Almost fifteen," I say. "Why?"

"Then you're fourteen," she corrects me.

"Yes, I guess I'm fourteen. Why?"

"You like to read," she says.

"How do you know that?"

"Young man, it's odd how you answer my questions with questions of your own. We'll never get anywhere if you keep that up," she says.

"Oh, sorry. Yes, reading is a favorite pastime of mine, ma'am."

"Dickens?" she asks.

"How do you know that—" I catch myself midsentence. "Yes, Dickens is one of my favorites."

"I thought so," she says. "See that guard over there?" she asks.

I cover my head, duck, and spin to the ground all in the same motion, expecting to be shot. After a second or two, I raise my head and look toward the guard. He's holding a square black object. Through the smoke it's difficult to tell exactly what it is.

"You're not on the ground, are you, Stephen?" Mrs. Gardner laughs.

"Yes," I say, standing and looking back through the hole. "I see the guard but thought you were warning me he was going to shoot."

"Oh, he'll do no such thing. He's my nephew. Items get in

and out of the prison through him," she says. "Nobody would dare shoot in my direction."

"He's holding something, but it's too far away to see what it is."

"It's *Great Expectations* by Dickens. It's for you. Don't worry; the guards won't take it from you." She can tell I'm puzzled. "There was a book in your hand the other day, when you walked through town. You clutched it tight to your chest like it was the most valuable thing in the world to you."

"It was a gift from the governor of Indiana." I haven't told anybody that except for Dorman the day we snuck into the prison in Indianapolis.

"The governor?" she asks. "You must know important people, then. They took the book from you when you arrived?"

"Yes, ma'am, they did."

"Don't fret about it none. You'll get it back when you leave. I'll see to it. It must be very valuable, getting it from the governor and all."

"It is. The governor gave it to me on one condition."

"What was that?"

"He ordered me to personally bring it to him at the end

of the war. He wants to borrow it. He told me Abe Lincoln himself recommended it for me. It's the president's favorite book."

"Well, I came to let you know Dickens will keep you company for a couple days. My nephew may not be important like the governor, but just return it to him when you're through. Don't give it to anybody else."

She stares at me for a few seconds, and I shift on my feet to relieve the uneasiness. "Your mother's worried about you," she says.

"I bet so."

"One bit of advice, Stephen. Don't trade any clothing to the guards."

"Lots of fellows in here are without shirts," I say. "They said they traded with the guards for an extra piece of beef or a stack of playing cards."

"Don't do it. Alabama winters can be crippling."

A cloud of smoke smothers us, and when it clears, Mrs. Gardner and the spoon are gone. In the hole, instead of a bent spoon are two sheets of paper rolled into a tube. Inside are an envelope, a stamp, and a pencil.

CHAPTER TWENTY-NINE

This morning, prisoners and guards seem motionless; some appear to be in deep slumber. A tap on the paper and pencil hidden in my shirtsleeve lets me know they're still there, safe and sound. Getting up, careful not to step on anyone, I search for an area to hide them. A spot beside the privy, where nobody goes because of the odor, works perfectly.

I dig a shallow hole and cover the paper and pencil with a thin layer of dirt. While spreading dirt with the palm of my hand, footsteps approach from behind me.

"Whatcha doin', Stephen?"

"Uh ... nothing," I say quickly.

"Don't look like nothing," the voice says. "It looks just like you're doing something."

"I ... uh ... lost something." It's not a good lie, but it'll have to do on such a short notice.

"Want some help?" he asks.

"No," I say quickly. "I guess it's not here, after all." I stand, put my hands on my hips, and look at where my stash is planted. One corner of paper sticks out of the dirt. A push with the edge of my boot dumps soil on top of it.

I turn around to find it's Charles Evans, a bugler for Company A. Charles is a huge boy. I wouldn't stand a chance against him in a fight. "Want some help looking for it, Stephen? There's nothing else to do," he says.

"Naw, Charles, there was a picture of my mother I smuggled in. It got lost, and I remembered looking at it over here a couple days ago. I thought maybe it was dropped but probably not." I shovel more dirt with the toe of my shoe while Charles looks me dead in the eye. A quick glance down shows only dirt and no sign of the paper.

Charles shrugs. "It's getting cooler at night," he says. "Have you noticed?"

I'm thankful for the change in conversation. "Yeah. It is getting cooler. They'll have snow back home soon now that it's nearly October."

"I'll be glad when it cools a bit during the day here, too," he says.

"Yeah, me too." I walk away, glancing back to make sure everything is still buried. If anybody sees it, there's sure to be a fight—and some explaining to do.

I walk over to the shallow water trench running through the middle of the camp, bend down, cup water in my palms, and splash my face. I look back to see if Charles has found my stash. He's gone. I'll go back early tomorrow morning and retrieve it.

The water's cool on my face, but it smells like rotten eggs; we were told it's sulphur. I'm amazed how quickly fresh fish get used to it. The first couple days, it bothered me. But now, not so much. It washes the dirt off my fingers and cools my face, and I'm thankful for that. One fellow from Ohio said the water flows out of a spring in town and runs along the streets of Cahaba before coming to the Castle.

"I bet they traipse their dogs and pigs through it. And we get what's left," he said.

Three sunken barrels, their rims inches above ground level, catch the water and serve as reservoirs. A story retold in camp is that in August a man, drunk from Alabama's heat, climbed into one of them to cool himself. "We drink that, soldier. Get out now!" a sergeant yelled at him.

"Going to float across the Jordan River," he sang.

Everyone thought he was kidding, but the man knew his time on Earth was up. Minutes later there's a dead body in everybody's drinking water.

Death visits us almost every day. Though it's taking me longer to get used to than the smell of the water. I've heard stories of a place in Georgia where there are so many deaths that everybody knows somebody who dies every day.

The next morning I wake to a thin line of blue painted low in the eastern sky. It's not light enough to see well, but ample. There are a few quiet conversations, not unusual because many soldiers, not used to the Southern heat, sit up all night and sleep in the roost, out of the sun, all day. I step over men on my way toward the privy and duck around the corner. I clear the dirt with my toe, looking for my secret stash.

It's gone. Charles, that no-good river rat, took it.

I wake Big Tennessee and tell him everything: how I had met Mrs. Gardner, how she gave me paper, how I buried it, and how Charles saw me hide it near the privy.

Big Tennessee raises on his elbow and squints his eyes. "Where's he at?" The two of us tiptoe around groups of sleeping men while making our way across the compound. When we find him, Big Tennessee kicks Charles's foot like he's knocking mud loose from his boots.

"What?" Charles says as he spins on the ground.

Big Tennessee straddles above him, one leg on each side of his body. "You have something that belongs to my friend," he says in a hushed voice. "He would like to have it back."

Charles's eyes dart first at Big Tennessee then to me and back again. "Maybe the guards would like to know what it is," he says.

"Maybe the guards are overworked and couldn't care less what you have," Big Tennessee tells him. He bends down, puts his knees on the ground, and sits on Charles's stomach. "If you want to see the day break, you'll do the right thing."

"Can't breathe," he manages to get out. When Big Tennessee's full weight is lifted off his body, Charles fishes into his pocket and hands over the paper, envelope, stamp, and pencil.

Big Tennessee gently pats Charles on the hip. "Thank you, young man. Now please, go back to sleep."

I sit against the privy wall and, with just enough light from sunrise, write a letter to Mother.

Dearest Mother,

I'm fine, but in a southern Alabama prison. Don't worry. I'm eating enough, but always want more just like at home.

Sound familiar? I'm able to write due to the kindness of Mrs. Gardner. She reminds me the world of you. I miss you more than words can say.

Please write to me at Castle Morgan in the town of Cahaba. Any news concerning home is welcomed. The Alabama River runs beside us. One hundred Paddy's Runs could fit in it with no worries.

I lost one of my best friends and fellow bugler, Henry Dorman, at a place called Sulphur Branch Trestle. I can't bring myself to tell you the whole story on this page, but perhaps one day I will tell you what a great friend and soldier he was. For now, it is enough it to say he died serving this great country.

Send my love to friends. Save a share for yourself,

Stephen

The letter folds neatly into the envelope. I seal it, address it to my uncle's house, and put the extra sheet of paper and pencil in my pocket. They won't be safe there for long with pickpockets taking things from people while they sleep. The only place nobody will think to look is inside the hole of the privy. I wait for the last man to leave, go inside, and stick my head deep into one of the openings. Although not well lit, a thin stream of light does reveal a shelf of sorts tucked along one side. Something is odd, however. A gold glittering speck reflects light back at me.

I grab for the light and discover it's a metal frame. Somebody has stashed a picture of a young woman. Her hair, dark and pulled to the back of her head, is crowned with a black bow. She sits sideways in a tall wooden chair, her hands folded gently in her lap. On the back of the picture is a handwritten note. "Dearest Matthew, I'll be waiting for you. Hurry home."

I replace the picture along with my single sheet of paper and pencil. One secret will keep the other safe and out of sight.

★★★

Tonight's a good one for food. We have beef. Every ten days or so real meat finds its way to us, or so I hear. Chicken is rare. Rotting pork is more common. Before gathering rations, I pat the letter in my pants pocket to make sure it's still there. I hope Mrs. Gardner comes to the hole so I can give it to her to post. I start the fire and begin boiling water for the ground corn. Hopefully, when it's cooked into a mush and the meat's added, everything will be edible.

I keep one eye on the pot and one on the opening in the fence. Soon, the sign appears. I wait for the guard to turn away and dash for the wall. "Mrs. Gardner?" I call.

"Yes," she answers. "How are things in the Castle this fine day?" she asks.

"Fine, thank you, ma'am," I say, peering out of the opening.

"Ma'am?" she echoes my word in surprise. "You were raised right."

"Thank you, ma'am. My mama would love to know that."

"That's how my son was raised," she says.

"Your son?"

"Yes," she says quickly. "Do you have something for me?"

I had almost forgotten about the letter. "Oh, yes. Yes, I do."

Mrs. Gardner smiles at me and pauses. "Can you give it to me?"

"Ohhh, yes." The coiled envelope passes easily through to her. I have no idea where the boldness comes from, but I need to ask her for more. I feel there are two debts to be repaid. "Is there any chance to get two envelopes and one more piece of paper? I have one sheet left but need to write letters for two friends."

Without hesitation, she fishes into an apron pocket and

passes me two envelopes, already stamped, and paper. Did she expect the question?

"Thank you, ma'am."

"You're welcome," she says quietly. Then five pieces of sliced pumpkin pie slip through the hole, one at a time. "Perhaps these will go well with the feast you're having in the Castle tonight."

"Indeed, they will," I tell her. "Bless you, ma'am, bless you."

Mrs. Sarah Dorman,

Today is painful as pen is put to paper to write you. I do not know you personally, but feel I do through your husband. Henry served in the same company with me. He was a fine man, and his passing is a great loss to the Union. When we arrived at training, he could only make what might have been called goose sounds with his bugle. But he worked at it, sometimes after drills were over, to make sure he was an asset to the army. It may not be of any comfort, but Henry died experiencing no pain and was holding a bugle in his hand.

He spoke of you often, and his son. His comments were always kind and gentle. Every soldier he met could tell by how Henry talked about you all that he was a good family man.

Henry is surely with God, looking upon the two of you as you read these words.

Although I do not know your grief, my only brother was lost to the war two years ago. The pain of your loss will never go away and things will not be the same without Henry, but life can still be good.

Please know that Henry said he loved you to the moon and back. He said those words often. If it's not too much to ask, I'd like to borrow those sentiments and use them when speaking of the ones I love. As I do, I'll also think of my dear friend and your husband, Henry Dorman of the 9th IN Cavalry.

Yours,
Stephen M. Gaston,
Centerville, IN

CHAPTER THIRTY

Six weeks after arriving from Sulphur Branch, a bugler calls assembly. Colonel Jones appears on the walkway above the gate. "Men," he begins, "before I share some news with you, I trust your stay at Castle Morgan has been adequate."

"If you like sleeping with bedbugs and eating corncob soup!" someone yells.

A roar of laughter erupts from the compound.

"Be that as it may, you could always have it worse," the colonel says.

"We could be sleeping with corncobs and eating bedbug soup?" the same man retorts.

"What's the news?" another man yells.

"Abraham Lincoln was reelected," the colonel announces.

"Three cheers for Abe!" somebody shouts.

"Hip, hip, hooray."

"Hip, hip, hooray."

"Hip, hip hooray!"

The cheering and clapping lasts several minutes.

"Also, as of tomorrow, I'll no longer be in charge of Cahaba prison."

A thundering cheer rings through the compound and bounces from the walls, making it sound louder than it should be. "Three cheers for the colonel leaving."

"Hip, hip, hooray."

"Hip, hip, hooray."

"Hip, hip, hooray!"

"My replacement will be Captain Henderson. I trust you'll show him the same respect you've shown me." His remarks sound sincere, but I detect a stream of anger flowing just beneath his words. "He's a Methodist minister, so I'm positive he'll bring the good word with him when he reports."

"Amen!" somebody shouts.

"A-men," Big Tennessee says, stretching each syllable like bread dough. Several more Amens are said, a few at a time at first, like corn beginning to pop in a kettle. But other voices join in louder and louder until the colonel retreats from the platform.

When we break ranks, I seek out Big Tennessee. With the uncertainty of a new commander, things might get worse. Mom says the devil you know is better than the devil you don't. I'm afraid Mrs. Gardner won't be allowed near the compound wall in a few days.

"Can we talk?" I ask my giant friend.

"Yeah, let's stroll up the road a mile or two for some privacy," he jokes.

I laugh, then quietly say, "I have paper and an envelope. Do you want to write your wife and let her know you're okay?"

"Where do you keep getting paper and envelopes?"

His voice, a bit loud, might bring unwanted ears. "Shhhh, don't ask," I whisper. "Do you want to write a letter home?" I ask again.

Big Tennessee looks down at the ground. "I, uh, I would, only . . . I can't."

"What do you mean you can't? I told you I got everything you need. I got pencil, paper, envelope, even a stamp."

"I can't write," he says. "Never learned how."

"Oh," I say. "Well, I can write it for you. Just tell me what to put down on the paper, and I'll get it sent to her for you."

"You'd do that for me?"

"Sure," I say.

★★★

Later that afternoon, we sit near the corner of the privy with our backs to the prisoners. I use the copy of *Great Expectations* the guard gave me to support the paper. I write exactly what Big Tennessee whispers.

Dear Mary,

Hope you are fine. Doing well here. Last you heard from me we were in Tennessee. Now in Alabama. Being detained awhile. Hope to return to you and the mountains of Tennessee soon. I've lost some weight, but you often said my waist has grown a lot since we married.

Love, your husband

When I finish the letter, Big Tennessee takes the pencil. "I sign my name with a check mark crossed along the longer side," he says as he puts the mark at the bottom of the page.

"She'll know it's mine from that," he says as he taps the X. I turn the envelope over. "Where do I send it?"

"Mary Pierce, Cumberland Gap, Tennessee," he says.

"We live a few feet from the Virginia line."

"I bet it's beautiful there."

"It is. It is," he manages to say, a catch in his voice. "And she is too."

★★★

The next day before noon, there's a terrible row near the gate. Commotions are not unusual, as two or three prisoners will trickle through the gate every other day. The call of "fresh fish" lets everyone know we have company.

"Don't go past the deadline!" a guard shouts.

The reply comes from a female voice. I recognize it immediately as Mrs. Gardner.

"I'll go past the deadline if I like. *And* you can shoot me if *you* like," she argues. "You shooting a woman with only shirts to defend herself may not hold up well with General Lee."

A man, obviously Captain Henderson, follows her into the compound. She walks quickly to the edge of the deadline.

"Ma'am. We have procedures to follow," he pleads.

"Oh, then shoot me," she says. "Go right ahead and get it over with."

"You know I'm not going to do that, ma'am."

"Then make yourself useful and help me pass these clothes out to these men." She drapes several shirts across the captain's arms. "Some of the men don't have a single shirt to wear."

The compound is silent as a stone as we wait to see how this scene will end. "Look at these men," she says in disgust. "Many only have rags for clothing."

"Ma'am, there is this thing called a war going on. We don't have—"

"A war? Really?" she interrupts him. "You, sir, should not insult my intelligence." Mrs. Gardner drops a pile of shirts onto the ground. She spins on her heels to face the prisoners. "You," she says, and points to a bare-chested William Peacock. "Stand up."

He does as he's told.

Mrs. Gardner looks at him, cocks her head one way, and then the other. She reaches into her mound of clothing and grabs a brown shirt. "Try that one on for size." She throws it to William. Three weeks ago the shirt would have been too small for Peacock. But he's so skinny now, it fits perfectly.

Without skipping a beat, she adds, "So, there's a war going on, huh, Captain Henderson?"

"Yes, ma'am," he says.

"A man died here this summer from the heat, and winter's just weeks away," she says. "So, instead of killing soldiers with bullets, your plan is to hold them up here and let the weather kill them for you. Is that right?" she asks.

"Well, no, ma'am," he says. "This prison has an excellent record."

"Sir, you are a man of the cloth. Maybe you can help me out. I don't know the New Testament very well. What was it Matthew said regarding the naked?"

"I don't know what you're getting at, ma'am."

"Chapter twenty-five I believe it was. Yes, in chapter twenty-five, Matthew said something about being naked. But it escapes me now *just* how that part of the Bible goes. Do you remember? Being a man of the cloth and all."

The captain studies Mrs. Gardner a long while before a smile creeps onto his face as he realizes what she is getting at. "*I was naked and You clothed me.*"

"Ahhh, yes, that's right. It's coming back to me now," she says. "And I've missed a Sunday or two in church, but didn't he say something regarding being in prison?"

"*When I was in prison, You came to me.*"

"So, the Bible says I should clothe the naked and visit those in prison?"

"Yes, ma'am, it does. But, if you'll just come outside, we'll talk it through."

Mrs. Gardner lowers her voice to a fake whisper, clearly wanting as many of us to hear her as possible. "My Bible tells me, 'Jesus said, "*What you do for the least of your fellow man, you also do for Me.*"' Those are Jesus's words, Captain Henderson."

Sergeant Survant has a thin stream of tears flowing down each cheek. "Why should she care so much about us?" he asks nobody in particular.

"Just come outside so we can talk," the captain pleads.

Mrs. Gardner nods in agreement. "Just a second. Stephen Gaston," she calls.

I jump to my feet. "Here, ma'am."

"Give me that rag you're wearing and put this new one on," she demands.

I cross several platoons of men to get to where she's standing, and I unbutton my shirt along the way.

"Stop right there and turn around," she orders. I wonder who's really in charge of the prison now. She walks up behind me and holds the shirt, making it easy to slip my arms into the sleeves. With her back to the captain, she whispers, "Check the pocket later." I turn to face her and am shocked to be greeted by the smell of Mother as my fingers slip the first button through its hole. It's one of my shirts from home. I press the right sleeve to my nose and look at Mrs. Gardner. "How did you get my—"

"Shhhh," she says softly, and winks.

I glance into the pocket before returning to my spot. A piece of paper is tucked deep into the folds of the fabric. I feel like a spy, receiving a message slipped to me by a Southern contact.

The captain helps her hand out the rest of the shirts and motions with his palm faceup toward the gate for her to leave. She nods and leads the way, and they depart.

I think about heading straight to the privy to see what the paper is, but recent bouts of dysentery keep the doors swinging like flags in the wind. Some unfortunate souls spend half their days in there.

Cooking time is my best option for seeing what Mrs. Gardner passed me. While gathering wood, I slip into a grove of cedar trees, knowing nobody will come near here for firewood.

The shirt pocket holds a letter.

★★★

Dearest Stephen,

Centerville and I are proud of you. An angel named Mrs. Amanda Gardner wrote me by way of Governor Morton. She said you were safe, but we should pray for you. Rest assured, we do so every day.

Mrs. Gardner said she speaks to you from time to time when a relative of hers is on guard. She said you are a gentleman and that I raised you right. I thought I'd never hurt again as much as I did when Robert died. I was wrong.

Mrs. Gardner asked if there's any way to send clothes, especially long-sleeved shirts since winter's coming on. With war still raging, God only knows if the clothing gathered from neighbors will make it to you. When Governor Morton was in town, I gave him a sack full and asked him to get them to Selma, AL, if he could.

If you are reading this, it's a miracle and is with God's blessing. Everyone in Centerville read your letter. I do mean everyone. Reverend Collins recited it in church. Dutch said you are a hero, and he has something for you when you return. Sorry, I don't know what it is. He said you'd have to guess.

Praying for your safe and quick return,
Mother

CHAPTER THIRTY-ONE

November 29, 1864

Amanda Gardner is back in the prison today. I think her talk with Captain Henderson opened the gates of kindness a bit, because she's carrying a crate of books. She strolls into the compound and sets the box right on the deadline. I think about the time she had to smuggle *Great Expectations* to me through her nephew. I rush to the box, wanting to be the first to choose a title.

The collection is as varied as the men inside Castle Morgan. There are books on poetry, religion, and history as well as biographies. "These will do more to take our minds off the lice and bad food than anything else," I tell a fellow rifling through the selection with me.

A guard announces, "Want a book, take it. Done with it, put it back. Mrs. Gardner will come on Sundays to check the crate. If there are no books in it, she'll return with a few more from her house." In an hour, men are sitting in small circles listening to one or another of them read books by Washington Irving, Charles Dickens, Jane Austen, or Walter Scott.

★★★

A week later, after roll call, Captain Henderson directs everyone to sit on the ground. A guard enters the compound, carrying a stack of papers. Nothing like this has happened since I've been here, and everyone's confused. The guard walks to the center of the prison and finds an area with a bit of space. "Sergeant Survant," he calls. When the sergeant approaches, the guard hands him what looks like an envelope.

"It's a letter from home!" he yells, flashing it over his head. He is so overcome that his hands shake violently as he attempts to tear open the envelope without doing too much damage.

Many men receive letters that afternoon, including some of us captured at Sulphur Branch. Most letters wonder why previous notes haven't been answered. But if any of us had gotten mail in the past, it never made it into our hands.

On Sunday I rush to greet Mrs. Gardner at the book box

to find out why I got a letter smuggled in my shirt several days before the rest of the men got theirs. The timing seems coincidental.

"Did you sneak my mother's letter from the captain's stash?"

"Heavens, no, son," she says. "There'd be no way to do such a thing."

"How did you get it to me, then?"

"That letter came straight to me, mother to mother. Would a sane person then place it in just anybody's hands to deliver?" she asks. "It would have to be somebody I trusted one hundred percent. The captain never laid eyes on your mother's dispatch."

"What about the letters delivered the other day?" I ask.

"Perhaps somebody shamed the captain into delivering those." She gives me a Sunday-morning smile and adds, "Pass the word around that there are pencils in the box for the men to use. They can write on the same letters they received from home, on the backs or perhaps squeeze their writing between the other lines."

Stamps are a minor problem because not all families included stamps in what they sent. Some prisoners trade food for stamps, since the guards are not fed much better than we are.

December 11, 1864
Cahaba, Alabama
Dear Mother,

    Some things have improved at Castle Morgan. In more important ways, they've gotten worse. My old shirt, the one you sent from home is looser. We have joked there are two ways out of Castle Morgan: lose ninety pounds or die. A few men who weighed less than one hundred pounds have been sent home.

    In June, we got word from General Grant that he would not authorize any more prisoner swaps. He had been trading a general for sixty men, a colonel for fifteen, a lieutenant for four, and a sergeant for two. We were told Lincoln ordered Grant to stop the exchanges. "It's only extending the war," we were told were his exact words.

    My paper's run out. Thanks for the shirt.

    All my love to friends. Save a share for yourself,
    Stephen

Sharp pains in my stomach wake me in the middle of the night.

Sergeant Survant, who is dozing nearby and sees I'm restless, asks, "What's wrong?"

"My stomach hurts real bad," I tell him.

"It'll pass," he says.

But it doesn't, and three nights later Sergeant Survant has to wake two men to take turns nursing me through the night. One of them, a private, puts both hands on my arms and feels me trembling. He removes his shirt and drapes it over me to keep me warm. "You'll freeze," I warn him.

"Don't worry about me," he replies. "I'll be fine."

The private shakes his head. "Dysentery," he whispers to Sergeant Survant. "When I had it, the privy was my only friend for three days."

Somebody dips a cloth in water and wipes a cold swath across my forehead. "We need to keep you bundled and warm, but this will cool your fever down a bit," he promises. He holds a cup to my mouth.

"No," I say, and turn my head away.

"Drink it. You need to drink."

I'm shaking so hard that when my lips touch the tin, half the water spills onto my shirt and the ground.

"Guard," Sergeant Survant calls. "We need to take him to the hospital."

I grab his arm. "Don't let 'em take me there. That's where they take us to die."

"You've been sick for a week, Stephen," Big Tennessee says. "We can't take care of you here. You're not eating, and now you have chills."

"How many of the sick have come back from the hospital?" I ask. He doesn't say anything because we both know the answer. "Not many."

"Leaving the prison is the last thing you want, Stephen, but you're skin and bones," Sergeant Survant says. "You've drifted in and out of consciousness for a day and need to get out of the freezing air."

"It's not your call anymore, Stephen," Big Tennessee says. "Grab his arms, Sergeant, and I'll take his legs. Let's carry him over to the gate and wait for the hospital to send somebody to come get him."

I lie on the ground, staring up at ominous clouds. They block most of the sky but part slightly, revealing a bright golden moon. I wonder if Mother is looking out her bedroom window at this very same time. "Maw," I say softly. "If this is the end, I love you to the moon and back."

I don't know how much time passes, but the gates finally rattle open. Two lanterns slide through the air on either side of my head. Floating between the lights is Mrs. Gardner's face. She leans over and asks a guard to hold a lantern closer. She studies me for several seconds, tugs at the corner of my eye, and nods to Big Tennessee. "Will you two gentlemen mind taking him to my house?" she asks.

We pass through Mrs. Gardner's front door. "Place him here on the sofa," she says.

Big Tennessee and Sergeant Survant position me on a sofa and put a pillow under my head. A young lady stands in the doorway to the next room, staring at me. "Stop gawking and put some water on for hot tea," Mrs. Gardner snaps. "And cut up what's left of the bread into small bites."

Mrs. Gardner dabs a wet cloth across my forehead. She looks behind the sofa at the men who brought me here. "Your name?" she asks.

"Sergeant Survant," he replies politely.

"Has he eaten anything?" she asks, this time without looking up.

"No, ma'am. Not for two, maybe three, days."

She looks toward the ceiling above my head and raises her eyebrows at the man towering above her.

"Uhhh, everybody calls me Big Tennessee."

"Suits you, I suppose," she chuckles. "Well, Stephen,

they say the darkest hour is just before dawn."

I want to say something, but can't. There's not enough strength in my body. I moan, and she pats the side of my face like Mother did when I was sick back home. "You'll be all right, Stephen," she says.

"He's a fine boy, ma'am," Big Tennessee says. "Anything you can do to help him would be most kind of you."

"He'll do better here than with the two hundred in the hospital," she says. "Every bed there is taken."

The girl enters from the next room carrying a tray and sets it on the table in front of the sofa. It holds three steaming cups, a polished round tin, and a spoon. "Here, Mother," she says.

"Thanks, Belle." Mrs. Gardner takes the tin and removes the lid. She takes the teaspoon, digs sugar from the tin, pours it into one of the cups, and stirs the water. "Those are yours," she says to my friends while nodding toward the two remaining mugs she leaves sitting on the tray.

The thought of a hot, fresh cup of tea instantly makes me feel better. It's been almost a year since I've had one.

Mrs. Gardner props my head a bit more with the pillow. She sinks the teaspoon into the tea and then holds it to my lips. The smell and warmth of the spoon rushes into my body, my lips part, and I drink down the hot liquid.

"That's right. That's it," Mrs. Gardner says. "We're going to get you through this," she whispers. She takes my left hand and wraps it on the outside of the cup. The warmth flows through me like water flowing through Paddy's Run.

Mrs. Gardner looks at Sergeant Survant. "Do you have children?" she asks.

"Yes, ma'am, I do." The question brings a wide smile to his face.

"You know, your family needs you. They think about you a lot."

"He has five children, ma'am," Big Tennessee offers. "All boys."

"Five? My goodness," she says. "There's five blessings right there."

Sergeant Survant chokes back tears but manages to say, "Yes, ma'am, I miss them terribly."

"I'm sure you do," Mrs. Gardner says, smiling. "And, Stephen, you have to get better too. You have a mother waiting for you at home." She turns to Big Tennessee. "Finish your tea. The two of you need to head back. Henderson granted me permission to take in a few guests in dire emergencies. A full hospital fits the bill, I'd say."

Sergeant Survant notices something across the room.

"May I ask who that is?" He indicates a picture of a soldier on the mantel.

"My son," Mrs. Gardner says. There's a tinge of pride in her voice.

"Where is he?" Big Tennessee asks.

Mrs. Gardner pauses before answering. "He's gone. He was nineteen when he was taken, almost three years ago. May '62."

"Where, ma'am?" Sergeant Survant asks.

"Near Richmond," she says. "He was killed near Richmond."

Big Tennessee lays his cup on the table. "I'm real sorry, ma'am, for your loss. I'm sure he was a brave and capable soldier."

"And a fine son, ma'am," Sergeant Survant adds.

"Thank you," she says, her voice dropping off. "I'll have Stephen back to you as soon as I can. He's going to be fine." Mrs. Gardner closes the door behind my friends and turns to find me staring wide-eyed at her. "What's wrong?" she asks.

"Mama sent my shirt to you."

Mrs. Gardner nods. "Colonel Jones wouldn't allow shipments from the north into the Castle, and nobody knew how long he'd be in charge. So I had her send a couple of things to me."

"It's my favorite shirt."

"Is it?"

"You told Mama," I say.

"Told her what?" she asks, squinting like she's puzzled.

"I'm here. I'm okay. That we needed clothes." It takes a lot of effort, and I'm exhausted from fighting to get that many words out.

"Of course," she says.

"Even though your son died in the war?"

"Stephen, worry about resting, getting better. Don't concern yourself with what goes on between two mothers. Leave that for the two of us," she says.

"My brother died in Kentucky, so she's lost a son too. Just like you."

"I didn't know that," she says. "She only mentioned you in her letter."

★★★

Over the next week, several other men arrive at Mrs. Gardner's house. She and Belle nurse us in her living room and kitchen. "Captain Henderson arranged for a steamship to deliver clothes, blankets, and shoes to Cahaba yesterday," she tells us one afternoon as she passes through on her way to the kitchen.

"He seems to be a good man," I tell her.

She stops for a second. "He is."

Belle, standing at the end of the sofa, crosses her arms firmly. She glances toward the kitchen to make sure her mother can't hear. "The shipment won't help much."

"What do you mean?" I ask.

"Have you seen what the guards wear?"

"Not really."

"They haven't had new uniforms in months. They'll end up with much of what was delivered."

"How?"

"They'll trade coats and shoes for rations. Your buddies from the north don't know how cold it can get here."

"It's cold now."

"It'll get worse. Right now your friends want food more than warmth," she says. "But when the weather turns—"

"That's enough," Mrs. Gardner says, entering with a tray of mugs. "The water bucket's empty. Fetch some from the pump."

"Yes, ma'am," Belle says, and leaves.

"How are you feeling?" Mrs. Gardner asks.

"Fine," I say. "Feeling much better, thanks to you."

"I think it's time for you to head back to your friends in the Castle."

"Why?" I ask.

"I need to make room for others. I hear there are more on —"

"No," I interrupt her. "Why are you helping Union soldiers? You have a good reason to hate us."

"What can be done to bring my son back, Stephen? Nothing. I can't make decisions for others. I can only control my own thoughts and actions."

CHAPTER THIRTY-TWO

December 20, 1864

When I return to the prison, a group of men are sleeping beneath the rug from Mrs. Gardner's living room. Every window in her house is bare. She's taken down each curtain and given them as well.

Nobody's immune from the bitter cold. The guards may get enough to eat, but they pace back and forth, their arms wrapped tightly across their chests, or rub their hands together briskly. The Deep South is not a harbor from cruel temperatures.

By mid-January, rations trail off, and we're only getting a pint of cornmeal a day. Most of it is padded with ground corncobs. We're lucky to get a quick bite of pork. The only times we feast are at night, in our dreams.

"What did you have to eat last night, Stephen?" Big

Tennessee asks one morning as we're still lying in the roost.

"That's an easy one. But you have to guess it in ten tries," I tell him.

"Plant or animal?"

"Plant."

"Garden?"

"No."

"Dessert?"

"Yes."

"Well, it can't be pumpkin pie because they come from gardens."

"Correct."

"Shrub?"

"No."

"Tree?"

"Yes."

"Did you have apple pie last night?" Big Tennessee asks with a wide smile.

"You are correct."

"That's one of my favorites," he says. "I dreamed of venison stew with carrots, potatoes, and biscuits."

"No butter?"

"Always fresh butter," he replies. "That's understood, isn't it? I dreamed I walked all the way home and when I got there, I didn't even hug my wife and kids. I headed straight for the root cellar and ate every potato we stored for the winter ... raw."

"Would she recognize you now, you think?"

"I doubt it," he says, lifting his shirt. "She might mistake me for one of our two scarecrows and make me stand out in the garden."

"There's something I miss almost as much as food or Mother," I say.

Big Tennessee turns over onto his elbows and looks at me real serious. "There's something you miss that much?" he asks.

"My bugle," I say softly. "Music was an escape. It took me away from all my troubles and worries."

"Like what?"

"My father getting sick and slowly dying, my brother Robert's death, and my uncle beating me. The songs I played carried me away from all that and filled my mind with joy, at least for a while. I guess that's why I got so good at playing it. Then, when Henry Dorman died holding my bugle, I thought I'd never want to touch it again or play another note."

"Why?"

"It caused his death."

"It didn't cause Henry's death, Stephen," Big Tennessee says. "Henry wanted to die. He said so before he walked toward the middle of the fort. You know that, right? I was there and heard him."

"I know that now, after I've had so much time to think about it. But that's not how I felt at the time. I left the bugle on the ground at Sulphur Branch and walked away from it. I wish I had it back now."

★★★

As winter marches on, a bitter cold swallows the prison, and more and more of us get sick. Corporal Horton Hanna spends three weeks in the hospital and comes back looking better than he ever looked in camp. "At least it was warm there," he says. "Out of the cold with a roof over my head made all the difference. It almost makes me want to get sick again." He sounds half serious.

One Ohio man lacks the strength to turn over or sit up on his own. His breathing is shallow and quick. A sergeant comes over with a few buddies to see if they can take him to the hospital. "Leave him where he lies," his friend demands. "He does not want to be taken to the hospital."

"He'll die for sure if he's left here," the sergeant insists.

His friend covers him with another blanket. "Philip, do you want to go to the hospital?" one of them asks. He puts his ear near Philip's mouth in order to hear his reply. "He says no. He doesn't want to go to the hospital. He stays right where he is."

We often pass the time by betting on lice races. We take a silver plate and set it on the ground. We put three or four of the critters in a cup and on the count of three, the cup is turned upside down over the center of the plate. When the cup is lifted, the first louse to reach the edge is declared the winner.

We sprinkle their backs with different colors. We grind charcoal, cornmeal, and dried leaves to a powder. It's entertaining to see those small specks of black, tan, and orange race for the edge of the plate.

"I bet a piece of cornbread on the black one," a man might say.

"My shirt says the tan one will whip," another will answer.

"Gathering wood on the plain one," a third man may yell.

Today, betting is at fever pitch. A man places the plate

near Philip's head, inches from his nose. "Philip, you want to watch?"

Philip nods ever so slightly.

"One, two, three," the sergeant counts, and turns the cup upside down onto the center of the plate.

"Before I pick the cup up and release the critters, which one do you pick, Philip?" the sergeant asks.

"Tan," Philip manages to say as he lifts his head.

Sergeant lifts the cup, and the lice crawl around in circles for several seconds before heading toward the rim. Eventually, the tan one crosses the edge and falls to the ground.

"You win, pard," the sergeant says, patting his sick friend's shoulder. "You win." Philip smiles, lays his head down on the blanket, and closes his eyes. He never opens them again.

CHAPTER THIRTY-THREE

January 18, 1865

Today we get word that prison command is changing immediately. Rumors spread quickly that some of our freedoms may be taken away. Will letters to and from home be stopped? Will Mrs. Gardner be told to keep her books at home? What about the food she occasionally surprises us with?

We are told nothing beyond "Captain Henderson has been reassigned and Colonel Jones is in charge." Now the new commander is strolling the compound, a guard at each side. One escort signals toward the cooking area, but their words are too low for me to hear. From time to time the colonel kicks the foot of a soldier who is so still and lifeless, he appears dead.

A guard shows the colonel how the flow of water makes

its way through the center of the camp and ends at the privy. They continue walking through the compound, and as they near me, I hear the colonel say, "It's crowded, but I'd rather be here than in Andersonville, Georgia."

"We get their escapees from time to time," the taller guard says. "They're happy when they end up here."

"I believe it one hundred percent," the colonel says.

The colonel makes immediate changes to the prison— for the worse. Shipments of clothes stop arriving. Those without shoes go barefoot across frozen ground. Mrs. Gardner no longer comes into the compound to see how she can be of assistance. It doesn't stop her from meeting me at the hole, but that becomes infrequent too.

"He might forbid me from coming inside the prison," she says one day as she passes pieces of pumpkin pie through the hole in the wall, "but he cannot control me outside those walls."

"Aren't you afraid of getting shot?" I ask.

"Humpth," she answers. "I'm not afraid of the guards. Colonel Jones is as bad to the guards as he is to the prisoners."

Under Colonel Jones's command, we are colder, hungrier, and more ready for the war to end than ever.

"One heck of a 'summer war,'" Sergeant Survant says in a

rare lighthearted moment. "It's been four summers now, and we're headed for a fifth. Nobody thought the Seseches would last this long."

"Word is the blockades are working," says a fresh fish.

"Makes sense. We're getting less and less food," Big Tennessee offers. "Less food for the guards means no food for us."

He's right. Six months of almost no prisoner exchanges have meant the rebs have more and more mouths to feed.

After William Peacock's recent trip to the hospital, many of us have taken him under our wings to make sure he gets home alive. "If I die, my parents will have lost all five sons to the war," he said today. "We lost two of my brothers the first fall, another the following spring, and then a fourth last summer." He's so thin, I can barely remember the stout boy he was a year ago in Indiana. He says he weighed one hundred eighty pounds then and was strong as an ox. Now, in late January, and after three trips to the hospital, he's as helpless as a newborn calf.

CHAPTER THIRTY-FOUR

March brings warm temperatures to Cahaba, along with rain. The storms begin slowly, like a pot of water wanting to boil. First, a fine, misty rain soaks everyone to the bone. Rain soaks everything: the ground, our skin, clothes, and fires.

The rains become steady, and cooking is impossible. We huddle over the wood and do our best to light tiny pieces of dried grass and leaves to start the fires. The wood's too wet. The ground inside the prison turns to mud. Castle Morgan becomes a pigsty. Our feet sink into the ground up to our ankles, and our legs feel as anchored as fence posts.

Nobody moves in the compound unless absolutely necessary. Some choose not to move even when necessity calls. We answer nature's need where we are or trudge only to the trench and let the flow take it on out to the Alabama River.

After three straight days of rain, rats start abandoning their holes along the riverbank and make their way inside Castle Morgan. The rats zigzag past groups of prisoners, dodging attacks as the men try to catch them for supper. Six months of rancid pork and thin corncob mush makes me look at the rats in strange ways. The mud slows them down a bit, and we manage to catch a few. But even with the windfall of fresh meat, we pray the rain will stop. The water chills us through.

The one silver lining in the sky of gray is that the lice are held in check. By the fourth of March there are no signs of graybacks in Castle Morgan.

Sergeant Survant sees the Alabama River is rising within feet of our eastern wall. When night falls on March fourth, the river is inside the compound and captures the privy, the lowest point in the prison. The roosts along that wall are threatened, too.

By morning the river has seized half of our ground. Men sit hip-deep in water as it passes slowly over their legs. The water swirls past shivering soldiers and flows out the southwestern wall.

The top levels of the roost are crammed with men because they are the only sections that remain above water. Not an inch of air can be found between anyone there. The sick, too ill to stand, are now forced to muster enough strength to sit up or drown.

Thick raindrops pelt our heads, making it difficult to hear. One guard yells at the top of his lungs, "You can cross the deadline and rest against the wall. Don't lean on the gates." We prop the sickest against the walls, shoulder to shoulder so they won't fall over.

"Would you ask Colonel Jones if we can leave for higher ground?" Sergeant Survant asks.

By midafternoon, a concession is made. Private Johnny Walker, from the Ohio 15th selects a team of eight men to gather timber and scraps of wood. They grab everything they can get their hands on and bring it inside the prison.

"The whole town is flooded," one of the men reports upon his return. We drag everything they collect to the center of the yard and create a shallow island. As long as the river stops rising, one large group of men can sit on the pile of debris to stay dry.

By evening, every inch of land is covered by a foot of water. The only places to get out of the cold water are on the top shelves of the roost or on the makeshift island.

Those on the island sit up, back to back, or risk slipping into the water. In morning's first light, the men in the roosts rotate. Men elbow one another and punches are thrown to gain one of the spots where sleep can be peaceful. In the daylight we can see that the river has risen more. Now, at its lowest point, the water in the prison is knee-high.

Some are exhausted to the point that they can no longer stand. Sitting means only our shoulders and heads are not submerged.

"We'll get the colonel to let you out until the water recedes," the sergeant of the guards says.

"Where will we go?"

"There are a couple of hills two hundred yards southeast of here," he explains. "They will hold all of you."

When the sergeant returns, he looks pale. The expression on his face says it all. We know the answer. "I'm sorry ...," he begins. "The colonel denied the request."

Caleb Rule, who was with us at Sulphur Branch Trestle, tries to reason with him. "If you opened the gates and gave us permission to walk home, none of us could do it. Heck, we're in no shape to walk to Selma."

The guard nods. "I know," he mutters. "I know."

"Did you tell the colonel that?"

"Yes."

"And . . . "

"He said every last one of you could die in here, for all he cares. I'm sorry. Fifty guards signed a petition for you to be moved, and he still refused."

We appreciate the guards' kindness, but it feels like the last breath of air has been sucked out of us. Caleb Rule flashes the palm of his hand to thank the guard, and walks away.

Early the next morning we hear horses neighing just outside the prison wall. We watch as, one by one, each guard leaves his post from around the top perimeter. We hear the horses ride off.

"Guess they don't think we have the strength to escape," someone offers. "No guards. No deadline. And nobody cares."

Thirty minutes later we hear horses again. And ten minutes later they ride off.

"How many horses were there?" somebody calls out.

"Couldn't tell. Twenty or more."

"What are they doing?"

Nobody has a reasonable guess.

Near noon, the gates slowly open. A stack of wood, as tall

as a Conestoga wagon and twice as wide, is piled a few feet from the opened gate. It includes logs from full-grown trees and boards of freshly cut lumber. Just beyond the pile I see the river has swept into all of Cahaba, including the porch line of Amanda Gardner's house.

The sergeant of the guard rides five feet into the prison. "I'm calling every Confederate guard away for several hours," he yells. "We have a very important meeting." He spots Caleb Rule and says in slow, measured words, "If we come back and every scrap of log and limb happens to have floated inside, I'm sure none of the guards will be upset."

"What about the deadline?"

The sergeant looks down from his mount. "I don't see one, soldier." Then he turns to a guard behind him. "Sergeant Williams, do you see a deadline?"

Sergeant Williams shakes his head. "No, sir. Haven't seen one of those for days."

"What about Colonel Jones?" a prisoner shouts.

The sergeant produces a slow smile. "The colonel was called to Selma for the day," he says.

The guards pull their reins and slosh away. We are left totally alone, the gate standing wide open. It takes four hours for able-bodied prisoners to drag the wood inside the prison.

We pile it crisscross fashion into small islands all around the camp. Sleep is once again possible for many of us.

Nobody stands for roll call the next morning. We simply stare up at Colonel Jones when he appears. He paces back and forth on his perch, seemingly unable to begin. He glares at the islands of logs scattered before him.

"Something's up," comes a voice from behind me. "He's never this quiet."

Colonel Jones coughs to clear his throat. "Sergeant Rufas, I gave orders for the prisoners not to leave."

"Yes, sir, you did," Sergeant Rufas replies.

"And yet, they did," he barks. If I were closer to him, I'm sure I'd see the veins popping across his forehead and neck.

"No, sir, I assure you the prisoners never left their area. They are all accounted for, sir. We checked last night, but we can count them again if you like."

"Then explain to me, Sergeant Rufas, what are some of the prisoners sitting on, when the ground should be covered in two feet of water?"

Sergeant Rufas leans over the wall and peers down at us. He studies the scene for several seconds, perhaps unable to make eye contact with the colonel. "It appears to be timber, sir," he finally says.

"Timber?" the colonel yells. He pauses, then steps closer to Sergeant Rufas. "And how, if they did not leave, did it get inside the prison?"

"That, sir, is easy to explain. The wood floated along the Cahaba and Alabama Rivers with the floodwaters."

"I see."

"Yes, sir. The logs piled up against the gates, and . . . I . . . ah, opened them to release the pressure. If it hadn't been for that, the force would have torn the gates plum off their hinges, and every single man would certainly have escaped."

I start smiling and turn to look at Sergeant Survant. He's buried his head between his legs and is laughing so hard, his shoulders are bobbing up and down.

"So by opening the gates and allowing the logs to float in, you prevented the prisoners from escaping?"

"Yes, sir, I believe so. And it worked, sir, because all the prisoners are still here this morning."

"I see," the colonel mutters.

PART THREE

HOMEWARD BOUND

CHAPTER THIRTY-FIVE

The colonel surveys the scene for a while longer and finally turns to the prisoners. "While in Selma, early this morning, orders came down that when the waters of the Alabama recede into her banks and we're able to get a steamship to Cahaba, seven hundred of you will be released to go home." The colonel turns and walks down the steps and out of sight.

Every prisoner, even some with hardly any energy left, lifts his head and smiles. Soon the walls of the prison are shaking with cheers. Nobody seems to believe what we've heard. Seven hundred of us are going home!

Johnny Walker jumps on top of the roost and begins dancing. He flicks his legs into the air, puts one hand on his hip, and thrusts the other over his head. He twirls counterclockwise slowly and taps his feet against the roof of the roost. Everybody claps to keep him on rhythm.

"What's he doing?" I laugh.

"*That* is called a Scottish jig," Sergeant Survant explains. "Private Walker's originally from Scotland."

Rumors spread as to who is being released and why.

"They don't have enough food to hold us here any longer," someone argues.

"True. They cut rations in half this last month."

"Perhaps the war's ending," someone suggests. "No sense in keeping us here if there's no war."

I can hardly allow myself to think the war may be over. Seven hundred of us are going home, and it doesn't matter why or how. Only who.

The floodwaters recede over the next few days and leave behind a field of mud. It's thick and clings to everything.

Before the prison ground is totally dry, the commander sends word for all the men from Ohio and Michigan "well enough to carry themselves on their own power" to be in formation in two hours. An hour later we hear a prolonged steam whistle. An Ohio man calls up at a guard standing on the southeast corner, "Is that the boat taking us home?"

The guard cradles his musket in his left arm and gives a thumbs-up sign with his right hand.

In another hour, the men from Ohio and Michigan are in formation, as best as they can be among the debris and logs, eager to leave. Colonel Jones appears on the walkway. "We'll do this as quickly as we can . . . ," he begins. "We have rolls organized by company. When we call your company's name, line up at the gate and give the guard your last name. He will direct you to one of five tables outside. You are to step up to the table. You'll receive an envelope with all the items taken from you when you arrived. Take the envelope, check the contents, sign your name, and walk toward the dock at the end of Capitol Avenue."

Colonel Jones salutes, turns, and leaves the platform.

A guard steps forward. "We'll begin with Michigan's cavalry. Everyone else, at ease." We watch in envy as the line moves through the gate. Occasionally, men stop to hug friends being left behind.

As the Michigan boys file out, the men left inside sing "Battle Cry of Freedom," the very song I played as a solo for Governor Morton when he visited Centerville. We look more like filthy pigs in a sty than proud soldiers from war, but there's nothing that can wipe the smiles off our faces. After the Ohio fellows leave, the prison looks spacious. An hour later the boat's whistle blares again. We sit in silence and wait to hear what we know is coming: Michigan and Ohio boys cheering loud enough to wake snakes. They are going home.

With hundreds of men gone there's ample room for sleeping. I lean against a log and stare, for what seems like hours, at the sky. Even after closing my eyes for twenty minutes, sleep doesn't come. I reposition myself multiple times. "Still awake, Stephen?" Sergeant Survant asks.

His question makes me laugh. "You too?" I ask. "Guess everybody's too excited."

"Yeah," he says. "But all the Indiana boys are still here."

Sleep finally catches up and overtakes me. Mother is quick to appear, and we walk arm in arm away from Castle Morgan. She's so happy to see me. I turn for one final glance at the horrific place that held me captive for six months only to discover my brother, Robert, is the only prisoner left inside. He's standing just beyond the deadline inside Castle Morgan, two guards blocking his escape with their rifles. The dream scares me awake.

The exodus does not end with the first ship. Several more groups leave over the course of the next ten days. Each batch gone opens more space in the prison and in the roosts.

Three weeks after the first release, I hear my state's name

called. "Indiana and Tennessee are next to leave," a sergeant announces. I lie back onto the dirt ground, stare up at the gray clouds, and begin thinking about leaving the foul water, the starvation, the filth, the cold, and the death of Castle Morgan and swapping them for home. I'll never think of the word "home" the same way again. I close my eyes and imagine Mother's arms around me. I can feel her warmth and hear her heart pounding in her chest. I see Mrs. Gates on her porch, sewing tiny American flags, her famous pumpkin pie cooling on the banister nearby. She's baked the pie just for me. Dutch is waiting on the steps of the Mansion House, an orange behind his back. But this time, he doesn't make me guess what it is. He tosses it to me in the air and welcomes me home with a hug. Home. Home. I'm going home. I begin to cry, quietly at first, but I can't control myself and it builds to an uncontrollable sob.

★★★

The steam whistle blows, as the other whistles had, near ten a.m. By noon, all able men are in formation. Nearly one hundred of us from the 9th Indiana file out the gate and into tents to claim our envelopes.

"Name?" a sergeant asks when I enter my assigned tent. "Stephen M. Gaston. S-T-E-P-H-E-N," I spell loudly, remembering my first day here.

The Sergeant thumbs through a box. "Check the contents," he says, pushing an envelope across the small table to me. My name's written across the top. It's the same one I was given and that I signed when we arrived from Sulphur Branch Trestle.

After picking up the envelope, my heart sinks. "It's light," I say.

"What do you mean?" the sergeant asks.

I open the flap and see it contains only my pocket watch, comb, and two dollars. "There's no book in here. One was put in when I came." I don't know where the courage comes from, but my voice grows tall and thick. "I surrendered a book in October."

"Calm down," the sergeant says. He points to a line scribbled across the front and reads the writing. "One book taken by"—the sergeant pauses and brings the envelope closer to his eyes—"the name's smudged." He turns it for me to see.

The name is impossible to read. "Nobody had a right to take the book out of here. It was mine."

"It's a lousy book, Sunday Soldier," he snaps. "Move on to the boat and be glad you're going home."

My body tenses and shakes from anger. What right did anybody have to take it? I could leave without the watch or the money, but not without the one thing I was ordered to bring home.

A second line has formed outside the tent. It's not headed in the direction of the boat, but toward Mrs. Gardner's house. As the line shortens, I see everybody's hugging her, and I take my place at the end.

"God bless you," she says to each soldier.

"No, God bless you," the soldier in front of me says. "Half of us wouldn't be alive without all you did."

When he moves, Mrs. Gardner reaches for me with both arms. Dirt covers the front of her light blue dress so thick, it looks as if she's used it to clean a stall. She notices my glance. "It's from the men saying good-bye," she explains. "It must have been terribly muddy in the Castle."

I nod and try to force a smile.

"What's wrong, Stephen?" she asks. "You should be overjoyed. You're going home. You'll see your mother soon."

I show her the nearly empty envelope. "My copy of *David*

Copperfield. Somebody signed it out and didn't return it. Nothing else in here mattered to me."

Mrs. Gardner points to the steps leading to the porch. "Yes, yes. Here it is," she says, picking my book up and patting the cover with her hand. "I'm sorry you worried so."

"You took it? Why?"

"Colonel Henderson entrusted it to me. I knew it must be something very special by the way you carried it through town six months ago. I never saw anybody hold a book like you did, and I didn't want anything to happen to it. I told the colonel I was sure they'd return all the items when the soldiers left, but, as a special favor, I asked if he would let me watch over the book for you"—she pauses—"just in case."

"I never thought I'd see any of my things again," I confess.

"To be honest, I didn't trust all the guards either. That's why keeping the book safe for you was important to me. I've been waiting a long time for your release," she says. "When it was announced that the Indiana boys were going home today, I kept an eye out so I could give it to you personally."

A wave of guilt swallows me. I don't know why, but I start crying, again. Union soldiers had taken her son near Richmond. Yet she did so much for all the men in Castle Morgan. Mother once told me that the best thing to do when someone has been kind to you is to look them in the eye and say, "Thank you."

Mother's voice whispers in my ear, *Simply say, "thank you." It will be enough, Stephen.* I take the book, wipe away the tears with the back of my wrist, and say, "Thank you, Mrs. Gardner."

She tries to speak, but her jaw quivers so much, she can't. I wonder if she's thinking of her son and how he won't be coming home. She touches the side of my face, collects her skirt with her hands, and runs up the stairs and into her house.

CHAPTER THIRTY-SIX

March 28, 1865

The boat pulls away from Cahaba's dock at four o'clock in the afternoon. William Peacock wraps his arm about my neck and whispers, "We're going home, Stephen. We made it." The ride upriver to Selma is slow and uneventful. But for the first time in six months, we see signs of normal life— barns, roads, large trees bursting with splotches of green, and people turning the soil for spring plantings.

I sleep next to Peacock and Big Tennessee on the boat that night in Selma. The next morning we walk from the boat to the train depot between two rows of armed guards. "You're headed to Vicksburg," one of them tells us. A short lady with tangled hair and hard rough hands gives each man a small cloth sack just before we board. Inside are four pieces of hardtack and a handful of dried meat, two days' rations, enough to last us through Alabama. After so long, it feels odd not having to work for food.

Until yesterday, most of our thoughts were of survival. We'd gathered firewood, cooked meals, tried to stay warm, and nursed one another back to health. Every day our thoughts were: *What has to be done to stay alive one more day?* Now each hour is filled with joy. We rest, have rations handed to us, and realize every minute takes us closer to home.

There are two small windows on each side of the train car. We take turns staring out the windows or between a few cracks in the walls. It's hard to turn away from the sights passing by. We overtake Southern town after Southern town: Potter, Browns, Faunsdale, Gallion. A half-burned barn appears in one field. A pile of rubble where a farmhouse once stood emerges in another. Some of the buildings have pockmarks from being struck with artillery shells. Every village looks aged by the war.

The train rolls to a stop just beyond the town of Demopolis. When our car door opens, an officer explains the situation. "We had a derailment late last night. A small section of rails split from the cross ties. Five cars from that train tipped over and are no longer usable. We loaded as many of those passengers as we could onto the train's remaining cars. However, we still have eighty men left to board with you."

We're crowded already. But not as bad as at Castle Morgan. And eighty more people, evenly spread across fifteen cars, means each car will get just five or six additional men.

"Sir!" someone yells from the next car. "How far to Mississippi?"

"Near 'bout forty miles," he answers.

A "Hip-Hip" rings out and is quickly followed by a loud "Hooray!"

"I'll never be so happy to leave a place," Sergeant Survant says.

Our joy is tempered when Big Tennessee sees the first man coming to join our train. "My God, Stephen," he says faintly.

"What?" I ask.

Big Tennessee doesn't answer. He jumps from the boxcar and hurries toward a man walking our way. When we look out to see what caused his alarm, we can't believe our eyes.

If we'd had it bad at Cahaba, these fellows had walked straight out the gates of hell. Their cheekbones jut above hollowed jaws. Their eyes are dark as pitch and sink deep into narrow skulls.

Although he's able to put one foot in front of the other, the man appears to know little of what's going on around him, where he is, or where he's going. He's staring through unfocused eyes.

"Help this fellow up, Stephen," Big Tennessee says. It doesn't take much to lift the man onto the train, and eight others soon follow. They're as light as leaves and brittle as fine pottery. One boy from Rushville takes pity on the fellow sitting beside him. "Here," he says. "I saved a little of the hardtack they gave me in Selma. You can have it."

"Here's some pork," Sergeant Survant says, quickly breaking a piece into two parts. He hands a piece to the two men sitting on either side of him.

The man looks up at Sergeant Survant, confusion written across his eyes. "I have nothing to give you in exchange."

"I don't want anything in return. Don't care much for pork anyways," Sergeant Survant lies. He ate it for six months in Cahaba and was happy to have it.

"Can't remember the last time somebody shared food," the man says. He takes the pork, and it's gone in double-quick time.

"Slow down," Sergeant Survant insists. "You don't want to eat too fast." He breaks his last piece into smaller sections and slows the man's eating by handing him one tiny sliver at a time.

The man swallows each piece as fast as it's offered.

Soon the soldiers added to our car are settled in, and each have had a bite to eat. Several manage slight smiles for a split second. We know they're grateful to be with us and to have something in their stomachs.

We sit, staring at the strangers, unable to take our eyes off them. It's impossible to understand how they can still be alive. Everyone at Cahaba who looked this bad died. Sergeant Survant asks one of the men, "Where were they holding you fellows?"

"Andersonville," one says softly, "Georgia." I remember Colonel Jones's comment about that prison just weeks ago.

Repairs on the damaged rails take longer than expected. Our stop turns into an overnight stay. In the morning we chug west, making our guests as comfortable as we can. How any of us have food to spare is a miracle, but pieces of food appear periodically from ration sacks. Two hours later we pass a sign that reads, KEWANEE, MISSISSIPPI. Somebody says, "We're out of Alabama, boys. One state closer to home."

A little while later the train slows to a crawl as we

approach Meridian. Just beyond town, we pull onto a side track to refuel.

Someone yells the word "rations," and it is repeated down the row of the train car. Men pour out from where they have been resting in order to stretch their arms and legs. We tell the men from Andersonville to stay on board and save their energy. Only a few men from each car are needed to get the food. Two other men and I walk toward the designated area, a church on the edge of town.

Before the church we pass a house with a yard framed by a fence made of split timber. A boy, about my age, stands in the side yard, digging soil. He turns a batch of red clay dirt and knocks it loose with his spade. He examines it and tosses a rock from it onto a nearby pile. When the boy sees the line of men passing, he stops, turns, and rests his arms on the top of his shovel. By the looks of the growing pile of rocks, the soil is half stone.

When the Confederate guards who are leading the way pass by, the boy wipes his brow with a handkerchief and gives them a quick tip of the hat. He smiles warmly and nods their way. When those of us who have been in Castle Morgan come by, his smile withers. He glares at us as if we're worth less than the rocks he's discarding from the soil.

We arrive at a church where a long table is piled with sacks tied with string. Each one contains enough hardtack and pieces of salt pork to feed ten men.

When we return to the train, the Andersonville men frantically grab for the bags. "Hey, hey, hey, slow down," Sergeant Survant warns. "Only give them half of a hardtack and a bite or two of the meat," he orders.

"We were down to almost no food back in Georgia," one of them says. "We think that's why they let us out." We hand them only a share of their rations, and they're as grateful to us as we were to Amanda Gardner. In seconds their portions are gone.

"Hey, slow down," Sergeant Survant repeats to a fellow near him. "I'll tell you what I'll do. When your rations are gone, you can have half my meat," Survant says, tearing his chunk into smaller pieces. "But I'm going to save it and give it to you in an hour or so."

★★★

The train refuels, and we rest in Meridian overnight. The guards allow us to walk as far as a nearby creek. This is the first time we're able to get farther than a few feet from another human being, and it feels glorious.

We leave the next morning for Jackson, slowly following the sun across the sky. A Confederate sergeant tells us, "You'll have to walk the final miles from Jackson to Vicksburg. A boat will take you up the Mississippi from there."

"How far's the walk from Jackson to Vicksburg?" Big Tennessee asks.

"Several days," the sergeant answers. "Depending on how fit you are. It's near forty miles, but you'll have to do it all on foot unless you absolutely can't walk. There are a few Union ambulances for the critical."

There's no way most of the Andersonville men can walk one mile, let alone forty.

"They'll be able to rest as long as they need in Jackson before starting out," the guard assures us. He glances at those from Andersonville and pats one on the knee. "There's no hurry, fellows. Stay there until you have the strength to make it to Vicksburg."

Late that night, we make Jackson. A guard opens our door and says, "Don't get out for any reason. These townsfolk will shoot you in a heartbeat if you get on their property."

"Why did we stop?" someone asks.

"Another derailment ahead," he answers. "The tracks go on another eight miles past Jackson. That's where the holding camp is. While we're stopped here, stay inside the train. Don't get out while we're this close to town," he warns.

We sit for a couple hours before the wheels start turning. An hour later, we come to our final stop. This time, when we look out, campfires and crude shelters dot the landscape.

A guard comes to our door. "You can sleep in the train if you like or hop out. Makes me no never mind. The engine won't start up before morning, so suit yourselves for the night." He points into the darkness. "Over there is the road leading to Vicksburg. Just stay on that road for three, maybe four days, and you'll be in Vicksburg."

Excitement and reservations wrestle in my mind as I think about seeing Mother soon. Every night, hour, and minute brings me closer to home. Centerville is a long ways off, but a three days' walk is all that stands between me and Vicksburg—and the ship that will carry me home.

The next morning those of us who were at Sulphur Branch Trestle and have gained enough strength to begin the journey decide to travel together. The commissary issues us everything we need to bake cornbread for the trip. Once it is out of the fire and cool, we divvy the bread up along with three days' worth of pork and strike out for Vicksburg.

"Don't wander far off the road," we're told. "Ten miles to

Clinton and then ten more to Bolton. With luck, you'll make Bolton the first day. Union control doesn't begin until Camp Fisk, just before Vicksburg."

We haven't walked twenty minutes when a cold rain begins—and we're all reminded of the flood at the Castle.

"It's a sign, Stephen!" Big Tennessee yells out.

"A sign?" I ask. "What kind of sign?"

"It's a sign the good Lord doesn't think we got enough water back at the Castle."

"Couldn't care any less," William Peacock says. "As long as we aren't forced to spend another second sitting in river water."

Our goal is to make Clinton before lunch, which we do. But by the time we arrive, Peacock is exhausted. "Never thought I'd say this after all that time in the Castle, but I'm too tired to eat."

"You and me both," Sergeant Survant says as we pick out spots and spread rubber blankets on the ground. We agree to nap for two hours before heading out again. As we settle in, I call over to William, "What's my first meal going to be back home? You have ten guesses."

"Is it a meat?" he guesses first.

"No."

"Vegetable?"

"No."

"Is it sweet?"

"Yes. That's three."

"Fruit?"

"No. You have six more guesses."

I wait for several seconds before opening my eyes. Peacock's sound asleep, too tired to play the guessing game.

It's after dark when we arrive in Bolton at a makeshift camp, but we're excited to be one day closer to home.

The miles pass more slowly on the second day as we stop frequently to give Peacock time to rest. "Go on," he urges. "I'll catch up later."

"Nope," we all say. "We stay together."

★★★

Even at our slow pace, it doesn't deter our resolve to make Camp Fisk in three days. We know we're close when we approach a pontoon bridge spanning the Black River. A neatly printed sign reads, UNION TERRITORY: CAMP FISK (7 MILES). We quicken our pace.

The scent of smoke thickens the air, and the clattering

sounds of the camp increase the farther we walk. We suspect Camp Fisk is hidden just beyond the next hill. Big Tennessee notices something appears to be rising up from the ground.

"Look, fellows!" he yells, and points straight ahead. With each step toward the crest of the hill, a patch of blue and white rises higher and higher until we're all able to view the American flag in all its splendor. We crest the hill and take in the sweeping scene before us: a vast field, dotted with hundreds, maybe a thousand soldiers, surrounded by a wire fence. And topped with that brilliant flag.

None of us are able to contain our feelings. Peacock falls to his knees and weeps. "I've done it," he says. "It's finally over."

Sergeant Survant says, "If death gets me here, at least it will be within sight of that flag."

I sit for a good long while, powerless to move, unable to comprehend that I've survived Sulphur Branch Trestle, Castle Morgan, flooding, and have finally reached the spot where a ship will take me home.

★★★

Negro soldiers stand guard at the gates. Their dark faces nod and smile as we enter. They seem as glad to see us as we are to see them. One older man with a white beard pats me on the back. "Thank you, soldier," he whispers.

Another guard, seeing how exhausted Peacock looks, rushes to his side. "It's a miracle I'm here," Peacock tells him.

"It'll take four or five days to get rosters ready before you can leave on a steamer for home," a major informs us at a tent inside the gate. "When the rolls are complete, you'll be transported by rail to the Vicksburg dock. We'll put five hundred to one thousand men on each ship headed north. Until your group is called, rest up and get food. We have new uniforms waiting for you, along with plenty of hardtack, pork, good coffee, and cabbage."

They issue us new clothes, but mine are too big. "I'm swimming in these," I tell the quartermaster.

"You want them to be loose because you're gonna fatten up some," he says. When he's satisfied that I'm dressed properly, he tells me, "Go toss those mud-stained rags into a fire." I feel like a real soldier again for the first time in a long while. There are huge barrels of pickled cabbage at the commissary. And the vegetables are a welcome addition to our diet. We eat large portions with our fingers and lick every drop of juice as it runs down our forearms.

The boys from Andersonville have it the worst. For some

of them, their minds are like wild horses that refuse to be tamed. As hard as anyone tries, nobody can stop them from overeating. They don't listen when they're told their stomachs can't handle the amount of food they're trying to take in. One fellow stuffs his mouth so full, he chokes to death without putting up much of a struggle. Three others die from overeating. How odd it is that the thing these prisoners want most—food—is as lethal as a bullet if they're not careful.

Because of the massive number of people at Camp Fisk, everyone competes for wood to heat coffee and wrangles for spaces inside a limited number of shelters. But in a few days I notice a change in my body, as I'm able to walk through the camp and gather firewood without being out of breath or having to stop and rest. The immense number of people also overwhelms the roll-making process, and it takes longer than expected for the rosters to be created for groups leaving.

We're told to assemble on the parade ground to learn who will be heading home first.

"The first batch to head to the docks in Vicksburg," Captain Speed announces, "are Ohio boys." It's easy to see where these fellows are standing when the announcement is made. However, their hopes are tempered when he adds,

"Only certain regiments are on the list—not everyone from the state."

When the first regiment's name is called, one man wraps me in a bear hug and weeps openly. "I'll see my wife and daughters in a few days," he says in disbelief. "Home," he says over and over. "Home." A couple of his friends pat him on the back. "I can't believe it," he weeps. "Simply can't believe it."

Each man's name is called to make sure he's in attendance. "Desmond Adams?" the captain calls.

The man who gave me a bear hug jumps up and waves his arms in the air. "Here, here, here," he yells at the top of his lungs, "and ready to travel, sir!"

Two hours later, 650 Ohio soldiers have responded. Three boxcars and several flatcars are stuffed with grateful souls. Camp officers decide to add 150 more names to the list, men from Indiana.

My hopes soar in anticipation that the Indiana 9th will be chosen. A man complains loudly to Captain Speed, the officer in charge of assigning transportation, that the trains are already crowded. Captain Speed disregards the complaint with a wave of his hand and boards 150 more.

The Indiana 9th is not chosen.

The soldiers left at Camp Fisk begin a tradition of

sending each group off as it leaves. We stay on the parade ground and cheer that day's departing comrades with chants of "HOME ... HOME ... HOME," and punch our fists into the air with each word as the train lurches west toward the docks.

A few days later, on April 6, word reaches Camp Fisk that Richmond, Virginia, has fallen to Union troops. Seven days later, on Palm Sunday, we learn of Lee's surrender. The dogwoods are in bloom, the creeks are full from spring rains, the war's over, and we are days from home. Can anything be more perfect?

★★★

A celebration of unequaled magnitude is set for the next day. Rebel soldiers, stationed nearby, are told not to be alarmed when we fire off a two-hundred-gun salute to commemorate the end of the war. They canvass the troops and put together a band. I volunteer, and I'm handed a battered old horn to play. To hold that dented piece of metal brings the most joy I've experienced in months.

At first, my mouth hurts as I press my lips hard together and force air through the horn. I'm out of practice, but slowly, it all comes back and feels right. I play better than I have at any time in my life. We decide to play "When Johnny Comes Marching Home."

When Johnny comes marching home again
Hurrah. Hurrah.
We'll give him a hearty welcome then
Hurrah. Hurrah.
The men will cheer and the boys will shout
The ladies they will all turn out
And we'll all feel gay when Johnny comes marching home.

There's not a dry eye anywhere in Camp Fisk.

CHAPTER THIRTY-SEVEN

April 17, 1865

Illinois prisoners are told to assemble for departure, and the rest of us sit nearby ready to give them a fond farewell. It's apparent when the Illinois boys are in formation that something's different. The sky may be clear, but the atmosphere seems cloudy and unbalanced.

My group has been at Camp Fisk for two weeks, waiting to leave. During this time, Confederate soldiers have worked every day in camp. They help prepare rosters for departures, bring in supplies, and assist in carrying wounded soldiers from Jackson in ambulances. They move freely about Camp Fisk, and nobody gives them a second thought. A Confederate officer and six of his fellow soldiers meet with a Union Major every morning to discuss departures. After their meetings, the major announces who is to leave that day.

Today, however, the Confederate officer calls his soldiers off to the side. He speaks to them privately for less than a minute. His hands, usually animated, are reserved today, his gestures slow. He dismisses his squad; they hurry out the gate and head east toward Black River without looking back. Several minutes pass, and after making sure his Confederate men have cleared camp, he speaks with the Union officers. We can't hear what's being said, but one Union officer grabs his head as if the news brings a stifling blow to his skull. Another officer reaches for the wheel of a nearby wagon and sinks to the ground.

Soon after, the Confederate officer leaves camp. He follows the same path his fellow soldiers took a few minutes ago.

We sit, waiting for perhaps fifteen minutes. We know something's amiss. "False rumors of the war ending?" Big Tennessee wonders out loud.

"I don't think so," Sergeant Survant says. "Their reactions were too strong for that."

"Worse than the war not being over?" I ask. "I can't think of anything worse than that."

Sergeant Survant nods. "Yeah, probably so, Stephen."

Major Fidler steps onto the wooden platform and raises a hand for quiet. He glances back to the east to where the

Confederate soldiers left camp minutes earlier. They are completely out of sight.

"Men...," he begins, "this is an important day for our brave men heading home to Illinois." He looks at his boots to gather his thoughts. "But before you leave, there's some news I have to share with you. Word arrived in Vicksburg today. A ship called the *Sultana* stopped on her way to New Orleans. With telegraph lines slashed, this is the quickest we could learn of... of... this news. The news is not good."

"We're going home, right?" a man shouts. "You got our hopes up, Major, that today's our last day here."

The major looks up. "Yes, you're going home today," he says too quietly.

"Then what's the news?" someone yells. "Spit it out."

"Three nights ago President Lincoln was shot in a theater in Washington." The major pauses. "Our president is dead."

The news crashes through camp like a boom of thunder announcing a storm. After the shock sinks in, someone yells, "Hang them rebels from trees!"

"Hang 'em thick as pinecones," another offers.

The major waits for the hatred to evaporate.

"We fought for nothing," somebody suggests.

"Is that why the Southern traitors ran from camp?" one asks.

The major raises his hand. "I asked the captain to leave."

"Ran like scared rabbits!" a man yells.

"We should raise a black flag and kill 'em all."

"It's not clear who shot our president," the major says. "One thing is for sure: The Confederate officers and soldiers at Camp Fisk had nothing to do with it."

"In for an ounce . . . in for a pound!" somebody shouts.

The major asks for quiet. "President Lincoln's death doesn't change the end of the war or the fruits of your labors. It doesn't change the fact that our Illinois brothers go home today," he explains. "I've asked the Confederates to return tomorrow to cut orders to release Wisconsin, Minnesota, and Iowa on Saturday."

The men from those three states are too shocked to respond to their good fortune with any signs of joy. Instead, some men start singing "John Brown's Body."

They will hang Jeff Davis to a Sour Apple Tree.
They will hang Jeff Davis to a Sour Apple Tree.
They will hang Jeff Davis to a Sour Apple Tree.
As they march along.

By the end of the first verse, almost every person in Camp Fisk joins in:

Now three rousing cheers for the Union.
Now three rousing cheers for the Union.
Now three rousing cheers for the Union.
As we go marching along.

The day's planned departure goes on as scheduled, and things are more quiet than I expect for the rest of the week. The only Confederate soldiers we see are a single officer and his secretary. The two of them come regularly, surrounded by Negro armed guards. With their work complete, they leave without pleasantries.

★★★

On Saturday, as planned, we get word that the *Ames* has docked in Vicksburg and she takes the Wisconsin, Minnesota, and Iowa men home. More and more camp space opens with each departing group.

Early Monday morning, with the ground still damp with dew, the Union Major in charge asks every man in the camp to join him at the stage for an important announcement. "It will take a lot of doing, but we're working on the final rosters. At ten o'clock, trains will arrive to take all two thousand four hundred of you home, beginning with Indiana."

If the Major says another word, it doesn't land in my ears. All I hear is the sound of Mother's voice welcoming me home. I'm already seated at the kitchen table, her at my side. To say the last group of men hug and cheer is an understatement. It's over—really, really over. We're headed home.

It takes two hours to call the Indiana list. Every five to seven seconds, a name is called. The person acknowledges it and heads to a boxcar or a flatcar on the edge of the parade ground. Soldiers too sick to leave with their companies in prior weeks, like those from Andersonville, depart with us.

At noon, the first train of the day lurches west for Vicksburg, with the Indiana 9th Cavalry and three hundred men on stretchers. Ten minutes later, the train pulls parallel to the river, and we see what we have dreamed of for weeks: the five ships that will carry us home.

Today's the first time I've laid eyes on such a massive body of water. Heavy rains across the last month, including the ones that had flooded Castle Morgan, have swollen the Mississippi beyond its banks. We're told war damage to levees have allowed waters to flood the plains to the west, spilling miles into Louisiana. The river appears more like an ocean, save for a row of treetops defining where the other riverbank would normally contain the river.

We've hardly had time to climb down from the boxcar when we watch the largest of the five ships pull away from the dock. "That ship's empty. Why is it leaving?" I ask Sergeant Survant.

"How would I know?" he says. "There're plenty of soldiers left to fill all five ships."

The boat clears the dock and turns upriver. Painted on her side, in letters taller than Big Tennessee, are the words "Lady Gay." Why would the largest ship at the dock leave without any soldiers on it?

We're funneled along the bank toward the *Sultana*. It is the same ship that had brought word of Lincoln's death last week. The closer I get, the more massive it appears. One small building sits on the top deck, smokestacks as tall as any tree on either side. A couple shipmates stand on wooden crates by the gangplank. One of them points to each head and counts to himself as we pass.

Another yells instructions. "The top level is called the Texas deck. That's where the pilothouse is located," he says.

"You may sleep on the floor there, but the pilothouse is off-limits to everybody except the captain and crew. The Chicago Opera Troupe's on board till Memphis, and they have been assigned the rooms on the main deck. Then we have the boiler and, finally, hurricane decks. We want the non-ambulatory soldiers to be near the cabin rooms just above the boilers. They will be warm there. Indiana men, claim a stake anywhere that's free other than the pilothouse or near the cabins."

"How big is the side wheel?" somebody asks the shipmate giving instructions.

"Thirty-four feet across. There's one on each side of the *Sultana*, and it takes four very large boilers to power them."

As we board the *Sultana*, loud poundings are heard coming from deep inside the interior of the vessel. Sergeant Survant grabs the arm of a boat hand as he walks across the gangplank.

"What's that pounding?" he asks.

"One of the boilers is being fixed," the shipmate says. "It started leaking after we left New Orleans. We limped in here to pick you guys up. Barely made it, too."

★★★

The huffing and yelling of a captain from a nearby ship catches our ears. Everybody turns to see him storm down the riverbank and board his boat. He flails his arms in the air and shouts cuss words back up the riverbank toward the command tents. Minutes later, after we've made our way to the second deck, I watch his ship back away from shore. Like the *Lady Gay*, not a single soldier boards the boat before it leaves.

William Peacock, Sergeant Survant, and I navigate a dimly lit hallway, its walls covered in wood stained dark as molasses. Doors line both sides of the passageway. Jiggling five handles to cabin rooms fails to open any of them.

"Hey, fellas!" a boat hand yells. "Those rooms are for paying customers like the opera singers—or for the sick. Find a spot on a higher deck."

We maneuver around men gawking at the richness of *Sultana*'s walls decorated with fancy pieces of art and carved moldings, and go up a set of stairs. Along this deck, cots are folded up and tied against the walls. "The cots will be lowered at night. During the day they stay tied to the walls to give more space for walking around," we are told.

By two o'clock the three of us find a spot on the hurricane deck to put our provisions and two days' worth of rations.

Cheers ring out as the next trainload arrives. "Hurry, more guys are coming. Let's spread your things out a little to save a place for Big Tennessee just in case he gets assigned to this boat," I suggest.

We stake our claim and hurry to stand at the rail to watch lines of men pour from the train's compartments. We expect them to board one of the two ships on either side of the *Sultana*. They don't. Instead, the men are channeled down the bank and onto the boat with us. One of the first on board tells us that there were six hundred on this second train.

The boat hand I had met earlier comes by with bed linens draped over his arms. "How's this thing going to float with so many people on it?" William asks.

He laughs. "Don't worry, pard. This beauty floats in thirty-four inches of water. She'll hold lots more weight than you'd think."

As hundreds of additional men file onto the *Sultana*, the pounding on the boiler deep in the belly of the ship continues and can be heard from where we stand.

"You fellas want to see an alligator?" a man calls to us. He's standing near the stairs flanked by two small girls, both holding a hand.

"Excuse me?" I say.

"An alligator. You want to see one?" he asks again.

"Are you serious?" William asks.

"Sure. I'm taking young Elizabeth Spikes and her sister, Susan, here to see him now," he says, shaking a hand as he says their names. "You lads can join us if you like."

"Is he in the river near the boat?" I ask.

"No, he's on board with us."

"Is he alive?" the smaller of the two girls, Susan, wants to know.

"He's breathing the same air as you and your sister," the man answers.

"You two, go ahead," Sergeant Survant says. William and I look at each other and shrug. "Sure," we say at the same time.

The man is quite young, has sandy-colored hair, and wears a cap with a shiny black leather brim. As I get closer, I notice the word "Captain" printed in gold thread across the front of his cap. "You're the captain?" I ask, surprised by his young appearance.

"The one and only. Captain James Cass Mason," he says.

Susan Spikes pulls the captain's fingers so hard, his shoulders dip to one side. "Can it bite us?"

"You bet he can," he says. "He has lots of teeth and a jaw that can open this wide." The captain demonstrates with his hands to show how massive the alligator's mouth can stretch.

The older girl flashes a large grin as if this is going to be the best treat in the world, but her younger sister pulls back. "I don't want to see it anymore."

"Oh, he can't get to you," the captain reassures her. "He's in a big wooden cage."

"I'm scared," she pleads.

He kneels in front of her, removes his cap, and places it on her head. Then he grabs her shoulders lightly and looks at her from eye level. "Miss Susan Spikes, do you think the captain of the *Sultana* would let anything bad happen to two of the prettiest passengers ever to step foot on his ship?" he asks. "The beast is in a crate and can't do you any harm."

She puts on her bravest face, and the five of us climb stairs until we step onto the Texas deck. We round the side of the pilothouse and find a large wooden crate nestled against the side wall. Nailed to the front is a sign written in bold white letters: GASTONE.

"Hey, Stephen, I think you're related," William jokes.

"What do you mean?" the captain asks.

"That's his surname," William says, and laughs.

"Louisiana gator Gastone, meet Union soldier Gastone," Captain Mason says with a flourish of his hand.

"My name doesn't have an 'e' at the end, Captain."

"Close enough," William says. "Close enough."

The captain points to the front of the crate. "Move by his nose so I can show you his teeth," he suggests.

When the four of us are standing directly in front of Gastone, Captain Mason taps the front of the cage with his knuckles.

The alligator opens his mouth and reveals a set of pointed teeth ready to bite anything that's unfortunate enough to get close. He bellows a long, slow, deep sound, and everyone except the captain jumps. Flaps of skin near the back of the reptile's throat vibrate, creating a deep roar. Susan and Elizabeth break free and sprint, screaming down the stairs to find their mother.

The captain laughs. "I shouldn't have done that without warning them," he says, and bends over beside the crate. "Gastone's nearly nine feet long. Come closer. He can't get out. The crate's built of sturdy wood."

"What was that sound he made?" William asks.

"He thinks it's time to eat," the captain explains.

A crewman rushes up to us. "Captain Mason, you have to see what's going on," he says. He motions toward the other side of the deck and to a man stomping down the riverbank.

A cigar hangs out of his mouth, and he's puffing like a locomotive engine. Smoke encircles his head of snow-white hair and trails behind him like a tail in the air. It's hard to see where his hair ends and the smoke begins.

We watch the man shake his finger in another man's face. "I'm already behind schedule!" he shouts. "I have to pull out soon and haven't time to sit around and wait." He turns and sees us watching along *Sultana*'s highest rail. He points directly at the very spot where we stand. "The government is paying five to ten dollars a head to take all these boys home. That's a godawful amount of money to pay to one boat when the rest of us are leaving empty!" he yells directly at Captain Mason. "You're no better than a river rat with what you're doing, Mason."

The man standing with the irate boatman shrugs his arms. "Captain White, my hands are tied," he explains. "There's nothing I can do."

Captain White tosses his cigar into a nearby puddle and stomps toward the boat docked next to us, the *Pauline Carroll*. Halfway across the gangplank, he turns back and yells, "I pulled in here to fill my ship, and I'm leaving with seventeen people? You haven't heard the end of this," he says, shaking his clenched fist.

"Hey, Captain White," Captain Mason says, and chuckles, "you best be pushing off so you can stay on schedule."

Captain White's feet seem nailed to the gangplank. He stares at Captain Mason, then says in a matter-of-fact tone, "You think I don't know why they're putting all these soldiers on your boat, Mason? I know. We all know, and you'll get what's coming to you. Mark my words, Mason, you'll get what's coming to you." With that, Captain White retreats inside the *Pauline Carroll*.

Slowly, as a long line of soldiers continue to file onto the *Sultana*, the *Pauline Carroll* backs away from Vicksburg's docks and heads north with seventeen passengers and one irate captain.

It's nightfall when the last train arrives from Camp Fisk, and Big Tennessee still hasn't made an appearance. The men make their way down a dark bank and head toward the only other ship still at dock. Somebody runs down the hill from the command tent and calls out to the front of the line, "There's smallpox on that ship! It's quarantined."

I know that's not true. Several families, some with children and large travel trunks bound with wide leather straps, boarded earlier. He points to the *Sultana* and tells them to get on with us.

The captain had said the *Sultana* weighs far less than anybody can believe because many of the walls and floors are made of flimsy wood. That's evidenced now, as the center of the floor we're standing on begins sagging. We are asked to move starboard while crewmen place beams strategically to support the floors on portside. Then we move portside to ease the load so the floors can be reinforced on starboard side.

"I feel like I'm back at Castle Morgan," a familiar voice says. It's Big Tennessee making his way to the Texas deck.

"You'll be home soon enough," comes a reply from a tired and sweaty deckhand. "We're doing exactly what we're told to do."

Big Tennessee's right. Just like at Castle Morgan, not everyone can lie down at the same time. "It's great to see you, pard!" I yell, and reach to shake his hand, but he pulls me to his chest and gives me a hug. "We saved you a place below. If it rains, we'll be dry."

We head below, where double-stacked cots take up most of the hallways and floor spaces. Men are untying the cots, and those without beds sit against the walls and along the rails. The last ones boarding take any remaining spots on steps, between decks, against rails, and in odd nooks and crannies. Every spot is filled with a body.

Big Tennessee sets his bag on the floor as a boat clerk tells an Ohio man that when the *Sultana* reaches Cairo, Illinois, she will hold the record for number of passengers on any river run. "Over two thousand four hundred," he says. "In addition to that, there are a quarter million pounds of Louisiana sugar and one hundred head of livestock in the hold."

The floor sags as we walk around the *Sultana*, even with the additional supports. It gives less above beams, but the farther away we step from support timbers, the more the floor feels like a soggy field after three or four days of heavy rain.

CHAPTER THIRTY-EIGHT

April 24, 1865

After the excitement of our new surroundings wears off, time passes uneventfully. We pull out of Vicksburg, the sick on cots, warmed by the boilers below them, and everybody else packed in like crackers in a barrel. Everyone gets as comfortable as possible under the circumstances, and there are few complaints. We're going home, after all.

The next morning, the captain sends word via his staff that we're making excellent progress. The river flows with no rhyme or reason. It meanders west a bit, then north, perhaps east for a while. The impression is that the river's course was made on a whim. It seems extremely random.

For the first full day on the *Sultana* our only entertainment is watching the flat lands of Arkansas drift pass. Many of the fields sit covered in brown water, flooded from winter's melt.

The landscape, although choked with water, looks calm and peaceful. Occasionally, Negroes appear on the higher banks to the east. When they see our Union blue uniforms, they cheer, clap, and break into song and dance.

A little after daylight on the second morning, we come to the first town of any size: Helena, Arkansas. We slip into the dock, and the crew passes word around that we will stay for several hours. Workers busy themselves, loading coal to feed the boilers and rations to feed the passengers. Since refueling will take a while and Helena is the last town we'll see before the Chicago Opera Troupe gets off in Memphis, the singers have enough time to cross the gangplank for an impromptu performance on the banks of the Mississippi. The show is mostly for our enjoyment, but word soon spreads through nearby streets, and a large population pours from the town to the dock.

"Our first song is from *The Merry Wives of Windsor* by Otto Nicolai," the director announces from atop a small wooden crate. He turns to face the choir, and with the motion of his hand, the song begins. I don't understand a single word being sung because it's all in German, but their voices blend together like silk. Men who are talking soon quiet down in order to hear the songs. The notes send a tingling up my spine. It's absolutely the most beautiful singing I've ever heard and makes me glad to be alive.

After five songs, the performers take bows through an extended ovation. When the ship's loaded with provisions and the opera company's back on board, word spreads that a fellow who makes pictures has set up his three-legged camera onshore. He wants to get an image of the *Sultana* to document the largest haul of people on the Mississippi. Big Tennessee, William, Sergeant Survant, and I are near the rail of the hurricane deck, so we know we'll be seen in the picture for sure. Hundreds upon hundreds of men have the same idea and shift to be in the picture. The floors creak and groan from the added weight on the landward side but somehow manage to hold.

The *Sultana* lists in the river so much, it feels like water is going to spill into the boat's hold and sink us all. It doesn't. We hear Major Fidler yell from up above, "Get back to where your gear is stored. Do you want to drown us all?"

After calm is restored, we pull away from the bank and head upstream. A group of twelve women calling themselves the Sisters of Charity pass through the sea of soldiers, handing out crackers they purchased in West Helena. "Nobody goes hungry today," one says proudly.

An "Amen, sister" follows close behind. Everyone's glad to have real crackers instead of hardtack.

One of the sisters leans over a particularly sick-looking fellow lying near me. "I've got a little salt pork, too, if it will make you feel better," she says quietly.

"Bless you, sister," he whispers. "Bless you."

"No," she says. "Bless you. Where are you from?"

"Southern Illinois," he says.

"Well, you'll see home in two days," she promises. "Two days."

The sun is heading to bed when bluffs along the east bank of the Mississippi River come into view. The cliffs rise like castle walls from a wide river moat. Just past the bluffs, the buildings of Memphis make an appearance. The flooded river spreads west into Arkansas for miles.

The ship's quartermaster climbs onto the pilothouse and yells for quiet. "Captain Mason is offering twenty-five cents an hour to eighteen volunteers willing to unload sugar in Memphis."

"Good workers only," the captain calls.

"Look at these men, sir. They're all good workers," he yells back. His boss flashes a thumbs-up and a smile to his man on the roof.

"It will take several hours to get it off," he says. "After pulling into Memphis, we'll unload the opera singers. Men going into town will be let off next. When the soldiers are out of our way, we'll unload." William and I are the first to volunteer.

"I'll help," Big Tennessee calls. Soon eighteen workers are chosen.

★★★

A spot on the top deck provides a view of the Chicago Opera Troupe heading across the gangplank and up the hillside into Memphis. The captain makes his way to the center of the gangplank and blocks the path of excited soldiers. He yells, "Men, it's seven o'clock! We'll unload every bit of that sugar in the hold, a few heads of livestock, all the cases of wine, and then be on our way to Cairo."

"We're gettin' off for a while? Right, sir?" It's Sergeant Survant bellowing from the hurricane level. "We've been stuck on this floating prison for two days now."

"Hold your horses. That's what I'm trying to say," the captain says. "If we shove off by eleven o'clock, the *Sultana* will stay on schedule. We'll ring the bell at ten thirty. You'll have thirty minutes to get yourself on board after the bell sounds. If you're not here in thirty minutes, we leave you in Memphis."

The captain points toward a bell perched on the bow. "This is what you'll be listening for, men." The first mate pulls a leather strap back and forth for five seconds. The bell, half the size of the one hanging in the church in Centerville, packs a whale of a clang. I have to duck my head and cover my ears.

Captain steps aside and with a wave of his hand invites soldiers to enjoy Memphis. Walking down the gangplank and off the ship, the men resemble a small river cascading over a waterfall. Some, unable to walk on their own, hobble with the help of comrades. Others, totally disinterested in leaving the boat, lay where they are, happy to have space around them for a couple hours.

William, Big Tennessee, and I join fifteen men near the door leading to the ship's hold. We peer into the darkness, barely able to make out the shapes of barrels sitting in shadows. They're twice the size of the ones Uncle Clem had in his livery back home.

Captain Mason points to a stout man standing next to him. "This is William Rowberry, my first mate. He'll explain the process."

★★★

The massive man pushes long wavy brown hair off his forehead. A thin, tight-fitting black shirt emphasizes muscles I've never seen on a human before. He must be the strongest man on the boat by far—with Big Tennessee coming in a distant second. Rowberry takes a length of rope hanging from a hook on the wall. "Each one of these barrels holds hundreds of pounds. Eight men lifting together can manage one hogshead of sugar. We're not going to use ropes tonight. Instead, we'll work smart. Three or four of you will push a barrel up a ramp, out of the hold, and onto the deck. Others will take over from there. They'll roll it to the gangplank and off into the street. The company that purchased it takes control of it once it's off the *Sultana*. Their men are waiting there. Don't strain yourselves," he warns. "If you feel yourself slipping, say something. You don't want to end up beneath one of these rascals. It'll crush you.

"Line up by size starting with the big fellow on the other end," he orders. Rowberry strolls along the line, pointing to each man. "Deck!" he shouts to the first, second, third, and fourth man.

"Hold, hold, hold, hold," he says to the next four.

He points to me. "Hold," he says. "You too," he says to William.

He divides the last eight, with Big Tennessee ending up in the hold. "It's an easy job to push a hogshead across the deck, so, men in the hold, rotate when you get tired below. Any questions?" he asks.

Silence.

Rowberry claps his hands. "Let's get started, men."

With each step I make toward the kegs, they seem to grow larger and larger. Two lanterns are handed down to light the hold just enough to see what we're doing. "Can we get more flame?" I ask.

"No," Rowberry answers. "We can't risk a fire down there. This ship is a tinderbox, and if it catches fire, she'll burn to the waterline," he warns. "Let's go, you fellows in the hold. Get to pushing. These teams up here are waiting."

Because of the hold's steep incline, it takes six pairs of hands to roll the first few barrels up, out, and onto the deck. When they reach the top, workers roll them to the edge of the boat and ease them straight over a gangplank to the street. When eight barrels are up and out, we're able to lengthen the ramp by using longer boards. The incline's easier to manage, but not by much.

After working an hour, half the hold is empty. William spots a broken keg in the corner, away from the two lanterns.

He taps me on the arm and points to a small pile of white crystals reflecting tiny specks of light. While four men are busy pushing one up, William and I scurry over and pinch some sugar between our thumbs and fingers. We tilt our heads back and sample the product.

It seems like years since I've had this flavor in my mouth. Thoughts of Miss Gates's pies flash through my mind, as I remember how she'd sprinkle just the right amount of sugar on top of the dough before slipping it into the oven. The heat would brown up the sugar into a crust of caramel that tasted like heaven. "Oh my," William utters. "This is so good." We take turns dipping into our find and blocking the view of our coworkers.

"Let's get back," I warn while removing my hat to cover the white pile. Over the next thirty minutes, William and I return often to our stash and secretly sample nature's sweetness.

When we get to the last row, including the one with the busted hogshead, it's time to let Rowberry know about the find. "Hey, pard!" I yell. "There's a problem here you need to see."

"You shouldn't blame the crew for this," I say, pointing to our treasure. "It's not been moved a single inch." Several cups of the white crystals lay spilled on the floor, seemingly untouched.

He agrees. "The barrel hasn't been moved, so the crew didn't do it." He studies the surrounding containers, then looks at me. "Bring one of the lanterns over here," he orders. He bends over, studies the nearby barrels, then looks at me again. "You know," he says, "some of the Louisiana sugar is known to have special properties that sugar from the islands don't have."

"Is that right?" I ask.

"Yes," he says, rubbing his chin and looking around the floor. "This just might be that special type of flying sugar I've heard so much about."

"Flying sugar?" I ask. "You're pulling my leg. I never heard of such a thing."

"It's rare, but I've seen it once or twice before." Rowberry looks at my shirt. "Don't move," he says in a hushed voice. "Be very still." He raises his hand and swipes his hand fast and hard across my chest several times. White crystals fly through the air and look like tiny shooting stars. "Seems some of this stuff flew plum out of the keg and onto the front of your shirt," he says. He gives me a quick wink to let me know there's no worries, and those gathered around have a good laugh at my expense.

Rowberry instructs us to save the damaged hogshead for last. He singlehandedly spins the barrel around so the hole doesn't show, trying to remove any temptation. We work another fifteen minutes until the hold's empty except for the last container. "Big Tennessee," he calls. "Tell the men working on the deck to come down." When we're all gathered, he tells us, "It's time for me to notify Captain Mason that the hold's almost empty and that you fellas need to be paid. It'll take me exactly twenty minutes to find him. While I'm gone, I'm sure river rats might dive into this pile and eat a lot of what's spilled."

"River rats?" one guy asks. "Never seen any river rats down here."

Big Tennessee nudges him with his elbow. "Shut up, Sunday Soldier."

"Ohhh," the man says quickly after catching on. "River rats are fierce this time of year."

"Whatever sugar is gone in twenty minutes' time won't be the fault of anybody standing in the hold right now." Rowberry pauses in silence. "Right, men?" he asks.

"No, sir!" everyone yells.

Rowberry takes a bar from the wall and pries a larger hole near the bottom of the barrel. Several pounds spill onto the floor. "*Bon appetit*, men," he says. "See ya in exactly twenty minutes."

I gorge myself until my stomach hurts. After eating all we can manage, the rest is stuffed by the fistfuls into our trouser pockets. My hat holds two double handfuls. "I'll hide this in my bedroll as soon as we get back up on the hurricane deck," I tell William.

The first mate returns twenty minutes later with Captain Mason. "Fellows, line up," the captain calls to us. He hands out a dollar coin to each man. "Three hours' work at twenty-five cents per hour is seventy-five cents if my math is correct. Keep the extra quarter dollar for a job well done. There are still forty-five minutes left before shoving off in case some of you want to see Memphis. Listen for the bell."

Big Tennessee sprints for the gangplank and disappears into the shadows of Memphis. I tell William I'm too exhausted to walk into town, so we return to the hurricane deck. The cots are lowered and filled with the sick. When we near where our provisions are stashed, William heads toward the stairs.

"Where are you going?" I ask.

"Before unloading the sugar I found two great spots smack in front of the pilothouse. I moved our things to save places for us there. Survant and Big Tennessee will have to stay here."

"We had good spots already, closer to the boiler," I insist. "It's warmer here."

"It's too hard to breathe here," he says. "Too stuffy."

"I don't like the idea of sleeping outside in the open."

"Well, I don't want to be near all these sick people," he says. "Hurry before everyone gets back and moves our things."

★★★

Our arrival on the Texas deck is greeted by a light rain. "Are you serious, William?" I plead. "We're going to get soaked."

"Use a rubber blanket."

"It's cold and wet up here."

"Stop being a crybaby, Stephen," William tells me. "There's an eave on the pilothouse. We'll be under it and in fresh air. Unless there's a thunderstorm with high winds, we'll be dry as well."

We reach the spot William saved for us and open our haversacks. We dump the sugar deep into the bottom of each bag. "Sweetened coffee will never have tasted so good," I say with a smile. I wrap *David Copperfield* with a pair of pants and move it to a safe, dry corner of the sack.

I place the bag against the pilothouse wall to use for a pillow, lie down, and toss the blanket over my legs. "What'll you do with your dollar?" I ask.

"Don't know," William says at first. But then as quickly adds, "I think I'll buy Mother a jewelry box in Cairo."

"She'll like that," I say. "She'll really like that."

I'm so beat, I nod off until the bell rings to call the troops back. A tired-looking fellow asks if he can join us under the eave of the pilothouse. He says he's tried to find a place beside the two smokestacks but with no luck.

"Most of the free spots are saved for others," he says. "Each time I ask about sleeping somewhere, I'm told, 'Sorry, pard, my friend's here.'"

I squeeze over closer to William and create just enough room for the man to lie down. "Make yourself at home."

A ruckus erupts just prior to shoving off. "Get up on the Texas deck and go to sleep," a voice commands.

An answer comes in slurred words. "If you didn't have that rifle and bay-net . . . "

"Well, I do have a rifle and a bayonet, and I'm telling you to get up on the Texas deck and go to sleep."

"Up on the top wooost?" The voice sounds familiar, but

I can't quite make it out with the slurring of his words. Whoever it is has sampled some whisky tonight.

"I'll get you some help getting up the stairs," the first man says sternly, losing his temper.

"Shhhhhhh, people seeping," the drunk says.

As the man emerges from the stairs, everyone turns to see who's causing the stir. Out of the darkness, a soldier propped under each arm, stumbles Big Tennessee. He trips over a man near the last step and bumps into the stair railing. He nearly tumbles back down the stairs but is caught when one of the two men helping him grabs his shirt collar. "Whoa," the man says loudly.

"Shhhhhh," Big Tennessee whispers. "Seeeeping." He takes two steps, trips onto the floor, and passes out. Nobody bothers to move him.

Big Tennessee was always such a mild-mannered soul for all those months in Cahaba. "It's the whisky." William laughs. "I guess a few drinks in Memphis did what the war couldn't do, bring down Big Tennessee."

After pulling away from Memphis's docks, the *Sultana* lists in the river. "Can you feel that?" I ask William.

"What?" he says, waking from a fast sleep.

"The boat," I insist.

"Yeah, I feel the boat, grayback," he jokes. "We're moving. Go back to sleep."

"No," I say. "The boat listed in the river, William. It tilted an awful lot. Like in Helena when everybody raced to one side to get in the picture."

"It's your imagination," William says, yawning. "Please stop talking."

The fellow next to me props himself up on his elbows. "Without the weight of the sugar in the hold the boat's top-heavy."

"Sweet dreams," William says as he pats the stash beneath his head. "Sweet dreams."

The last thoughts on my mind, before I drift to sleep, is that we're almost home.

Almost home.

The war's over, and we're hours from home.

CHAPTER THIRTY-NINE

April 27, 1865, 2:30 a.m.

Something shakes the *Sultana* so violently, it awakens me. It's pitch-dark, but my eyes open in time to see a shadowy object sweep across the sky behind my head and plow into the pilothouse. Whatever it is crashes with so much force, it destroys most of the pilothouse. My nose is instantly overwhelmed by the smell of burning coal coupled with a pain shooting through my left leg. An orange glow in the air is enough to illuminate a shard of wood, the length of my hand, sticking straight up out from my thigh.

Without thinking, I reach for the plank to yank it out but lose my courage.

"Oh my God!" William yells, throwing off his blanket and standing. "What happened?" He sees me in pain and gasps at the sight of the piece of timber protruding from my leg.

"Hold still."

He crouches and yanks the piece of wood out.

I scream as blood pours from the wound. I grab a shirt from my haversack to use as a tourniquet. I wrap it around my leg and use the sleeves to tie a secure knot.

"William, are you okay?"

"Me? I'm fine, but what was that?" he asks in shock.

"Don't know. Looks like one of the smokestacks fell over on the pilothouse." William kicks a few pieces of debris off my ankles.

To my right, not even the length of a kitchen table away, the smokestack has knocked an immense hole in the Texas deck's floor. Everyone sleeping there was crushed and pushed down to the next level of the boat, possibly beyond. The back half of the pilothouse has been blown to atoms.

Right beside me, the man I had made room for earlier has a beam the thickness of a flagpole protruding through the center of his chest. It had to have killed him instantly.

"She's sinking!" someone yells from below. I stand, but putting weight on my left leg reminds me of my wound.

A faint voice nearby says, "I can't move." A thick beam rests across the man's legs. William and I lift the end and try to free him.

We fail. The other end is lodged under a pile of debris.

The more we strive, the more my thigh hurts. "Somebody help us!" I yell.

As if from nowhere, Big Tennessee staggers over to the beam. "When I lift, the two of you pull him out," he says in a calm voice.

"We already tried that," William says, an urgency in his voice. "It's too heavy,"

"Just do it," Big Tennessee orders. "Each of you grab one of his hands and pull on my command." Big Tennessee's giant frame straddles the freed end of the beam, and he clasps his hands beneath it. He releases a deep grunt as the obstacle rises a mere inch or two. "Now!" he yells.

William and I easily pull the soldier loose, and he scrambles to his feet.

"We've got to get off the boat," William says. "Are you okay to move?" he asks the man we just released.

"Yeah," he say, testing his leg. And with that he hurries toward the side of the boat and launches himself overboard. We hear multiple splashes come from the river as other men have started abandoning the *Sultana*.

Someone yells, "Put out the fire!" I turn to see embers flying through the opening where the smokestack stood seconds earlier. A man whose legs are pinned by a support near the hole begs for help. Big Tennessee, William, and several men rush to where he lies. "Help me!" he yells. "I'm going to burn."

I limp over and add my assistance as well. I gain some leverage with my right leg and push off the best I can. But even with all our hands, the wood won't budge. It won't yield. It's simply too large for us to move. Escaping sparks ignite the jagged edges of the deck, turning it to flames. Fire that begins devouring the wood gets closer and closer to the man.

"Don't stop. For God's sake, don't stop trying!" he yells. But it's useless. No matter how hard we try, the weight of the wood and heat from the fire push us back. Everyone ducks lower to the floor, trying to avoid the heat racing out of the crater. We shield our faces with our hands. Being recent prisoners, everyone's too weak, and the far end of the timber appears to be buried by other debris. The flames get closer, and the group retreats.

William stumbles, drops to his knees, and vomits on what's left of the front wall of the pilothouse.

A voice whispers, *Be calm, son. Don't lose your head.* It's Mother speaking. *You'll be okay if you don't lose your head.*

"Out of the way!" Big Tennessee yells as he and another man carry a limp soldier toward the stairs. But when they get there, they find the stairs are gone. That portion of the Texas deck blew up with the smokestack. "We can't take him that direction," Big Tennessee says. They hurry to the side of the boat and dangle the man over the edge by his arms to the deck below. "Grab this man!" Big Tennessee screams at the top of his lungs. After the man is taken from their hands, Big Tennessee leaps over the railing and into the Mississippi River.

The smokestack's hole is now a volcano blowing embers and heat into the evening sky.

"Swim or burn!" someone yells.

A figure darts toward the edge of the boat, weaving around the debris. He takes off every stitch of clothing except his drawers and peers into the water, scanning left to right. Finally finding a clear spot, he jumps three stories into the black river surface.

Bodies are scattered everywhere, many bleeding, some missing arms or legs. The scene is far worse than at Sulphur Branch Trestle, and there are no nurses here to be of assistance.

I think the situation through for a minute. "William, we have to get off this deck. It may give way soon."

We race to the railing, me hobbling on my wounded leg. There's a rope dangling over the side, so we lower ourselves to the next level while men continue rushing into the water, some diving straight over us. The river that seemed so calm and peaceful a day ago is now a sea of bobbing faces in pitch-black water. Many of the heads go under and fail to come up again.

"I can't swim," a man says to me as we finally get footing on the lowest deck. It's Caleb Rule, the farrier who had begged the guards at Castle Morgan to let us leave the prison during the flood. "I can't swim," he says again. "Should I burn or drown?" he asks.

Caleb's hugging a four-by-four-inch post at the railing of the deck as if it's as dear to him as a child is to a mother. He looks at me again. "I can't swim."

"That's okay," I tell him. "It's going to be all right."

Steam shoots out a nearby window, scalding a man running by. I pull on Caleb's arms, but he's having none of it and refuses to let go of the post. His gaze does not leave the sight of the men floating in the water. "I can't swim," he repeats for the fourth time.

"Help me pry his fingers loose," I tell William.

William leans over and bites Caleb's fingers. Our friend

lets go of the post and we drag him to the edge of the banister. Men in the frigid water beg us to throw them anything that might help them float. Heads bob below the surface a dozen at a time—never to resurface. Others on the boat are pulling everything they can off the walls to toss into the water.

Coal boxes, shutters, bales of cotton, doors, and cracker barrels litter the river's surface. Somebody has managed to throw a massive flour barrel into the mix.

"Your choice is being made for you," I tell Caleb after seeing a man fly from the Texas deck, his hair on fire as he whizzes past. The flames on his head dissolve when he hits the water. "You're going in the river."

"I can't sw—"

"Can't swim, we know." A green shutter lies on the floor, blown off by the explosion. I pick it up. "Wrap your arms around this and don't let go. Even when you hit the water, don't let go of the shutter."

William braces himself against the ship's outer wall with both hands and kicks the three wooden rails free to provide an opening into the water. It's going to be difficult to get Caleb off the boat, so a nod to William tells him to help me push. I hold up one finger, then two, then three. On the third, Caleb Rule flies overboard with his shutter.

"Can't swim!" he yells midair.

Caleb hits the water hard, but the shutter breaks his fall. His chin barely gets damp as he floats away. A team of mules won't be able to pry that shutter from his grasp.

Sergeant Survant rushes by, a bedpost in his hands to throw over. "What happened to the *Sultana*?" I ask.

"Boiler exploded," he says. "I was next to the stairs when it blew. The banister saved me when the Texas deck came crashing down. The fellow six inches from me was crushed.

"Listen," Sergeant Survant says, panting. "I have a plan. Wait as long as you can before jumping in. Watch," he says, pointing to the water. "Too many of the men are pulling each other under. Those who can't swim are drowning those who can. Wait for the water to clear a bit."

I nod. "Okay."

"You can swim, can't you?"

"Certainly."

William Lugenbeal rushes by, dragging a large crate with GASTONE written across the side.

"Where's the gator?" Sergeant Survant asks.

★★★

Lugenbeal laughs and points over his shoulder toward the flames shooting out of a window. "He's on his way to hell by now is my guess. I stabbed him between the eyes with a knife and took his crate." In a heartbeat, Lugenbeal and the crate are in the river. Sergeant Survant walks toward the front of the boat, clutching a cabin door to chuck overboard.

When Lugenbeal mentions the alligator, I remember the hold contains livestock. Beyond the fire and smoke, the shapes of some of them can be seen being pushed into the water near the stern.

A loud splash catches my ears. A shape, larger than the roof on Uncle Clem's house, is buoying in the water. It's *Sultana's* gangplank. Instantly, pairs of hands, too many to count, appear from every direction and latch on to the edges of the wood.

"Help me, Stephen," William says. He's gathered a heap of spindles from a staircase railing. "Tuck half of these under your right arm." A few of them spill to the floor, and I stoop to pick them up.

"Leave 'em lay," William says. "The flames are getting too close." He takes off his suspenders, wraps them around the wood, and ties the four ends in a knot. "If God's willing, these will see us through. There's enough here for both of us. Take off your suspenders," he orders.

After tying the second batch and with blazes lapping out many of the nearby cabin windows, the time has come to jump. I think of the sugar we had hauled up to the pilothouse just hours before, now burning along with our blankets, with our few possessions in our rucksacks, along with my . . .

"I have to go back up!" I yell at William.

"Back up where?"

"To the pilothouse."

William grabs my arm. "No, you're not going back up there, Stephen."

I pull away. "The book! Governor Morton said I have to bring *David Copperfield* back home to him. He hasn't read it."

"He didn't mean it literally," William says, shaking his head violently, eyes pleading. "Look around, pard. My God, he'll understand."

"It was an order. Good soldiers follow orders."

"Let it go," William pleads.

But it's too late. My mind's made up. "Give me a boost," I say.

I latch on to the rope we had used earlier, climb up on William's back, and onto his shoulders. He places his hands, palms up, next to his neck for me to step onto. By pulling on the rope while he pushes me up another two feet, there's just enough room to get a good hold on the railing above me. Men jump over me and plummet into the river. I grab the deck and swing my good leg up and over onto the flooring.

The boat's top floor is mostly burned. I shield my face from the inferno with both arms and walk toward where the pilothouse once stood. A light breeze blows some of the heat away and toward the back of the boat. But at the same time, the wind is turning the vessel slowly to the right. This brings the flames straight back to where I'm headed. The entire spot where we had slept, fifteen minutes earlier, is now an inferno. My knapsack, sugar, hat, and copy of *David Copperfield* are gone.

I've failed.

CHAPTER FORTY

April 27, 1865, 3:08 a.m.

A second explosion rips at my ears. It's louder than twenty cannons on a battlefield all firing at once. It blows me, and most of the deck I was running across, into the coldest water I've felt since leaving the Alabama prison three weeks ago. It's hard to tell which way to swim, submerged in muddy water, struggling for my life.

So this is how it ends? I'm fifteen years old and this is how my life ends: at the bottom of the flooded Mississippi River?

Arms and legs thrash all around. Planks, churning water, legs kicking, barrels, fists punching ... everyone ... everywhere ... EVERYTHING fighting for the surface ... wherever that is. AIR ... that's where life is. If I could only reach it.

But which way is up? How far is it? One thing is for sure: I can't hold my breath much longer.

Just fifteen years? That's all I get? I'm younger than Robert was when he died in the war.

I've made it through too many dangers to die like this, sinking toward the bottom of a muddy river swollen with two thousand soldiers, countless horses, and one murdered alligator. After all I've been through, it can't end like this. Not when I'm so close to home.

Something kicks my thigh. The strike, a glancing blow, has to be a mule or horse kicking for the surface like the rest of us.

A boot kicks my chest. What little air I've managed to hold in my lungs shoots out and bubbles past my cheeks and ears. The boat must be behind me. My body twists easily in the red-black muck. I push both hands up through the water as if trying to catch the escaped bubbles. A fast stroke brings them down to my side. Somebody's hair tangles through my fingers. I push him away, expecting a fight. Whoever it is will latch on like a burr if he can. He doesn't. There is no grabbing, no fists punching, no legs kicking. Whoever he is, he isn't trying to find the surface anymore. He's already gone.

An orange glow in the water—a distant, faint spark—like a campfire's last hour appears above me. The shape grows larger, and shadows move toward the light. I reach above me, cup the water, and pull hard down to my side . . . and do it again . . . and again. The light gets rounder and brighter, and, at the same time, sounds grow in my ears.

My body slips through the water and breaks the surface of the river. When I gasp for breath, my lungs take in as much water as air. I cough violently. Somebody puts an arm around my neck and pulls down. The best thing to do is to stay under until he lets go. Don't fight. Play dead. Finally, whoever it is releases their clutch.

Returning to the surface, I see the *Sultana*—or what's left of it—swallowed in flames, making the sky glow like a sunrise. Orange and yellow light dance against a frantic hand nearby. I snatch at the hand and pull a flailing body back up. It's Charles Evans, bugler from Company A.

"Help," he says, and gasps between quick breaths. "Please! Please help." He's so disoriented, I don't believe he knows who he's talking to.

A barrel floats by. The word "flour" is written on it in large white letters. I grab Charles's hand, but he pulls in a panic. We both go under. Holding him underwater forces him to let go. I resurface in time to seize his hand as it sinks below the water, and pull him back up.

"Don't grab me!" I yell quickly.

His jaw chatters, but he manages a slight nod. "Okay," he says, but not convincingly.

I pull at his hands in quick bursts like I'm moving a hot coffeepot from one side of the stove to the other. I'm trying to gain his trust and keep his head above water.

"Charles, you're going to take my hand. Don't fight or lunge at me. Just hold it."

He grabs hold. With all my strength I'm able to raise his arm toward the black sky. This clears his head of the water. "See?"

"Yeah," Charles says, and manages a quick smile. His smile disappears quicker than a shooting star.

"If you fight, I'm holding you under the water, and only one of us will come back up alive. Do you understand?"

"Okay," he promises.

I struggle toward the flour barrel, but a trunk lid blocks my way. The top is light and moves easily with a swipe of my hand. I rest my fingers on the rim of the barrel for a second to regain some strength. Charles sees we've reached it and flails so unbridled, I have to let go. Somehow, he manages to clamp his fingers on the rim of the wood.

Within seconds the barrel is swarmed with several more pairs of hands. It sinks a bit in the water but buoys enough to support those grabbing its edge.

As the flow takes me away from the wreckage it's impossible not to look at the burning mass. A thin figure lies on the deck, near the railing of the boat. "Please somebody throw me in the river!" he screams. "The flames are getting closer!"

"Your leg is broken," another man still on board shouts over the roar of the fire. "You won't be able to keep yourself afloat in the water."

"You've got to do it. I'll die in the fire for sure!" he yells. "Don't let me burn alive."

The second man cups both hands in front of his mouth and hesitates. Is he praying? Is he thinking? Finally, he rolls the soldier to the edge, shields his face from the approaching flames and shoves with the heel of his boot. The soldier enters the water, but the splash cannot be heard over the roar of the fire. I search, but his head doesn't resurface.

Brave men faced death on the battlefield without flinching. But in the icy April waters of the Mississippi there are no privates. No sergeants. No generals. There are only men doing anything for their own survival. Some beg for life, others plead for a quick death. I don't recall such screaming and praying even in the heat of battle at Sulphur Branch Trestle.

"Gaston!" somebody yells out. "Grab hold." A leather strap from a horse's rein smacks the water in front of me. I see the shape of a horse from the corner of my eye.

I turn to swim in the opposite direction and call back over my shoulder, "Get away! One kick and that thing will kill us for sure."

"He can't kick, Gaston. Not anymore," the voice assures me. "He's got no head. That second explosion blew him plum into the river. Grab the damn strap if you want to live, boy."

It's Robert Talkington, a sergeant from Company A. He pulls the rein back and tosses it in my direction again. This time it lands across my right shoulder. My hands feel numb. Can I swim much longer in this icy water? Floating with Talkington, on a dead horse, is my best option at the moment, so I grab the rein.

Talkington pulls me to the carcass. "I'm getting cold," I tell him.

"Wrap the reins around your wrist so you don't float away," Talkington orders. "Don't worry. I've got the other end secure. Here, lean up on the base of his neck and shoulders. He's dead but still warm."

He's right. I nestle across the horse's shoulder, my head resting on its neck, and the horse's body warms mine. Wrapping the rein four times around my right wrist and twisting my left hand through what's left of his mane, I anchor myself to the corpse.

Talkington shakes his head, laughs, and says, "You know, trading a live horse for a dead one is the best bargain I ever made."

Then, slowly, everything goes dark.

CHAPTER FORTY-ONE

April 27, 1865, 4:20 a.m.

"Gaston, wake up. Stay awake, pard."

I wake from the splashing of water against my face. "What? Stop."

"Better stay awake, pard. You almost slipped away once already." It's Robert Talkington, and he's the one flicking water at me. He has a grip on my forearm with his other hand and shakes a finger in my face.

I lift my head slightly and see a bonfire floating on water. It's the *Sultana,* and it's illuminating the scene enough to reveal a river of human heads bobbing. Light from the flames dances on the faces near us. A crack like thunder causes every head to turn toward the sound. Men are hanging on to a round structure on the side of the boat. The form is now angled out like a tree branch jutting from the side of a tree.

"What's that?"

"That's the side wheel," Talkington says. "It's about to go."

The mighty wheel lurches sideways again but catches itself momentarily. The jerk knocks seven or eight men into the water. A few do manage to hang on to the wheel. Then there's another crack of thunder, and the entire mass of wood breaks free from the flames and crashes into the river.

"There goes the wheel," Talkington says, "and anybody near it."

I lift my head up farther. "Is that ... the ... *Sultana*?"

Talkington laughs. "You were out longer than I thought," he says. "Yeah, that's the *Sultana*. Or what's left of her. She's burning down quickly."

"It exploded ... the *Sultana* ... There was an explosion," I say.

"Correction, two explosions," Talkington says.

My thoughts weave backward in slow motion through a thick fog of smoke and steam. I piece together the series of events in my mind. Robert Talkington had tossed a leather strap to me to save my life. With my help, somebody reached a barrel of flour. I fought under the water to reach the surface. I*t was the second explosion that tossed me into the river*, I say to myself.

"I saw awful things, Talkington," I say.

"Everyone did," he replies. "I saw a man put life belts on a woman and girl. I told him it was too low on the little one's waist. Others tried to tell him, too. But he would have none of it. He stared with this blank expression on his face, as if he were in another world."

"Do you think the girl's okay?"

"I don't see how she can be with all the fighting in the water and the belt being too loose on her."

The sounds of soft prayers mingled with singing drift into my ears. The mixture of voices and men splashing in the river float above the sounds of water lapping against debris.

"Talkington."

"What?"

"I came within an ace of being right above that second explosion. Why am I here now and not dead?"

"Stop talking like that," he says. "That's nonsense."

"No, I should have died."

Talkington laughs it off. "Well, there must be some reason you lived," he says. "You got every right to be floating down this river alive, hanging on to a headless horse. Now you'll have a great story to tell your grandkids."

"I can barely move," I say. "All feeling is leaving my feet. The water is freezing."

"Too long in confinement," he says. "Your muscles are not all the way back yet."

"My left leg hurts. A plank stabbed my thigh."

"We'll get you out soon and tend to the wound. Hang in there, pard."

A light rain begins pelting the river. A crate, buoyed enough to show the name Gastone on the side, floats by. Two pairs of fingers clutch a slat at the top, and a man is draped on the other side. I can't see who it is.

"Is the beast in the river?" Talkington calls out to him.

"Naw. He's burnt to a crisp by now." It's William Lugenbeal.

"How long have we been in the water?" I ask.

"Not sure, an hour, maybe ninety minutes."

That's hard to believe. I must have been passed out longer than I thought. It feels like time is standing still.

A pinging sound, like a hammer striking a train rail, drifts above the moans of men in the water. "Shhh . . . listen," Talkington says, "Hear that?"

"Barely. What is it?"

"Don't know. It's coming from downriver."

★★★

We drift another five minutes in silence. "It's the church bells from Memphis," Talkington finally says. "They know what's happened."

"Why do you think so?"

"Why else would bells be sounding now, Stephen? In the middle of the night? It's an alarm to send help." He sounds confident.

"Talkington, I should have done something to save others."

"Come on, pard. Stop talking like that. How could you do more? That was the biggest mess I've ever seen in my life. If the fire didn't get you, the steam did. If the steam didn't get you, the smoke did. If the smoke didn't get you, the fire did. I couldn't see where I was walking half the time. People running in every direction. Flames shooting from every cabin window."

"I tried to help. I managed to get one fellow who couldn't swim on a flour barrel."

"So there you go. You put a guy on a barrel, and yours truly put you on a headless horse. And here we are. Stop thinking about all that. We have more pressing issues to deal with now. We're not out of the water yet, and I'm not letting anybody pull me off this beast."

We drift, listening to moans and cries from strangers. A weak voice, too close to ignore calls out. "Help." It sounds like he's speaking directly to us. "I can't ... hold ... on ... much ... longer," he pleads. "Please ... help."

Although faint, I recognize the voice. "Caleb?" The glow from the burning ship is growing dimmer, but there's enough light to see it is indeed Caleb Rule. He's still holding on to the shutter, but barely.

"I'm ... numb," he says. "My fingers ... slipping. Can't hold ... on. ... "

The shutter teeters back and forth in the water, tipping to one side and then the other. I let go of the horse's mane and swim toward Caleb.

"Gaston!" Talkington yells. "Come back!"

I ignore him. There's no feeling left in my feet, but my thighs still pump. Pain shoots up my left leg with each kick, but I have two good arms and one good leg. "I've got to help him."

By the time I reach Caleb, he's slipped off the shutter. I dive below the surface and reach toward where his head disappeared. Groping wildly in the muddy water, my hand finds another. I pull it up.

Caleb sputters out a mouthful of water and coughs several times. I cup his chin in my hand and pull him back toward the horse. There's no fight left in him; he's no different than a log floating in the river. Talkington helps me to lift Caleb so his back rests on the horse's side. The carcass sinks a bit, but Caleb's face is totally out of water.

At about that exact moment everything in the water turns black. I look back to where the *Sultana* has been in time to see the final flickering flames disappear. Red-hot irons send hissing sounds into the air. Steam explodes to an immense height as the *Sultana* descends into the Mississippi River.

"She's gone," Talkington says. "She's totally gone."

"Talkington?"

"Yeah?"

"There's a new moon. It's going to be pitch-dark till dawn. It'll be after sunrise before anybody comes."

"Don't say that. We heard the bells, and I can see lights in Memphis now," he says. Streetlamps from Memphis appear as faint stars sitting on the horizon.

"That's miles away, Talkington. I don't know if I can hang on till dawn."

We float, saying nothing, for another hour, maybe more.

At one point, we get caught in a whirlpool and spin in circles. From time to time we hear calls from weak voices. Some men use their last breaths to beg the Almighty for mercy.

Something grazes the side of my head, and I flick at it to knock it away. It rustles, and I realize that it's a tree branch. "Grab that limb, Talkington!" I yell, but it's too late. We've drifted past it.

By now dawn must be near. I can see the outline of branches passing overhead against a deep purple sky.

"We are in a grove of trees on the Arkansas side of the river," I say. "The river is wide from flooding."

The horse's hind quarter lodges on something, causing it to roll over in the water. "It's a tree. Grab a branch!" Talkington yells. I use every bit of strength I have to reach for a thick dark shadow while Talkington snatches Rule. We let the horse float away. We'll be safer sitting in a flooded tree in Arkansas than drifting down the middle of the Mississippi River. Realizing it might be the last thing I do, I summon all the energy left in my body to position myself in a fork and collapse against a sturdy tree trunk. The limb's about as round as my wrist and juts out inches above the water. There's ample room for the three of us to perch.

Talkington positions Caleb's rear onto the same branch

between us. Exhausted, I lean against the tree's thick trunk. The two of them recline against another branch. Except for our lower legs, we're out of the freezing water and able to relax a little.

I feel myself drifting to sleep, flies nipping at my neck and the bells of Memphis ringing in my ears.

CHAPTER FORTY-TWO

I hear voices around me long before my eyes open. Commands are being issued by many people. The words make sense, but I can't respond. My lips won't move, and my eyes won't open.

"Keep rubbing him, he's almost awake," a female voice says. My body rolls one way on a hard surface and then the other, like a pin rolling pie dough. Hands and fingers rub my legs, arms, neck, and shoulders.

"Be careful of his left thigh," a woman says. "He has a nasty wound there."

Finally, my right eye pops open a little. A woman stands near my head.

Black fabric flows from the top of her head over her shoulders. Her entire body is covered in black except for white linen hiding her forehead, ears, and neck. A wide collar rests on her chest. I glimpse a chain of wooden beads hanging from her waist with a cross attached to the end.

She sees my eye open and smiles. "Try to drink this," she says softly. She cups the back of my head with one hand and lifts. In her other hand, she holds a tin cup.

I choke on the substance and try to spit it out. "What is it?"

"Well, it's not springwater, I can assure you that," she laughs in a quiet voice. "It's whisky, young man. Now, to be perfectly honest, I normally wouldn't provide whisky to anybody, especially somebody of your age. But, if the Saints allow, under these circumstances, I think it will do you best."

"Who are you?"

"We," she says acknowledging others around us, "are Sisters of Mercy."

A stinging on my leg makes me wince. "Sister Angelina is washing the wound on your thigh. You have a nasty gash there," she says. Her voice is calm.

"We rolled and rubbed you for ten minutes to get your blood circulating and get you awake."

My other eye finally opens on its own. "Where are we?"

"Cabin room on the *Bostonia*," she answers. "There are

five hospitals in Memphis. We'll have you in one of them in just a little while. Here, a drink will do you good."

A gruff voice barks from somewhere outside the cabin, "Bring that skiff in right here."

"More survivors coming in," she whispers to me with a brief smile. She sounds as calm as if we're playing cards around a campfire. "The *Belle of Memphis* passed us with over one hundred men earlier this morning," she adds. "Every rescue is a blessing."

"Earlier?" I ask.

"Yes, sometime around nine a.m., I'd say. They were headed to Memphis to unload."

"What time is it now?"

"Nearing ten thirty. Take another drink," she insists.

"My neck is stinging."

"They told us you were plucked from a tree like an apple. Your neck, face, and arms are covered in welts from buffalo gnats and mosquitoes. Insects are so thick this time of spring, you're lucky they didn't fly off with you."

I raise my right arm and see it's covered in bumps. The welts on my neck and face tingle.

The same gruff voice from outside yells, "We counted twenty-three on top of that stable across the river. It'll take several trips to bring 'em all in. Except for bugbites, they look like they're in good shape."

Another voice answers, "Most all the cabins are full. Bring the live ones portside. If you pick up any bodies along the way, store them in the hold."

The sister places the cup of whisky on my lips. "Take the last little bit," she tells me.

The strong smell reminds me of Big Tennessee staggering onto the *Sultana* last night. "Where's Big Tennessee?" I ask the sister.

"Yes, you're in Tennessee," she says. "Memphis, Tennessee."

"No, there's a tall guy who goes by the name of Big Tennessee," I explain. "Where is he?"

"Haven't got a clue, but he's not here. Don't worry about him for now. You need only to worry about yourself," she says. "We'll get you into town soon. They'll have a better look at your leg there. If it's infected, they'll treat it, and you'll be up and about in no time."

Most of the whisky is gone before I feel any of its effects.

CHAPTER FORTY-THREE

April 27, 1865, 10:35 a.m.

The *Bostonia* jolts as it docks in Memphis. I shift to my elbows and try to stand. I can't. I'm groggy and have no energy. "It's okay," a Sister of Mercy says, patting my shoulder. "Don't move. Let us do all the work."

The cabin door opens, and a man sticks his head into the room. "Keep these men in here. It will be a while before we get to them. We have to get the severely injured off first."

Sister Angelina smiles and says the wound doesn't look too bad to her. "I washed it out and put a bit of whisky on it. It's wrapped up now, and the doctors will have a closer look later."

A half hour passes, and two Negro men in Union blues bring a stretcher into the room and place it on the floor next to me. One man stands at my head and the other at my feet.

"Careful," a sister says. "Grab the edges of the sheet he's on, not his hands and feet," she commands.

One of the men counts down, "Three … two… one…" They lift in unison and hoist me from the floor onto the stretcher.

As we leave, I grab the doorframe. "Wait." I look back toward the lady who helped me the most. "I almost forgot to say thank you, sister. If it's not being too forward, what is your name?"

"Mary," she says quietly.

"Mary? That's my mother's name. Thank you, sister."

"You're very welcome, young man."

Ambulances take survivors two by two along a cobblestone road. The man with me is bloated to the point that his cheeks almost touch his eyebrows. He peers through thin slits. The ambulance driver says that the Gayoso House on Front Street, with its close proximity to the river, received injuries first. Minutes later, a metal sign tells me we've arrived at our destination. Six tall marble columns support a portico bustling with people rushing in and out of a four-story building.

Doctors are deciding which hospital will care for each patient. The grounds in the front of the Gayoso are nearly concealed with stretchers.

"It's a grand hotel," one of the men carrying me says. "Two hundred fifty rooms. Union generals been stayin' here since the capture of Memphis back in '62. Forrest rode his horse plum through the lobby one day searching for General Hurlburt. Can you imagine a horse in a hotel lobby?" He laughs.

"I met General Forrest in Alabama," I say.

"It wasn't the general who rode the horse here. It was Captain William Forrest, the general's brother." He points to the middle of three arched doorways. "He rode his horse right through that middle door right there."

"Did he get General Hurlburt?"

"Nah, Hurlburt left just hours before."

★★★

Three doctors walk down the line of stretchers, assessing the hurt. One of them points to the bloated man beside me. "Put this one on the first floor, here in the Gayoso," he orders. He then comes over to me, raises the sheet to look at my thigh. "This one has a thigh wound. He goes to the tents out back. He's not that bad."

A young boy with long blond locks trailing his head like

a flag in the wind runs up to the doctor. He pauses and plants a hand on each knee while he catches his breath. "Sir, Washington Hospital is nearly full. They have a hundred thirty patients and can't take any more."

"Well, we're expecting more!" the doctor shouts at the messenger. "The ships are still bringing 'em in, and they have to go somewhere."

The boy takes two long breaths. "Washington sent me to tell you not to send any more patients their way. Adams and Overton have a few rooms left."

The doctor dismisses the boy with a wave of his hand as if to say, "I don't have time for this nonsense, and I'll send them where I see fit."

I'm taken behind the Gayoso and placed in a well-manicured courtyard with other survivors. A Union nurse arrives shortly and says the bandage looks better than what he could do himself. He reassigns me to Overton Hospital and places me on a ward with a long row of beds lining each wall. There are too many patients to count them all. Nurses, Sisters of Mercy, and orderlies race down the center of the room, carrying bandages, pails of steaming water, and scissors.

A tall man standing straight as a ramrod introduces

himself as the chief surgeon. "Let's take a look at your wound," he says, bending at the waist. He gingerly unwraps the bandages from around my leg.

"You're not going to amputate," I plead.

"Doubt it. There's not much blood on the bandages, so that's a good sign." After the bandage is removed, he nods repeatedly. "This one's fine," he says to a nurse standing behind him. "We'll rewrap his leg this evening."

All around, patients call for help to deal with their pain. Nurses rush to their sides to see how bad of a shape they're in. If needed, they leave and return a short time later with aid. Some men are able to move, sit up, or talk. The man next to me doesn't move at all.

"He's in a coma," one nurse tells another. "I don't know if it's from exhaustion, being in the cold water too long, or a combination."

I'm glad to be left alone for most of the night. Occasionally a visitor stops to see if there's anything they can do to aid my comfort. After a breakfast of boiled eggs, corn bread, and stew, soldiers come around and hand out clean new uniforms. Few of us are well enough to get dressed. "Can we leave them for you so you'll have them when you're feeling better?" the soldiers ask.

I touch the fabric and rub it between my fingers and thumb. I pull a jacket sleeve to my nose, inhale deeply, and cry soft enough so nobody will hear. This is the uniform Robert and I fought in to save our Union. It smells clean, fresh, and new and makes me feel reborn.

Hours later, a chill wakes me from a deep slumber. My bed's soaked with sweat and my body aches, so I call for a doctor.

"It's a fever from your leg wound," a doctor says, nodding. He seems to have been expecting my complaint to come sooner or later.

"My leg is throbbing."

"Let's take those bandages off. We'll leave the thigh exposed so the air can carry the infection away. We'll see if that helps." The directive is given, and a nurse removes the bandages.

★★★

Sister Mary and Sister Angelina come by to check on my progress early the next morning. "Hello, young man," they say in unison. "We're making our rounds. We heard you'd taken a slight turn for the worse," Sister Mary says. "Did you sleep at all last night?"

"Every time I tried to move, the pain wouldn't allow it."

Sister Angelina fetches a wash basin and wipes my head, face, and neck. "This should make you feel a bit better."

A slight moan rises from the silent fellow in the bed next to me. Sister Angelina scurries to his bedside chair. She reaches down and cradles his left hand in hers. "Yes, dear," she says. "Are you okay?"

"He hasn't said anything since I've been here," I say. "Somebody said he's in a coma."

The man moans again. "What is it, dear?" Sister Angelina asks. "He's coming to, I think."

The man lifts himself with one arm but faces away from me. "Where are we?" he asks in a voice barely above a whisper. I hear his voice only because it's early, before the bustle of morning activities.

"You're at the Overton Hospital," Sister Angelina whispers, "in Memphis."

"Why?"

"An accident," she explains.

"Accident?"

"On the river."

He pulls his hand out from hers and points to the row of cots stretching to the far end of the room. "Who are they?"

"Injured from the *Sultana*," she says. "Do you remember?"

He falls back on the bed. "When it exploded," he says.

"That's right," Sister Angelina says. "Shhhhhh." She motions for Sister Mary to get a doctor.

"I remember the cold water," he says.

"Just rest. A doctor will be here soon."

"I sat in freezing water for a week."

Sister Angelina laughs politely. "It may have seemed like a week, but thank heavens you were in the river for a couple hours," she tells him. "If you were in the water that long, you'd be dead."

"In prison," he insists. "I begged the guards to let us leave. We sat in freezing water for a week."

Sister Angelina turns to me. "He's delirious."

"No, he's not," I say. "Caleb?"

He turn his head to face me. "Yeah," he says.

"It's Gaston here, Stephen Gaston. You made it out of the Mississippi River, pard."

"That shutter saved my life." Caleb lowers his head back on this pillow for a couple seconds. "Guess what, Gaston."

"What?" I answer.

"After a week in the Alabama and Mississippi Rivers, I still can't swim."

And I know that Caleb's going to be just fine.

CHAPTER FORTY-FOUR

"The army requested the rolls of the *Sultana* be brought from Vicksburg," a survivor says to his friend two beds away from me. "The lists arrived today but are not worth the paper they're recorded on."

"How so?" his friend asks.

"Remember how the rebs wanted every Yankee on ships and out of Vicksburg that last day, whether the rolls were completed or not?"

"Yeah," the fellow says. "They told us, 'Get on board; we need to get the *Sultana* on its way.'"

"The list has one thousand eight hundred names. We were on the last train leaving Camp Fisk, and they didn't record a single name from our group."

"That number can't be right, then."

"The crew bragged there were two thousand four hundred on board the *Sultana.*"

Union officers, with scribes in tow, appear at the door. They visit every hospital bed and ask a barrage of questions. "Who was on the boat from your unit? Besides your company, who did you meet on the ship? Did you learn the names of any crew members?"

★★★

Some survivors are refusing to board steamers home. They leave on trains or any other way they can besides by water. By the end of the first week, the official passenger list swells from 1,800 to 2,187 names. That list is light, too. Ten days after the explosion, over 1,287 soldiers, women, men, and children are reported killed or unaccounted for, and the list grows daily. Only two hundred lucky souls scraped by with nary a need for any medical attention beyond a swig of whisky.

Caleb gets much better very quickly. He seems itchin' and ready to be released. "I owe my life to you, Stephen," he says.

"You'd do the same for me," I say. "Besides, the doctors

say I'll be discharged in another week," I tell him. "They're still keeping an eye on the wound."

"The river was colder than the water in Castle Morgan," he says. "No comparison."

"I haven't told you, but we floated down the river on a dead horse."

"I wasn't on a shutter the whole time?"

"Not the entire time. I plucked you out of the water and set you on the horse's side. We came to a tree, and somehow we got you up there. I passed out from exhaustion. The last thing I remember, before the cold put me under for good, is latching on to a tree branch with you on one side of me and . . ."

"What?"

"Oh my God!" I yell. "I forgot about Talkington."

A Sister of Mercy doing needlework in a chair by the door hears me and looks my way. "Sister, can you check on a name for me? Actually, a couple of names." I'm embarrassed to not have thought of the names before.

"We'll find them for you," she says as she walks over to my bed, taking out a pencil and paper from beneath her garments.

"Sergeants Survant and Talkington," I tell her. "Both are

in the Ninth Indiana Cavalry. If you can find out about them, I'd be most appreciative."

"What's Survant's first name?"

"Joseph. And Talkington's first name is Robert."

"Any other names?"

"Two more. One is a tall fellow; everybody calls him Big Tennessee. He's almost seven feet tall. The other is William Peacock, and he's in the Ninth too."

★★★

Later, Sister Mary pays a call and looks at my arms. "Rotate them back and forth for me," she says, demonstrating by twisting her own arms. "Good. No signs of bugbites at all. Many of the fellows used spring growth of willow limbs to swat the buffalo gnats. They say it didn't help much, that there were too many of 'em."

We sit in silence for a while before she says, "Oh, I almost forgot, Stephen: a letter arrived for you." She slips her hand into a pocket inside her black garment and produces an envelope.

"Who's it from?" I ask.

"I don't know," she answers. "There's one thing on it I've

never seen before, kind of odd. There's a kind of X near the postmark of Nashville."

The envelope reads:

Stephen Gaston (Sultana—injured)
Memphis, Tennessee

Beside the postmark is a long check mark and a shorter straight line forming an X.

"It's easy to tell who sent this," I say.

"How?" Caleb asks.

I point to the X on the envelope. "I'd know that mark anywhere. I wrote a letter for him when we were in Cahaba Prison, and that's how he signed it. He didn't write this letter, though."

Hello, Pard,

With the help of God, Big Tennessee and I are back home. We left Memphis on the St. Patrick *headed for Nashville. We came by Overton Hospital to say good-bye. They told us you had a fever and shouldn't have visitors.*

The crew of the St. Patrick *treated us like heroes. They said we suffered through a war, a prison, and the* Sultana. *Anybody who did that was a hero in their eyes. They offered us real nice rooms to sleep in. I couldn't bring myself to sleep anywhere on the boat except one place. I spent the entire trip to Nashville hanging over the stern in the yawl. I wasn't taking any chances. Big Tennessee took them up on their offer and slept like a king on a real bed with fancy cloth draped over it. He said his feet stuck out past the end of it.*

Your buddy Caleb never came to while we were sitting in the tree. I kept one hand on a tree branch and the other hand on his shirt collar. We looked like three crows sitting on a fence row. You two were in bad shape when a skiff got around to taking you over to the Bostonia. *I don't know where Rule is now. Hope he's fine.*

Big Tennessee's headed for the mountains of Tennessee and I'm going north. I expect to see you back in Indiana when you're released.

Get well soon, Pard

Robert Talkington signed his name at the bottom of the page, and, right beside his name, as big as a silver dollar, is a large check mark with another line crossing the longer end:

The letter lifts my spirits and Caleb's, too. He gets a kick out his name being written in a letter coming all the way from Nashville.

The doctors visit Caleb and declare him well enough to make the journey home. "I'm not getting on another boat, unless Saint Peter is taking me to the other side of the Jordan River," he says as he shakes my hand to leave. "Besides, we both know that if I'm on a boat and it goes down . . ."

"You can't swim," we say together. Then we say good-bye.

That night the ward seems especially empty when the Sister of Mercy returns with the information I requested. "Your friends Robert Talkington and Big Tennessee survived and have left for home . . . ," she begins.

"I know. They wrote the letter you gave me," I say, smiling.

"William Peacock is in the Soldiers' Home, a hospital. He has scalds on his right side and a cut shoulder, but he'll be fine."

"There was another name," I remind her. "What about Joseph Survant?"

She shakes her head and closes her eyes. "He has not been heard from nor his body found," she says quietly. "It doesn't look promising."

I lie more quietly than normal, Sister Mary at my side. "What's wrong, Stephen?"

I start to speak but can't and shake my head instead. The words won't come out.

"It's all right," she says. "You don't have to say anything."

"No, I need to. It's just hard." Looking at her reminds me of an angel, like Mrs. Amanda Gardner. She has such a perfect smile. "I have to admit something to you."

"What's that?" she asks.

"I'm so ashamed."

"Of what? You've done nothing to be ashamed of, Stephen."

"I'm ashamed I'm alive."

She starts to speak, but I interrupt her. "There's one thing I'll always remember, sister ...." my voice trails off.

"What's that, Stephen?" she asks.

"I can't get the screaming out of my mind, Sister Mary. Those men were burned alive ... some scalded to death. I never heard men scream that loud ... and ... and the smell of burning flesh," I say. "I can't stop smelling that smell."

"You did nothing wrong by living."

"I'm being punished now for not doing enough," I say. "Sergeant Survant had five children. They need him, and he's probably not going home."

Sister Mary grabs me and buries my head into her chest.

She rocks us both back and forth. "It's going to get better. I don't know when, but it will get better." She turns her head and looks back over her shoulder toward the door several times.

After a period of silence I say again, "I'm ashamed."

"Of what? That you lived and others didn't?"

"I should have done more. Some of 'em in the river were so close to me that our bodies could have touched as their heads went under."

She pats my arm and continues rocking. "And how would you have saved them?" she asks. "How could you have helped another man? Where would you have put him?" she asks. "On the horse you floated down the river on?"

"No. There was no more room with the three of us."

"Well, there you go," she says. "The men who died near you did so with the same honor as if they lost their lives on a battlefield." Her voice changes to a measured cadence. "Listen to me, Stephen. Survivors have told me they were caught in death grips by drowning men. They were pulled under and would have died too had they not fought off the people pulling them under."

"I know. We watched some of 'em being pulled to their deaths. They were yelling, 'Let go.'"

"Good swimmers were also pulled under and are gone now," she says. "It wouldn't have helped to have you listed among the dead or missing."

Sister Mary turns toward the door. I glance just in time to see the tall silhouette of the chief surgeon appear. When she nods to him, he walks away. "I promise you, it's going to get better," she says softly to me.

"I hope so, but I don't know when," I say, trying to be agreeable.

"Well, how about right now?" she asks.

Seconds later, the tall shadow of the chief surgeon reappears in the doorway. This time, a much shorter figure, in a dress, stands beside him. Their arms are interlocked. Even in silhouette, I see the lady dab her eyes and nose with a handkerchief. She's wearing a black mourning crape over her head. *She's probably here to claim the body of a loved one,* I think. The only thing I can see clearly is a piece of jewelry fastened at her collar. It reflects the light ever so faintly. It's a neck brooch.

CHAPTER FORTY-FIVE

The shadows walk toward me.

"Stephen?" the woman asks. It's a familiar voice, one I haven't heard in two years.

"Yes," I answer, and sit up in bed on my elbows. Sister Mary tucks a pillow behind my back as I strain to see through the darkness.

"Stephen?" the shadow asks again, as if not believing my first answer.

Sisters Mary stands, gathers her dress in her fists, and hurries out of the room.

"Yes," I say again, louder this time.

The two visitors stop at the foot of my bed. The only thing illuminated well is the golden brooch fastened near the woman's neck. It's the size of a dollar piece with the shape of a quarter moon on it. My throat closes, and pressure rushes to my cheeks. Unable to speak, I nod and reach for her.

Mother.

We hug, sob, and stare into each other's eyes for the longest time. Mother bends over and kisses me on the forehead. She touches my chin and lifts my face toward hers. "Stephen, are you okay?" she asks.

"I'm fine, Mother," I say. "I'm fine."

"You look so good," she says. "And what a fine-looking soldier you've grown to be."

I wipe my eyes with the back of my hand and reach to touch the brooch. "That's the pin Robert gave you when he left."

"Yes. Was it four years ago? Once he—" Mother pauses abruptly. "Once Robert didn't come back home, I couldn't bear to look at it again. It reminded me of his death and not his life," she says. "That was wrong. When your letter arrived explaining the real reason you left, I took it out and wore it every day."

"Every day?"

"Every single day."

"Why?"

"It reminded me I still had a brave soldier in the army."

Mother chokes back a sob. "A soldier who needed my thoughts and prayers."

I start to speak, but Mother places a finger on my lips. "Some nights, if there was a full moon, I'd look up into the sky and wonder if you were looking at the moon at the very same time."

"I did too! A lot. But how did you get to Memphis?"

"Oh, we have so much to catch up on," she says, patting my wrist. "Governor Morton heard what happened and learned you were sending all your money to Clem. He hired me on when he found out."

"Hired you on? To do what?" I ask.

"Well, I said 'hired me on,' but all he really did was take me in. I did whatever needed to be done around the house and continued working for Dutch. Basically, the governor gave me a room and fed me so I wouldn't be indebted to your uncle. Your uncle Clem didn't do right by your brother, me, or you."

So she knew how Uncle Clem treated me.

"You always talked about traveling," she says. "Remember how you'd watch those wagons heading west through Centerville? You'd come home and tell me you dreamed of heading west with them."

I smile at that wonderful memory. "I remember."

"Want to join 'em?" she asks.

"What do you mean?"

"Do you want to join them and head west?" she asks again. "Just like you always dreamed?"

"How? Where would we go?"

"I think we have the money to do it. We just need to pick a direction and go," she says, a shy grin spreading across her face.

"What money?"

"I have it all," she says.

"All what?" I ask.

"All the money you sent home," she says, her smile deepening.

"I didn't send you very much money. Most of it went to Uncle Clem."

"Well, you may have sent it to him, but that doesn't mean he got it," she corrects me. "We caught on fast enough that you were sending money to Clem. So, Governor Morton directed the postmaster to intercept anything coming from you, including army pay, and forward it on to his house."

"You have it? All the money?"

She taps the handbag resting in her lap. "Your uncle never

received one penny from you. Dutch and the governor took care of me while you were gone. Your brother, before he left, said, 'Neighbors help neighbors in war,' and he was right."

I stare down at her purse and then back into her eyes. "Mother, how much of it?"

"Stephen, did you stand too close to the cannons when they were fired? I think they took your hearing. All of it," she says, laughing.

"But . . . but . . . ," I stammer. "That's way over one hundred dollars."

Mother taps her black purse again and puts one finger against her lips. "Shhhhh," she says. "It's all here. I saved every penny you sent. It's your money, Stephen, not mine. You earned it, and I figured you should have it when you came home. I also saved most of the ten dollars a month Dutch paid me."

"You told Clem he was paying you five dollars."

"I did." She smiles. "Your uncle's not as smart as he thinks he is. When Clem asked him why he was paying me such a low amount, Dutch told him five dollars was all I was worth."

"But Dutch didn't actually think that."

"Heavens, no. He said I was the best worker he ever had."

"But Uncle Clem didn't know that."

Mother shakes her head. "Stephen, the governor wouldn't take a dime of my money to board me. My needs were simple while you were gone. Once word reached Centerville that you were sitting in an Alabama prison, nobody would take my money when I purchased anything: shoes, dresses, bonnets. The only thing I lacked was having you back home." Mother smiles. "Nurse," she calls. "Is it possible for us to go outside and sit for a while?"

"Are you feeling up to it, Stephen?" she asks. "It's a nice, warm, spring evening."

I haven't been farther than the chair by my bed in a couple weeks. I decide to give walking a try. We find a bench in a small flower garden next to the hospital. We don't say a word for the longest time but never let go of each other's hands.

★★★

"Stephen?" Mother breaks the silence.

"Yes?"

"There is something else waiting for you back home, if you want it."

"What?" I ask.

"Your bugle."

"What? How?"

"Major Lilly said he found it on the ground in Alabama and carried it back to Indiana. He told the governor, 'Stephen, may not want it, but if he changes his mind, here it is. The governor has it if you want it back.'"

"That would make me very happy," I tell her.

"The newspaper says one thousand seven hundred people are dead or missing," Mother says.

"It was chaos. But in the middle of it all, your voice floated all the way from Centerville, found my ears, and whispered, 'Stay Calm, Stephen,' and I did."

"Following orders like a perfect soldier," she says.

Mother pats the middle of her chest several times and snittles. She's crying. I don't want to look at her and embarrass her more.

"How about Texas?" I finally ask.

"Texas?" she asks.

"I've always wanted to see Texas. Lets start there, and see how we like it."

"Sounds good to me," she says. "Texas it is. We'll leave as soon as they discharge you."

"Well, I have to get out of the army first," I say. "It might be best to serve a couple more years back in Indiana."

"After that, then," she says.

"Mother," I say quietly.

"Yes, dear."

"Thanks for coming."

Then Mother says, "I love you, and I'm so proud of my soldier."

The nearly full moon shines brightly in the sky. "I love you more," I tell her.

"Don't know how you could," she says, "because I love you to the moon and back."

★★★

AUTHOR'S NOTE

Several years ago, while discussing books about boat disasters, the topic of the *Sultana* came up. "Have you heard about the worst ship disaster in America's history?" I was asked. I admitted I had not. It shocked me even more to learn the event happened in my home state of Tennessee on the Mississippi River. After doing preliminary research, I became intrigued as to how such an important event in our nation's history happened and why it has remained relatively unknown for one hundred and fifty years.

Though *Crossing the Deadline* is a work of fiction, sadly many details and events are true. Stephen M. Gaston was born on January 11, 1850, in Centerville, Indiana, hometown of Governor Oliver Morton. He enlisted at the age of thirteen in the town of Moores Hill and became Eli Lilly's bugler in

Company K of the Indiana 9th Cavalry. Stephen must have been a very bright and talented young man to have been given that responsibility at such a young age.

Centerville is approximately fifteen miles from Fountain City, home of Levi Coffin, known as the "president" of the Underground Railroad. The typical distance covered each night on the Underground Railroad was fifteen miles, the same distance between Stephen's birthplace and Levi Coffin's house. An abolitionist once argued that humans who could speak English and French, as many slaves in the Deep South could do, were intelligent and not inferior to white citizens as some believed. The scene where Clay reunites with his mother in the governor's house is totally fictional. There's no evidence Governor Morton was involved in the Underground Railroad. This scene was written as a secondary reason to compel Stephen to join the war effort, the first being to support his mother.

Stephen's capture at Sulphur Branch Trestle near Elkmont, Alabama, was written exactly as the events happened, ending with him blowing surrender precisely at noon on September 25, 1864. It has been documented that the 111th Colored Troops were not shot or sent to prison following the surrender of the fort, but were placed on work details defending

Mobile, Alabama. Richard Pierce aka "Big Tennessee" stood nearly seven feet tall. He was from East Tennessee and was captured along with Stephen at Sulphur Branch.

Stephen arrived at Cahaba Prison the first week in October 1864. Just months earlier General Ulysses S. Grant convinced President Lincoln to suspend prisoner exchanges except for officers. Grant believed the practice prolonged the war, and Lincoln agreed. Prison camps, North and South, were dirty, often short on food, and filled with diseases. Stephen remained in Cahaba, referred to by the locals as Castle Morgan, until his release in March.

The number of men confined at the prison during Stephen's confinement swelled to 2,151, an area intended to hold 500. By the time the facility emptied in March, that number had grown larger. The average space per man was 7.5 square feet. Imagine the area of a football field, but only from the end zone to the 33-yard line (138.5' x 109' = 15,096.5 square feet). That's exactly the size of Cahaba Prison. Despite being the most overcrowded prison (North or South), records indicate that fewer than 150 men died there, one of the lowest death rates of any Civil War prison.

The town of Cahaba was located at the convergence of the Cahaba and Alabama Rivers and was the first capital of

Alabama. Constant flooding forced the legislators to move to Montgomery. Just before the prisoners were released, the town flooded again. The commander refused to allow the prisoners to evacuate to a nearby hill despite a petition signed by prison guards. Prisoners sat in cold floodwaters for a week.

After the war, many prisoners mentioned Amanda Gardner in documents, diaries, and books. Some called her an angel and said her generosity kept them alive through the harsh winter of 1865. Remarkably, losing her son in the war in Virginia did not extinguish her kindness toward the prisoners from the North.

Cahaba began emptying in March 1865, and men made their way by boat, train, and on foot to Union-controlled Camp Fisk, seven miles east of Vicksburg. They joined prisoners from other places, such as Andersonville, Georgia. Over the next weeks, boats carried soldiers home, and the population of Camp Fisk dwindled.

On April 21, 1865, the *Sultana* left New Orleans loaded with many barrels of sugar, passengers including the Chicago Opera Troupe, livestock, and other cargo. She headed north to Vicksburg to take former Cahaba and Andersonville prisoners home. However, hours before arriving in Vicksburg, one of the boilers began leaking, the result of a faulty design. The boat limped into Vicksburg, where repairmen urged a boiler replacement, a fix that would have taken up to five days. Captain J. C. Mason, knowing every soldier would have been loaded onto the other boats, demanded a quick patch.

While the boilers were rapidly repaired, all remaining prisoners from Camp Fisk crammed onto one boat, the *Sultana*. Why was that decision made with other boats waiting to receive passengers? Many people have the opinion there could only be one explanation. Steamboat companies earned between five and ten dollars per soldier carried home from the South. It is believed the assigning officers may have been frequently bribed by boat captains into putting as many men as possible onto the vessels they owned. At nine o'clock on April 24, Captain J. C. Mason's boat left Vicksburg with 2,400 passengers.

When the *Sultana* stopped in West Helena, Arkansas, to refuel, the Chicago Opera Troupe did, in fact, provide a brief concert for townspeople and *Sultana* passengers. This is also where the only photograph was taken of the boat with its massive load of people. Soldiers, knowing a picture of the boat was being taken, nearly caused the *Sultana* to capsize as they rushed to the side near the photographer.

The *Sultana*, with a capacity of 376 but carrying 2,400, exploded and sank about six miles north of Memphis in the early-morning hours of April 27, 1865. Most historians put the loss of life somewhere around 1,700. That eclipses the *Titanic* by 200.

There is much speculation as to why the *Sultana* exploded. One conspiracy theory is that a bomb was loaded on the boat with the coal in Memphis. Conventional wisdom states that the boilers exploded from a faulty design and from quick and shoddy repairs done while in Vicksburg.

Because of hastily made manifests in Vicksburg, nobody knows the exact death toll, only estimates. The clerk of the *Sultana* reported: 2,400 passengers with 100 fare paying, 85 crewmen, 200 horses, and over 300,000 pounds of sugar.

Why did so many die? One answer may be found in a letter written by Thomas W. Horan to his parents while waiting at Camp Fisk to board a steamer home:

When the gate was opened [Cahawba [sic] Prison], I felt I could march 50 miles as poor and as weak as I was. When I was captured my weight was 175 pounds and when I was released I weighed 106 pounds. Thank God I am spared to return to the land of plenty.

Sadly, Horan's remains were never found.

Commodore Smith wrote:

"My weight when captured was 175 pounds, and when I reached our lines at Vicksburg, Miss., March 16, 1865, my weight was 94 pounds, although I had not been sick a day while in prison."

Many soldiers were simply too weak to swim. They faced the choice of burning on the *Sultana* or drowning in the Mississippi River. Those who could swim faced a gauntlet when they entered the river. Spring thaws from the north swelled the Mississippi up to five miles wide in places. The water was extremely cold. Drowning men pulled (otherwise) able swimmers to their deaths.

On page 120, Jerry O. Potter writes in his book, *The Sultana Tragedy*:

"Dr. Irwin estimated that 530 survivors were placed in hospitals and another 260 in the Soldier's Home. (Dr. Irwin's estimate included a few civilian passengers.) According to published accounts in the Memphis newspapers, the Gayoso Hospital received 139 patients; the Adams, 139; the Washington, 143; the Overton, 90; the Officers', 6; and the Webster and the Soldiers' Home, a few more."

To this day, the *Sultana* remains the worst maritime

disaster in US history. However, the story of the *Sultana* is mostly unknown. There was almost no coverage in the newspapers at the time. John Wilkes Booth shot President Lincoln thirteen days earlier. The nation's focus was on the end of the war and President Lincoln's assassination and burial. Telegraph wires had been severed during the war to keep each side from communicating with troops, so information about the *Sultana* was slow to spread.

Many of the events in this book were taken from letters and diaries of survivors. For the sake of the story, different characters took on experiences that may have happened to other people in real life. For instance, Samuel Pickens (a survivor) actually wrote that trading a live horse for a dead one was the best deal he ever made. Stephen M. Gaston wrote that he saved himself by floating down the Mississippi River on a barrel of flour.

I don't know why Stephen came to hold the Lone Star State so dear to his heart, but he ended up moving there. He had several children and named one of his daughters Texas. Stephen M. Gaston died in 1910 and is buried in Sherman, Texas, beside his wife and one of his sons.

ABOUT THE AUTHOR

Crossing the Deadline is the fourteenth book from author Michael Shoulders and Sleeping Bear Press. Previous books include *Say Daddy!*, *M is for Money*, and *T is for Titanic*. Having been involved in education for more than thirty years, Michael now writes and travels extensively, visiting schools and speaking at conferences across the country. He visits nearly one hundred schools each year, spreading his message that "Reading IS Magic." Michael lives is Clarksville, Tennessee, with his wife, Debbie. They are the proud parents of two sons, one daughter, one very large standard poodle, and two very spoiled cats—and the happy grandparents to one grandson and two granddaughters.